Be careful what you wish for.

Tarot-reading Justice of the Arcana Council Sara Wilde has an avalanche of oppressed psychics crying out for her aid. How can she help them all? Despite the support of the formidable Magician, she's only one woman.

Worse, the Council's biggest rival, the Shadow Court, taunts her at every turn, defying her efforts to discover the power behind their elite operation.

Frustrated by the Council's unwillingness to act, Sara is tempted to take matters into her own hands. Especially when she uncovers ancient, mysterious references to a vigilante-style enforcer, the night witch, who does what Justice can't...or won't.

Then a new, mysterious ally emerges, a reclusive sheikh with tales of captured genies and impossible wishes who offers Sara his assistance—for a price. A price that may prove to be more than Sara ever expected to pay...

Shadows dance and demons howl when *The Night Witch* comes to call.

THE NIGHT WITCH

WILDE JUSTICE, BOOK 6

JENN STARK

For Sabra
You are more magical than a djinn could ever be!

Virgins never seemed to catch a break.

I leaned over the edge of the stone wall, peering down at the gyrating crowd that filled the amphitheater below. While music thundered from two-story-high speakers, some unintelligible mash-up of house rock and New Age hokum, the dancing revelers flashed enough glitz to be seen from space. Above and around them, a multimillion-dollar light show cut through the star-filled night sky.

Here in the ruins of Pompeii, Italy, a city overwhelmed by the eruption of its most famous volcano, Mount Vesuvius, the amphitheater had been restored to serve as the perfect party palace for some of the richest and most entitled magicians, sorcerers, occultists, and wanna-be wizards in the world. And if you were going to have all that mysterium together at once, it wouldn't be a party without a few virgins.

Beside me, the High Priestess of the Arcana Council stood with her characteristic regal hauteur, for once dressed totally on point in her deep-red toga and Cleopatra Barbie jewels. To me, Eshe always looked like she belonged on stage in Vegas, not occupying one of the soaring shadow residences of the Council far above the city, but even she wrinkled her nose as she studied the line of white-clad young women being marched up to the stage at one end of the party pit. Except the reason for her disdain wasn't what I expected.

"There would've been two dozen virgins in my day." She sniffed. "I don't know who is running this operation, but it's decidedly bare bones."

"What, not enough blood and circuses for you?"

She shot me a withering glance. "It's bread and circuses."

"Give it time." I tracked the progress of the young women. "Why so many of them? What's their purpose tonight?"

"Traditionally, the members of the priestess's court are selected to serve as vessels for divine magic based on their Connected ability and their virginal status. I seriously doubt most of these attendants qualify on either count. Simon has provided facial recognition for all but three. Most of the identified participants are daughters of famous politicians, government notables, and a few random celebrities chosen mostly, I suspect, for notoriety. The research he's completed indicates that their current locations are actually known, at least in general. They are all the guests of Stratosfaire."

I grimaced at her mention of the official title of this get-together. I hadn't been willing to believe it when word first came to us of the potential danger this exclusive celebrity music fest posed, beyond that of good taste. But Stratosfaire was billed as the first-ever techno-psychic music festival for the highly evolved. It wasn't exactly clear whether that evolution implied mental or supernatural abilities, or simply the flexibility of one's bank account, but it didn't seem to matter. To the rich and the bored, a new festival to show off their importance was the nectar of the finest flower. Celebrities had clamored for the exclusive invitations, paparazzi had swarmed the outskirts of Pompeii until a military presence had been required to shut them down, and the entire event was being live-streamed for the hefty price tag of fifty thousand dollars.

That's right. Fifty thousand dollars to see a video feed of a party you weren't cool enough to attend.

I couldn't imagine anyone shelling out that kind of cash, until Simon, the Fool of the Arcana Council and our head tech geek, had shown me the numbers. The conference had sold out within minutes. Everything was, to all appearances, top-drawer—from the light show that lit up the amphitheater with a retina-searing glare, to the temporary scaffolding that created eco-friendly seating areas above the original ruins. Even the catering that had brought the finest booze and food to the revelers all damned day and into the night, was top of the line.

All that was well and good, but we weren't here to give the show a Yelp rating. Several days earlier, back in Las Vegas, distressing calls for help had started to come through my office at Justice Hall. I hadn't even been aware of the upcoming festival when the first complaint had landed quite literally on my desk.

As Justice of the Arcana Council, I was sort of the cosmic cop of the Connected world. Not even a police officer, really, more like a one-woman United Nations peacekeeping force. If someone with psychic ability was harming another

Connected, the call went up, and I came in to see what was what. Sorcerers, witches, occultists, and magicians generally tended to stay on the side of angels in their inter-Connected dealings, at least in full daylight. But when the makers of magic turned on each other, I got involved. Or that was the theory, anyway. In truth, there were so many calls for Justice that my office had cold cases dating back to the Bronze Age.

I scowled down at the gyrating crowd. "You got any line yet on who's behind all this?"

"For approximately the fifty-seventh time in the last three hours, no." Eshe breathed out a gust of haughty disdain. She must have lungfuls of the stuff. "I'm not a trained seal."

"You'd be a hell of a lot better company if you were. It's gotta be the Shadow Court, though. Has to be. Nobody else would be this tacky."

"Tacky, perhaps, but Jarvis isn't this sophisticated," Eshe pointed out. She gestured to the lights, the security, the state-of-the-art sound system. "And his family didn't amass the largest fortune in Europe by staging grandiose displays of largesse for no reason."

"Yeah, well. He also sucks at his job, and no one has stopped us from getting this far. That kind of incompetence has Jarvis Fuggeren written all over it." I'd pitched my voice slightly louder, hoping this area of the amphitheater was wired for sound. I needed the Shadow Court to make a move. The slightest push would do it—anything to justify the Arcana Council stepping in to ensure the balance of magic in the world was maintained. That was our reason for being, after all, and we'd been pretty good at it for the past few millennia.

Then the Shadow Court had slunk onto the scene, an organization dedicated to pushing the envelope on magic and using arcane powers to advance their position in society. The Council had been trying, albeit unsuccessfully, to kill the Court in the face for the past few months, and tempers were wearing thin. Particularly my temper. So when the Shadow Court's name had become attached to Stratosfaire, I'd been more than ready to check it out. Plus, apparently beyond the rich and gullible, some of the most powerful members of the arcane world had been tapped to attend the shindig. It wouldn't have been neighborly if I hadn't stopped by.

I'd been surprised and intrigued to discover that out of the entire Arcana Council, Eshe alone had received a formal invitation to attend. She didn't cut a very high profile when it came to the Connected community, and beyond her general disdain for pretty much everyone on the planet, she had no affiliation with the Shadow Court. To her, they were the consummate nouveau riche—broad, boorish, and well beneath her notice—especially Jarvis Fuggeren, the blond-haired, blue-eyed poster child for louche excess, who was supposedly the organization's leader. She wasn't wrong that this entire operation seemed above Jarvis's Mensa score, up to and including her invitation. Still, there was no denying her amusement at having been chosen out of all of us for her golden ticket. Figuring out why Eshe had been targeted was part of my reason for being here.

The other part was more straightforward. One of the calls for help that had rattled into my office this past week had been a desperate summons by a low-level wizard whose daughter had been gulled into attending the event. She was an innocent, unaware of the power within her, and one day, she had simply left a note that she'd found new friends. The wizard had used his scrying abilities to locate her, but dared not go further. The faire, he warned, was guarded by forces too dark and powerful for him to breach.

I didn't have a problem with dark and powerful. What was good for coffee was equally good for enemies. Besides, when a member of the Connected called out for Justice to help them, Justice was obligated to act. And this time around, Justice got to wear cool clothes.

"How long did it take Nikki to pick that out for you?" Eshe asked now, her gaze raking over my party attire. Her heavily painted lips curled with amusement. "You look like John Wick."

"I feel like John Wick," I agreed, adjusting the collar of my knee-length black leather duster, the perfect accompaniment to the black silk tank top and black leather pants I had underneath, finished off with boots meant for kicking Shadow Court minions in the face. She was right, of course. My attire had been selected by my right-hand woman and best friend, on the Council or off it, Nikki Dawes. Nikki had been sorely put out that she couldn't attend the gig with us, but we didn't want to draw too much attention, and attention was Nikki's stock-in-trade. Besides, she had her hands full with a private gig back in Vegas, and I was technically here as Eshe's muscle, her one-woman bodyguard to make sure the Shadow Court didn't pull anything stupid...and secondarily, well, as bait. Because the Shadow Court seemed compelled to pull something stupid whenever I was around.

So far, however, no one had given me much notice. Simon's facial recognition wards were being put to good use, which had allowed me to pass through the basic security around the event as Eshe's burly male sidekick, but this was the Shadow Court we were talking about here. I had to believe they'd be able to identify me, no matter how good the Fool's particular combination of magic and tech was.

No one had so much as blinked. After some initial fawning over Eshe by the coordinators of the event—conspicuously not any members of the Shadow Court that we'd identified—we'd been left pretty much to our own devices. We'd made our way to the high walls surrounding the amphitheater, which allowed us a bird's-eye view of the circular structure, lit up with a pulsating technicolor light show.

Beyond the pretty lights, however, the party itself had proven to be kind of lame. A lot of loud music and flashing glitterati, not much in the way of real magic or magicians. There was a fair amount of money changing hands, but for what, we couldn't exactly tell. At least not until twelve young women in white had been led out into the crowd.

"They're spelled," Eshe murmured, and I shot a look at her. She'd noticeably stiffened, her dark eyes narrowing as she stared down at the stage, her perfectly arched brows drawing together across a smooth expanse of creamy skin. Eshe had once been an oracle in residence at Delphi, and she retained her lush, ethereal beauty all these millennia later. "The women. Spelled and drugged. And I was right. There are only three with abilities, the three Simon could not identify. They've been placed in the middle of the line, as pretty as the rest, but not as pampered. Their hands will be careworn, even at their young age, and their bodies will have known hunger."

She spoke with a strange resonance to her voice that made my skin prickle. The High Priestess of the Arcana Council didn't speak much of her own youth. I'd never really thought that it'd been all that bad, but then again, she had willingly ascended to the Council rather than stay an oracle. She'd given up worldwide fame, something she seemed uniquely positioned to crave, for relative anonymity. There was probably a good reason why.

"You think they're Connected?" I asked. "Here against their will?"

Eshe nodded. "The Shadow Court needs to make a show of power. Ergo, they need people of power, Connecteds. But any Connected who actually *had* money wouldn't be a willing vessel for the kind of magic they're going to want to display tonight. For that, they need somebody who can't complain and who can't say no. And who doesn't have anyone to look out for them."

She said this last without rancor, but I picked up the accusation all the same. As Justice of the Arcana Council, looking out for the most vulnerable members of the Connected community was literally my only job.

"Look, I'm here, all right?" I huffed. "You're here. And unless I miss my guess, the real heads of the Shadow Court are here. So let's get this rolling."

"Or what?" She turned to me, her expression hardening unexpectedly. "Or you'll actually do something on your own? Serve the Connected of this world the way you were supposed to all these long centuries?"

I blinked. "I haven't had the job all that long, Eshe. Don't flake out on me here."

But there was something wrong with High Priestess's eyes. They were turning milky white, and the skin of her face had grown paler beneath the sheen of her makeup, her stance now unnaturally rigid. Her lips parted and her words, when they came, were low, sonorous, and damning.

"You have been summoned and summoned again, and you do not listen. You do not care. You are so certain that Justice walks only in the light, but it wasn't always so. It cannot always be so. Darkness draws down, and the night witch stirs."

"Well, of course she does...." I dropped my voice to a murmur. "Simon?"

The Fool's hi-tech communications bud crackled in my ear. "I didn't catch that," he said. "Can you repeat?"

"Not a chance." Eshe's words slipped away from me as I lifted my hands and edged carefully toward her. "But turn up your speakers in case it happens again."

The High Priestess's quick hop onto the crazy train was not supposed to be part of tonight's festivities, and I couldn't tell if the show was for me or for whoever might be watching us. I had a sinking suspicion it was for me, and as her milk-white eyes widened, her breathing growing harsh, almost guttural, a whisper of fear curled through my gut. I'd never dealt with a Council member in full-on meltdown. This wasn't especially a good time.

"Hang tight with me, Eshe," I tried, reaching out to touch her bare arm. "Snap out of—whatever it is you're doing. We can chat."

She jerked back from me, twisting toward the crowd again.

"It's starting," she cooed, drawing in a deep, satisfied breath as the music leapt and toga-wearing bodybuilders lit torches surrounding the young women, now arranged in a semicircle on the stage. Her smile curled, and a level of profound pleasure creased her lips. "Oh, it *has* been too long."

Okay, this wasn't necessarily an improvement. There was something new in Eshe's voice, something new and unhinged. In my ear, Simon hummed with concern. "Remember, Eshe, you've gotta—"

I didn't get a chance to finish my warning. With a grace

that would have been breathtaking if it wasn't so insane, Eshe stepped up onto the stone barrier and swan-dived off the edge of the wall, straight into the roaring, chanting crowd.

"Eshe! Dammit, *no!*" I shouted, dashing forward to throw myself after her.

Smoke and fire exploded in my face.

2

"**E**she!" I staggered back as the billowing cloud shot skyward, pushing me away from the wall. A scream, loud and long, rent the air around me, but it didn't seem to be coming from the crowd. If anything, it only added to the frenzied excitement.

I lurched forward once more, my mind focusing sharply on the chaos in front of me. I'd never been to Pompeii before, certainly never to this amphitheater, but it was a wide open bowl that I could easily take in at one glance, despite the knot of dancing people and the jittering lights. My ability to hop from place to place, one of the perks of being a member of the Arcana Council, didn't need much more nav support than that. Unfortunately, there was an element of combustibility required, so I flipped on my burners, then focused on the process of shifting the atoms in my body slightly apart from each other just enough—

A thick, heavy force shoved into me from the side. I went sprawling to the stone walkway, landing hard before rolling several paces. My current pack of Hello Kitty Tarot cards spilled out of my pockets, but I ignored them for a second as my hands shot up instinctively.

A second perk of my developing powers was being able to generate flaming projectiles in my palms. I'd never taken the time to fully master the rest of my magical abilities, but throwing fireballs always proved to be a good opening salvo.

Only, it wasn't happening this time. Like, not even remotely. It wasn't that the spirit wasn't willing, but the flesh barely sizzled along my fingertips, and nothing appeared in the palms of my hands but a puff of smoke. In fact, there was a whole lot of smoke happening along the base of the stone walkway, it seemed, only a small percentage generated by me. Worse, that smoke now seemed to be what was flattening me to the floor, my face driven hard into the stone surface. *Ouch.*

I peered around, trying to see who'd hit me, but no one emerged from the billowing clouds. Anger spiked deep in my gut, but unfortunately, it didn't fire up the ol' hands. Instead, I focused at the pile of cards I'd sent flying, barely visible through the smoke from the...from what? Had Eshe turned up the stage torches to max or something?

I needed to get down there, but right now, I could barely do more than squint at the cards. Three of them were faceup, only one fully visible in the mist. The rest remained facedown, a parade of white kittens in pink bows looking back at me accusingly. Since when did Hello Kitty get so judgy?

The first card I could see was the Ten of Swords, betrayal, featuring a guy flattened on his stomach, swords pinning him to the ground. I could relate, but enough was enough. I struggled to push myself to my hands and knees. It was like shouldering up through wet concrete.

Again, the problem wasn't simply that my magic fireballs had been dampened. Something else was weighing on me, and not just existential angst. There was a dead zone in play here that hadn't been moments before.

"Who the hell is running this show," I muttered, crawling to the wall again. If it was Jarvis, he'd definitely upped his game.

Through a split in the rock, I watched Eshe. She stood in the center of the stage and lifted both her voice and her arms to the heavens, her exultant cries echoed by the white-clad minions surrounding her. The three young women in the center actually seemed to know what they were doing, but even the celebutantes were getting into the act, studying their neighbors and trying to mimic their actions like freshmen cheerleaders at the first home game. Around the High Priestess, a dozen torches flared with enthusiastic bursts, which explained the smoke, and the crowd in the mosh pit was starting to take notice. How was she doing all this when I couldn't light a cigarette?

I grunted as I pulled myself up to my feet, the mists finally clearing enough that I could make out the second visible card. The Devil. Somehow, I didn't get the sense of the actual Arcana Council Devil in this mist, unfortunately. There was something else going on here.

I saw it then, a new swirl of pink-and-blue smoke snaking over the far balcony of the stone walkway. I couldn't see anyone in the smoke, yet the mist seemed to hold a curious sentience, as if there was something inside, watching me. *Suppressing* me.

Who, dammit?

I pushed on, glancing down as the third faceup card came into view. Only a corner was visible, a swirl of colors I couldn't quite make out. I staggered forward another step and the card revealed itself—the Seven of Swords.

Man, I hated that card. It could be read in far too many ways, the most obvious being the employment of strategy and deception. Well, the Shadow Court certainly was being strategic, given whatever was screwing with my mojo. Maybe it was time for me to turn the tables.

I staggered a little as I widened my stance. The weight on my shoulders and legs felt like a lead blanket. It didn't hurt, but I could definitely tell there was the potential for hurting a great deal. Hurting at a level that went far below the surface. What kind of magic was this? I shot another glance down to the stage, gratified to see that Eshe had drawn the three virgins closer to her. The High Priestess's ways were subtle and elegant. I had no doubt she would carry off her role stupendously and protect the girls at the same time. I spared the briefest consideration for which of the girls was the daughter of the wizard who summoned me, but that hardly mattered in the end. None of them would be hurt on my watch. Or Eshe's, better stated.

More smoke billowed up from the amphitheater floor, spilling over the wall, swirling toward me. I squinted down, trying to keep my focus on Eshe and the girls, fixing on their position so I could bolt over the wall and wink out of this location, then onto the stage below—

A shriek right out of the Jurassic age exploded from the smoke, followed by a rush of wings. Not just wings, but beaks and claws and beady little eyes and leathery squawking maws. They lunged for me, a horde of squawking...*pterodactyls?*

With nowhere else to go, I hurtled over the edge of the stone walkway, the horde hot on my heels, both jaws and claws straining for me. They swarmed around me and, like some Technicolor Hollywood movie from the 1950s, I found myself stepping, jumping, and lurching from body to body, racing down the stairway to hell as I tried to clear the mass of creatures before they ripped me to shreds. Fire boiled inside me, but my hands remained encased in their gloves of magic-suck, so my flames had nowhere to go. I'd never thrown fire out my ass, but I was seriously considering it—

"*Caw!*" screeched the nearest creature right in my ear, and I used my distinctly unmagical hands to crack the leathery lizard bird in the jaw, sending it hurtling end over end into its fellows as three more latched onto my back—

Looking like a one-woman pterodactyl clown car, I crashed into a swarm of drunken, screaming revelers, their designer-decorated bodies providing a million-dollar bouncy house for me to land on and stagger back up to my feet.

As soon as I hit the floor of the amphitheater, though, I felt the restriction lift from me. I was no longer in a dead zone, no longer repressed. How could I be? Eshe was standing on the stage not thirty feet away, sending a ring of fire from the torches straight up into the heavens, the women around her practically levitating in their oracular thrall. There was *way* more magic here than I needed, so I flung my hands wide.

"Get *back*," I snarled. Instantly, the air was filled no longer just with lizard birds, but a hundred bands of silver. They exploded out from me in all directions, wrapping themselves around beaks, talons, legs, wings.

I grinned. Typically, when Justice used her fancy faux friendship bracelets to bind some misbehaving Connected, it was to expedite transport of the bad guys straight to Judgment. I saw no reason to break that tradition now. A second later, every manacled creature disappeared, leaving me spinning and disoriented, all the flying monkeys off my back.

I plunged toward Eshe, struggling through flailing, writhing bodies that were still caught up in the dance. Eventually, I hoisted myself up on someone's shoulder, trying to push myself out of the throng. Around me, screams of surprise turned into alcohol-soaked howls of delight and pleasure as the glitterati lifted me up and shoved me forward, my first and hopefully last experience of crowd surfing. I wiggled out of my duster to move faster, and a second later, I reached the stage.

Even as I vaulted toward it, though, another curtain of smoke bloomed in front of me, multicolored and smelling suddenly of...sulfur?

I plunged into the murk, half expecting round two of the bad birds. But this was different. Far different. These were *demons* standing in a thick line, complete with pointy-toothed muzzles stretched wide, eyes glowing red, and trails of saliva dripping from their jaws and streaming from their snouts. Their breathing was labored, almost frantic with excitement, like dogs held back at the leash. The moment I entered the roiling smoke, they burst forward.

This time, I didn't hesitate. I whipped my arms wide, sending a swath of fire out in both directions. The howls of the creatures were gratifying as they lurched back, black goop flying.

Little known fact: no human can kill a demon. Your best shot, your *only* shot, was to send them back where they came from, and generally only witches could do that. That meant that I had no way of terminating these bastards for good, and that bothered me more than I wanted it to. It was time for new rules against demons. There surely had to be a better way, even if the Council hadn't been in the demon-blasting business for the past thousand years.

Well, I might not be able to kill these bastards, but that

didn't mean I couldn't hurt them. And as with most demons, even those under someone else's control, hurting was enough. The moment they were wounded, they disappeared in a puff of smoke, leaving behind their thick black demon blood that would be visible to everyone once the smoke cleared.

A new shout emerged behind me, a rising cry not of fear, which was what it should've been, but of unabashed delight. The Stratosfairians were apparently happy for any expression of magic rolled out in front of them, no matter the danger to themselves. *Freaks.*

I burst through the last line of demons, rushing into the center of the stage as the music built to another crescendo, then crashed over the amphitheater, sweeping the frenzied crowd along with it. Then I staggered to a stop, gaping as I finally registered what I was seeing.

The stage was empty. No celebutantes, no kidnapped virgins, no Eshe. Instead, the dozen torches spouting blue-white flame belched a new blaze of fire all around me, making me whirl. Eshe was no longer the target of the roaring cheer that erupted behind me. I was. I had become the show.

As wild-eyed, terrified, and ultimately furious security guards rushed at me from every corner of the stage, I drew in a shaky breath.

"They bought it," I said into my mic, hoping like hell Simon could still hear me. "Eshe is in."

Then I started running.

3

I stood in the middle of the Arcana Council's conference chamber fully eighteen hours later, aghast at the news I'd just been given. I pointed a slightly wobbly finger at Simon, who sat at the far end of the table. "What do you mean you still can't find her? How is that even an option?"

We were assembled in a chamber far above the Luxor casino in Las Vegas on a brilliant sunny morning. Far beneath us, the Strip stretched to the north, the glittering casinos somehow managing not to look out of place and tawdry without the backdrop of night. Even under the harsh light of the desert, they beckoned with their siren song of clacking and ringing slot machines, the fan of shuffling cards, and the tinny canned music celebrations that indicated that someone had just gotten seriously lucky. I wasn't interested in that kind of luck.

"It's already evening in Pompeii now," I continued. "How could the tracker have failed so badly? She should be up by now, moving again." After I'd crashed back into my own bed in my private rooms at the Palazzo Casino Hotel, it had taken me most of the night and well into this morning to feel remotely human, but come on. I'd been attacked by mini pterodactyls. Eshe hadn't been doing more than serving as the life of a very exclusive party, feted and fawned over. Or at least that had been the plan. "What happened?"

Simon sat back, looking equally perturbed. Lean to the point of being almost gaunt, the Fool still possessed a remarkably youthful baby face, his light blue eyes serious beneath pinched dark brows. The pale glow of the computer screen reflected on his even paler face as he rotated his chair back and forth in front of the table. Today, his curly black hair was stuffed under a Minions knit skull-cap, and his thin body was draped in a long-sleeved orange T-shirt and worn blue jeans. His version of business casual, all the way down to the neon-green Chucks that were shoved, untied, onto his rapidly bouncing feet. He looked like he was about one and a half Red Bulls shy of levitation. "Honestly? There's only one reason that tracker isn't working. And that's if she took it off."

I scowled. That idea had occurred to me, but surely Eshe wouldn't be so stupid. "She did? Or somebody helped her out of it?"

He shook his head. "It's not that kind of tracker. And Eshe isn't exactly a slouch when it comes to protecting herself. If she wanted to take the thing off, it would go; otherwise, nobody could get near her. Her power lies in prophecy, for sure, but also in illusion and persuasion. Nobody would've ever seen it if she didn't want them to. She's that good."

I nodded. I'd only seen the High Priestess in action a few times, but then again, I'd watched her appear in the center of a dozen white-clad virgins and disappear again with the entire lot of them, leaving behind a wide open stage with only glowing torches to mark their passage. Given how angry the security guards had been when they'd pounded onto the stage, they hadn't been in on the joke, at least not then. That meant that Eshe had succeeded in disappearing behind the Shadow Court's glittering curtain, a sorceress apparently ready to be tempted.

When the High Priestess hadn't shown up on any of our radar screens, and had, in fact, gone completely dark, I'd at first celebrated—at least I had early this morning, when I'd finally awakened out of the stupor that had cocooned me post bird fight and gotten my first update from Simon. To all appearances, Eshe had successfully infiltrated the Shadow Court's lair, acting as a spy. That'd been the plan all along.

The Court had already tried to get the Emperor to play their game. He hadn't, as far as we knew, but we couldn't trust him not to cave going forward. Eshe, however, had been ready, willing, and able to step up, and had seemed more than a little flattered when we'd asked her to volunteer for Shadow Court duty.

Now I was beginning to rethink that idea.

"Sooo...you're thinking she's deliberately blocking your ability to track her? Is there any reason why she would be doing that? At least a reason that's not bad news?"

A knowing chuckle slipped through the room, oddly intimate, a second before its owner appeared in the doorway. Aleksander Kreios stood framed with sunlight from the room beyond, looking like a fallen angel. The truth was slightly more complicated.

Kreios was the Devil of the Arcana Council, the ultimate deceiver ready to beguile the truth out of the unsuspecting with a glance. He was also, as of very recently, the Council's leader. Today, he wore his typical work outfit, which served as his typical day-off outfit as well—a long, tunic-style white cotton shirt, ragged khakis, and open-toed sandals that would have looked out of place in a business meeting on anyone but him. His long, tawny hair fell to his shoulders, framing a face made for sin, and his green eyes flashed above an easy smile. His long lean body seemed to shift forward sensually, even when he stood still.

"Eshe has never been one to fall strictly within the lines of black and white," he said now, sauntering into the room. "She is, first and foremost, accountable only to herself. She wishes never to serve another again."

That caught me up short. "Wait a minute, you're saying she took off the tracker simply to give us the message that we're not the boss of her? Didn't somebody think maybe that might be a problem before we assigned her as a spy?"

Kreios shrugged. "It was a risk, but a risk we were more than happy to take. The leaders of the Shadow Court have nothing that Eshe truly wants. She has no need of money, no need of adulation from a group such as they are, and no need for any supplier of delight. These are all already at her fingertips. The only need the Shadow Court could fill was to assuage her curiosity. I guarantee you, they will not be able to hold her interest for long."

"Uh-huh," I said. "So if I have this straight, your plan is that we're simply going to wait until she gets bored enough to make a report."

Kreios spread his hands. "Exactly."

Simon spun in his seat, a flash of uncharacteristic annoyance crossing his face. "You think maybe you might've let me know that up front? I've been losing my mind trying to track her down. The best I could do was confirm that the entire cavalcade of Shadow Court members stayed put the rest of the night in Pompeii partying their asses off, then took off for points farther east and south. I have no idea if she's with them, though."

He looked genuinely upset, and Kreios lifted his brows. The curiosity in the Devil's expression was enough to send Simon spinning back to his computer station, his irritation morphing into wariness. He scooted forward while Kreios glanced out over the Strip and lifted one long, elegant finger to tap his lips.

"Southeast," the Devil murmured. "Excellent. We have no idea where the Shadow Court's new base of operations lies. We'd thought Hamburg, of course, as they had been based there in the past, but that's what they wanted us to think. They are nowhere in the United States, to be sure, not with the Council based here. But that leaves quite a bit of territory to explore."

I nodded, though I still wasn't happy. Eshe's entire purpose in this little charade was to get us more information on the Shadow Court. There was too much about them we didn't know, including who funded them, who they were funding, and where they put their heads down at night. It was maddening. "So we wait."

"We wait," Kreios agreed.

"But we do not remain idle, surely." Another smooth-toned elite chimed in with this protest, one whose voice I knew as well as my own. I turned, trying to hold on to my entirely justified mad as Armaeus Bertrand stepped into the room. As usual, I was not up to the task. The Magician and former leader of the Arcana Council was as devastatingly gorgeous to me today as he'd been when I'd first encountered him back when I'd been an artifact hunter and he'd been my rich, eccentric client.

Dark hair winged away from his face and skirted the edges of his classically beautiful face, rich with the heritage of his French father and Egyptian mother. His folks hadn't been able to take many family photos, since both of them died in the early thirteen hundreds, and that truly was a pity. I could only imagine how beautiful they must've been. Beautiful and arcane, as Armaeus's mother had been a priestess in her own right, while his father had served as a knight in the Crusades.

That mystery-shrouded upbringing was nowhere in evidence other than the slant of the Magician's eyes and the cast of his skin, however, as he strolled into the conference room in a four-thousand-dollar suit and gleaming wing-tipped loafers. Platinum glinted at his wrists and neck, and his suit jacket flared wide to reveal a deep-blue jewel-toned shirt, open at the neck. He looked very much the billionaire in residence, which was his preferred attire. Just as the Devil's attire uniquely suited him, Armaeus looked comfortable enough in his flashy suit to start a pickup volleyball game.

He glanced to me briefly and smiled, something less than recognition lighting his eyes, but more than simple curiosity. I'd met him nearly three years ago, while he'd only met me a few months ago. Our relationship was...complicated.

"There is much we need to learn here, surely," he said to Kreios. "Miss Wilde's concern for Eshe is not unfounded. The High Priestess knew the parameters of her assignment. She agreed to them and, in fact, helped shape the nature of the gambit. Her concern for the kidnapped girls was real. Her experience in her own childhood was not pleasant, and she has not forgotten."

Kreios nodded, then turned to me. "Eshe's youth was spent in poverty, her startling beauty making it almost assured that she would be sold into marriage at an early age, until she expressed an ability that allowed her parents to set their bar a little higher. Even then, they beat her into submission before she would agree to the horrible strictures involved with being an oracle at Delphi. She never forgave them for that."

That sounded a little ominous. "Why do I get the feeling that Eshe would be the type to hold on to a private grudge?"

Kreios inclined his head. "She waited until the most opportune time, then she appended a requirement to one of the supplicants seeking answers. A requirement the individual was more than happy to meet. Her father fared worse than her mother, but she held them both accountable."

I rolled my eyes. "And *this* is who you trust going into the Shadow Court, knowing she could go dark?"

Kreios chuckled. "Eshe, perhaps more than all of us, does not need to color her acts with duplicity. She is who she is. We simply had to allow for that in our calculations."

I made a face. "Oh, right, so this is where you tell me it was part of the plan all along?"

Beside me, Simon snorted. "I was thinking the same thing."

"Based on your assessment of the Shadow Court's trajectory," Kreios asked Simon, ignoring us both, "where do you anticipate the Shadow Court is traveling?"

"Honestly," Simon said, rolling back to his computer, "my first thought was Cairo. Then Damascus, but now I'm kind of thinking it might be Dubai." He wrinkled his brow and peered up at the Devil and the Magician. "Does that make any sense at all?"

Both Kreios and the Magician glanced my way as a ripple of uneasiness washed through me. I'd kept my mental barriers locked down tight after I'd returned from Pompeii, needing my own time to process the crazy I'd endured. But

Dubai was smack dab in the Middle East. Like Arabian Peninsula Middle East, and I knew very little about that area. Was it known for pterodactyls?

"Dubai," Armaeus murmured thoughtfully, drawing my attention. "As far as I know, there are no strongholds of Connected in the city, but communication from that area is notoriously difficult to track. We've not focused on it, but now that I consider that, I'm not entirely sure why. The area has a long history of involvement with arcane practices regardless of its present dedication to Islam. But as a stronghold for the Shadow Court? I have a harder time believing that."

"A very hard time," the Devil agreed. "However, there's no denying that it is one of the richest areas in the world, with a leadership whose religious and arcane practices are very much held close to the chest. It's possible there is a connection...and there are all those virgins to contend with."

I winced. "Any word on them? Particularly the ones who weren't flush with cash?"

"Not the three we couldn't identify, but as for the celebrities, some of them have returned home, some haven't," Simon said, turning to a different screen. "The ones that have, though, haven't been saying much. Everything from official news channels to their private social media accounts have been quiet. At least, as it pertains to their little jaunt to Pompeii. Whatever party they signed up for, they apparently all pinky swore not to say anything about it."

He blew out a long breath and glanced toward the Devil. "We probably should track a couple of them down and see how dedicated to that cause they really are. Could be they just had a memory block applied. If someone applied the right lever, they may be persuaded to spill. It would give us something to go on while we're waiting for Eshe to resurface."

Opposite me, Kreios smiled. "I think that's a very good idea."

Simon leaned forward to his laptop, his fingers flying over the keyboard. "Closest and most accessible is Kymberlee Aines, social media influencer, LA heiress, beauty sponsor," he said. "She's got a gig today, looks like, in an LA hotel—lemme get her schedule. And her contacts. And what she ate for breakfast this morning."

As Simon mined Kymberlee's private and public media feeds, Kreios glanced my way. "Justice Wilde? Would you care to join me?"

"Have a care, if you do. You don't have a great deal of time," the Magician put in, his admonition making me blink.

"I don't?" I asked. "Why? Is Eshe in some kind of real danger?"

He arched a sculpted brow at me. "You cannot tell me that you've forgotten your compatriot's event this evening. She'll never forgive you if you miss it."

I stared at him, completely lost, then I felt Simon's gaze on me. The Fool grinned at me as I glanced toward him, leaning back in his chair.

"I don't think she forgot so much as she didn't compute what today is. It happens, especially since you're jumping time zones on the regular. But it's the fourth, Sara. Remember? Nikki emceeing the show?"

Sudden awareness burned through me, and I flinched. "That's *tonight*? I thought she was still hip-deep in prep. How is this already Thursday?"

"I can assure you that I will get you back in plenty of time before Miss Dawes's triumphant performance," the

Devil said smoothly, his mouth twitching with amusement. "In addition, I will personally see to your wardrobe. You truly can't ask for a better deal than that."

I opened my mouth, then shut it again. As usual, the Devil was right. I'd pretty much planned on wearing my John Wick outfit again, minus the leather duster, which I lost in the crowd in Pompeii. I was going to miss that coat.

I turned back to Simon. "You got this Kymberlee person locked down?"

"Oh yeah," he said. "Kymberlee Aines, nee Denise Glaston, YouTuber, fashion model, makeup heiress of LA. She no doubt came back because she's launching a new beauty line on the rooftop of the Carlton Hotel in downtown LA tonight. It's the hot ticket for everyone who's anyone."

"We can't wait for that," I said. "I've got to be back here by...when does it start?"

"Ten o'clock," Armaeus supplied.

I gave him a pained look. "Seriously? She couldn't have started it any earlier?"

"What are you, my mom?" Simon chortled, and I blinked. I'd never before this moment actually considered Simon as having a *parent*, let alone a mother. How old would she be now? Was she even still alive?

I shook off the question as he continued. "The party in LA will start around ten as well, but Kymberlee's booked solid with promo and pool parties at the same hotel until she has to go slither into her evening-wear tube top. You'll have plenty of time to chat her up and get back here."

"And take a brief detour while we're in the city," Kreios put in. "I have found their wardrobe selection is eminently more sophisticated than what we have here in Las Vegas."

I grimaced. "You know, I don't think we need to go that crazy—"

"And I think we do," Kreios said. "But we also can't continue flying blind with the Shadow Court. Why are they in Dubai? Where is Jarvis Fuggeren in all this—and if he is simply a front, who stands behind him? The Shadow Court is moving, and they are picking up speed. We would do well not to be caught unawares when they finally strike. We need to know who they are, and what they are. Once and for all."

"Agreed," Armaeus said. He moved over to where Simon was typing furiously, but his manner was distracted, his jaw set. The sight couldn't have pleased me more.

The Shadow Court was a mystery whose time had come to be solved, and the Arcana Council was on the case.

Finally.

4

Once Simon had his initial query underway, the Magician did Kreios and me the favor of transporting us to a hotel near where Kymberlee Aines was set up for her fashion show. He brushed a kiss across my lips as he left, the movement so quick, I wasn't sure it'd actually happened...except for the Devil's knowing smirk. Those two were the worst.

We emerged from a quiet alcove into the glitz-and-glam lobby, and I glanced around, confused. "Why didn't we just go directly to the Carlton?"

The Devil's smirk shaded to an indulgent smile. "Because the Carlton is not a friend of the Council, while the Rosewood makes itself available to us for whenever we have a need for its services, no matter how obliquely. We try to make a point of making an appearance whenever we're in the city."

I looked at him with some surprise. "Really? The Council cares about things like that?"

Kreios nodded. "You'll find, once you're forced to pay attention, that there are any number of things that the

Council does that don't seem to be quite necessary given our status and stature in the world. We maintain appearances, however. We nurture relationships. Not with very many people, and not in a very obvious way, and yet with an undoubted purpose to our actions."

"Really." I sensed that Kreios was trying to tell me something important, but in such a way that it couldn't come back on him later. It was one of his most charming attributes, but I wasn't getting the significance. That said, I did pick up on the subtle jab in his verbal gymnastics. "You don't think I pay enough attention?"

"You most definitely do not," he assured me without hesitation. "Admittedly, you haven't needed to for the duration of your time with the Council. That situation almost inevitably will change. When it does, try not to be too surprised."

I narrowed my eyes at him. "Why do I get the feeling that you know something I don't?"

His grin only broadened. "That, without a doubt, is certainly true. I would be embarrassed if it weren't."

While I was mid-eye roll, a manager emerged from the back room behind the gleaming reception counter, his entire expression lightening as he recognized the Devil. He was a small, tidy man with dark hair and dark skin, and he glided toward us in a bespoke pinstripe suit, beaming with excitement.

"Aleksander! Welcome. Welcome to you both," he said, turning to include me in his air of bonhomie. "What brings you to the city today? And what can I do to help you? Truly, anything at all—I am at your service."

"As it happens, we will not be staying long, though you are welcome to keep that information to yourself. If it is to your advantage to tell people that we will be in residence for a few days, by all means, do so," Kreios said with a smile.

"Oh! Well, I am more than happy to take you up on your generous offer. It would very much be to my advantage to be able to share that we are entertaining you both." The manager turned to me. "I don't believe I've had the pleasure of meeting you, Ms.—"

"Justice Wilde," Kreios inserted smoothly. "She has done her level best to remain out of the public eye, but I have a sneaking suspicion that will be changing soon."

I studied him warily. "Oh?"

We'd be continuing that conversation later, apparently, as the manager turned in step to walk with us. "Is there anything I can do for you during your brief stay?" he asked, his expression as hopeful as a golden retriever's.

I just wanted the guy to go away, but Kreios deliberately checked his stride. "What sort of movement have you been noticing?" he asked.

The man shrugged. "Only the usual. After that business earlier this year, the covens in the city have been quieter, as if their wings have been clipped. They're still out and about in society, but not making a fuss. We've had an upsurge in devil magic, but that happens from time to time in the city."

I looked over at him. "Devil magic?"

He smiled. "Justice Wilde, I'm proud to say that I have been providing Aleksander with the best information available about southwestern coastal United States and Mexico for some years now. I guarantee you that if there's any movement in the Connected communities, whether through the arcane black market, the deeper magic, or the older families, I hear about it. I would be gratified to provide you with information should you ever need it as well."

I nodded. "You're, ah, affiliated with one of the houses?"

The four houses of magic—Swords, Wands, Cups and Pentacles—were mortal created and mortal focused, and deeply entwined in the actions of the global Connected community. Anything that happened in the arcane world, aboveboard or below it, they knew about.

To my surprise, a look of elegant horror crossed the manager's face. A second later, it was gone. "Ah! You would set me a test. It's good of you, very good. What we are hearing...well. It is good to be cautious. To watch, and to wait," he said. Before I could make any sense of that, he rushed on. "But to answer your question, assuredly, we are not affiliated with the houses. Our allegiance is to the Council. First, ever, and always. You can trust us."

The Council? My brows flew up, but I managed not to gape. So the Council had its own network of supporters on the side? How had I not known this? I sent a mental ping to Armaeus, but he wasn't picking up. The manager turned back to the Devil.

"We have noticed a lot of money coming into the district via arcane channels, not enough to alert the federal watchdogs, but enough to trip our wires. We're not sure what's been bought or sold, however. It almost seems like it's more to make a point, an impression, if you will."

Kreios nodded. "Somebody wants everyone to know there's money to be had."

"And in a city like this, reputation matters, but money still talks. We've made a note of it."

"Excellent," the Devil said. "What do you know about Kymberlee Aines?"

To my surprise, the manager hesitated again, a sudden, but decided, hitch to his step.

"Young and well liked, rich family, richer connections," he recovered smoothly. "Has attracted sponsors up to her carefully moisturized décolletage, which she's more than happy to display whenever there's a camera involved. I warn you, if you are heading to her little presentation today, you should be prepared to be photographed. It's the entire purpose of the event."

Kreios chuckled. "We'll be careful. Is she Connected?"

"Oh!" The manager seemed to be genuinely taken aback by the question, then shook his head. "No. No, I don't think so. Now, are her sponsors part of the Arcanum? That's a more interesting question, and one I also don't know the answer to. But it's worth looking into. I'll let you know. Is there anything I should be cautious of?"

"Just tipping our hand a bit," Kreios said smoothly, while my ears pricked up at the new word. Arcanum? Was that merely the manager's affectation, or was this some sort of new subset of the Connected?

"Anyone who's watching will see us at the Carlton. I'm not attempting to make a secret of it," Kreios continued. "But we appreciate the information. There are...actors we are interested in tracking."

An unexpected spurt of irritation riffled through me at the Devil's subtlety. I didn't see the point in dancing around the subject. The manager seemed eager to talk, and I was eager to learn.

"What do you know about the Shadow Court?" I asked bluntly.

If I'd thought I'd catch him off guard, I was mistaken. "Only what they've wanted known," the man said with a genteel shrug. "Their money is old, but everything else about them is new, which is curious. They want to give the impression they've been around long enough to *deserve* respect, not merely to buy it, but they've given no indication as to why. In part, that's a good thing. Other groups would simply end enough lives to make a splash, but the Shadow Court seems to be playing a subtler game. To what end, though, we don't know."

"Who are they?" I pressed. "Do you know the principals?"

"Again, only those who have been set up in public roles. If you mean the house of Fuggeren, certainly they are the bankers of the organization. They have been bankers to the powerful and arcane since the Middle Ages. But as to decision makers..." The manager waved an elegant hand. "Doubtful. We're watching the entire family, of course."

"Consider watching them with a little more interest," Kreios said. "The Court is close to making an important move. That movement may not involve dead bodies, and it may or may not involve the pile of money that's been circulating, but it's possible it will involve both."

"Well, then," the manager said, his eyes flashing with the renewed interest of the inveterate gossip. "You do manage to keep things interesting."

The Devil smiled, and we were out the door.

The walk to the Carlton was brief and uneventful, and we blended into the crowd easily enough. In LA, clothes definitely didn't make the person. In fact, it was a city that prided itself on looking for a lower rent than it actually was.

That situation changed the moment we stepped into the Carlton boutique hotel. I'd never heard of the place before, and it was clear that at some point, it had served another purpose than that of an expensive hotel. The interior of the first floor looked more like it had once been a bank, down to the teller stations and the brass bars. But there was no doubting the rarefied air surrounding the celebutantes gathered in the lobby. Dozens of beautiful young women and men in sleek summer minidresses and open-collared shirts and slacks drifted around the space and pointedly ignored us as we entered. Even discounting the fact that the Devil had been born in the early 1900s, we were definitely older than most of the crowd. Nobody paid us any attention, and we moved quickly through the front to the back of the lobby.

Once we reached the security station, things picked up. One of the men looked our way, stiffening as he clearly recognized Kreios. That struck me as surprising until I glanced over and nearly tripped over my own feet. From all appearances, I was walking next to Benedict Cumberbatch in full Doctor Strange winged eyebrows and bespoke British suit.

"Seriously?" I muttered. "You couldn't at least have given me Tony Stark? Thor?"

"Regrettably, I must play to the audience I am given," the Devil murmured back. "However, I would be more than willing to arrange a private performance for you. That could prove quite...distracting."

Even knowing the Devil as well as I did, I couldn't stop the shiver of awareness that skated through me. He knew it, too, if his smirk was any indication. *Asshat.*

"Noted." He tipped his head.

When he spoke next, it was with a flawless British accent. "The Kymberlee Aines gala?" he asked with an admittedly adorable air of bemusement.

"Of course," the security guard blurted. "Do you have ID, special passes?"

"Yes, indeed," the Devil said, producing both with a flourish of his hand. The High Priestess wasn't the only Council member given to illusion. In fact, I was one of the few Council members who sucked at it, now that I thought about it. Something I'd need to look into.

The security guard barely gave me a glance, apparently satisfied that I was a suitable plus one for Mr. Cumberbatch, or simply too starstruck to care, and a moment later, we were through the line and to the elevator, the carriage complete with its own operator. We were taken to the fifth floor, not the penthouse, because, as the elevator monitor informed us breathlessly, that was where the pool was.

Once we were out on the deck, a pleasant breeze cut through the heat of the day, and plenty of eye candy gathered everywhere we looked, albeit of the decidedly airheaded variety. The one exception was Kymberlee Aines herself. She stood at the front of the staging area, wrangling products and cameramen as if she were born to the job. I didn't recognize her as one of the young women in long white gowns from Stratosfaire, but I didn't *not* recognize her either. She had that certain Instagram-ready cast to her face and makeup that made her look like any of the three dozen models doubtless posing for pictures elsewhere in the city at this exact moment. Such was the world we had created.

As we approached, the young woman looked up and gave a tiny squeal of surprise. "Paolo! You came!"

She dashed over, and I barely had time to notice the Devil's new glamour before he opened his arms wide and gathered the young celebutante into a warm embrace. I didn't recognize him as an actual celebrity, but his almost shockingly good looks made me think he was possibly a model the young woman knew.

He drew her away, and she went willingly, while I sort of floated in their wake, a discarded party favor off the back of the boat. I didn't mind. I just needed to know what the woman had to say.

"I tried to get ahold of you earlier today," the Devil

murmured in a voice I didn't recognize, solidly Mediterranean. "They said you were sick."

"I wasn't sick, I was wiped out," Kymberlee said breathily, with a voice like an invitation to sex. "Oh my God, the jack they had at that party was like nothing you've ever seen, Paolo. I've already got lines out for it. What it made you see, made you feel..."

"But it wiped you out?" Kreios pressed, soul of concern. "That seems kind of dangerous."

"Only because I took way more than I should've for my first time. But you know how I am about first times." She giggled, and the Devil nodded sagely. He stepped closer to her, tucking his hand under her chin.

"So tell me, what did you see?" he asked. "What truth would you like to share?"

At least here, it seemed, he was willing to get to the point.

Kymberlee blinked back at him, her eyes wide. "Only the most *amazing* witch in the world, and they told us she wasn't even a witch, but a *priestess*. A priestess!" She legitimately squealed. "There's real magic, Paolo, and we can buy in. I'm not talking sponsorships, either. I'm talking buying in at the very top. Having the kind of power to influence not with social media, but with a glance or a smile."

The Devil wearing Paolo chuckled. "Seems to me you've already got that power."

Kymberlee beamed at him. "Over *you*, maybe, over my fans, sure, but I want more, and I can get it because I'm the right kind of person with the right kind of ability. I can be trained to make it all happen with the snap of my fingers. They said so, and she did too—and she's a *priestess*."

Kreios gave her a concerned frown. "Hey, are you sure this isn't some sort of scam?"

I was seriously enjoying Kreios's younger, looser approach to conversation, and to her credit, Kymberlee didn't take offense. "I know it sounds like that, but that's not it, I promise. I *saw* things at that party. And I'm not the only one. I'm the first and only wave—well, that's what they said, but I don't believe them. I can give you a list of a hundred people right now who would want to be where I was, want to see what I saw. I'm going to have to act fast."

Listening to her, I grimaced. The Shadow Court certainly was upping their game if they were going after the gullible super-rich and promising them Connected ability. How far had they gotten, though? Did they have enough whales lined up to start gambling at the VIP tables?

I glanced back to see that Kymberlee and Kreios had moved on from chattering to engaging in a passionate embrace. I didn't care—I'd gotten what I'd come for. I waited with barely restrained impatience for them to finish, and even less restraint as Kreios and I then threaded our way back through the hotel, this time bypassing the security checkpoint altogether and exiting out the back of the building through a doorway I was pretty sure was never supposed to be opened.

"Okay, so what is she going to do when she figures out it wasn't actually Paolo who showed up?" I asked Kreios as we stepped back into the sunshine.

"I happened to know that Paolo is currently enjoying the favors of a woman who looks remarkably like Kymberlee on the other side of town. When she expresses her delight at his appearance today at her gala pre-party, it will be up to him to determine how to play it. I have every faith in the young man. Bottom line, however, Ms. Aines's presence at Stratosfaire was designed for her to receive an ironclad assurance that she could buy her way into Connected ability."

"So, technoceuticals?" I asked, referring to the arcane black market's product of choice, a mixture of pharmaceutical ingredients and pure magic, the latter often gained in the most brutal way possible.

"Technoceuticals and potentially true magic. There's no real telling what the Shadow Court is up to, especially since we don't have a full understanding of who is behind the curtain."

The cramp in my stomach was back. "All right," I sighed. "Then let's get home."

The Devil chuckled. "Oh, I think not. At least not before we shop."

I stared at him. "Kreios, we do *not* have time for that."

"And I assure you, we have nothing but."

He gestured, and a limo purred up beside us. "Trust me, this will only hurt a little," he promised.

5

"Welcome to magical Las Vegas!"

I wasn't so much surprised to see the thigh-high-slit gown that greeted the open door of Kreios's limo, his conveyance of choice from the Las Vegas airport given the trunk full of purchases we'd brought back on the Council jet from LA. What did surprise me was that I didn't recognize the muscular leg of the goddess who greeted us—or the voice.

"Oh!" the stunning redhead exclaimed as she reached into the car and grasped my hand in a powerful grip. "Nikki is going to be *beyond* thrilled that you made it. The show starts in twenty minutes, so you've only just got time to get to the bar. And honey, you're gonna *want* to get to the bar before things get started."

She said all this in a breathy rush as she pulled me to the pavement, barely giving me time to register her gorgeous red wig, million-dollar makeup, and a dress that plunged halfway down her torso in a sea of emerald green.

"Where's Nikki?" I asked, and she gave me a broad wink.

"Girl. She is up to her ass in paparazzi and loving every

minute of it. Don't you worry, she's got you guys set up right at the VIP table, and she'll be joining you as soon as the festivities begin. She'll be spending most of her time on stage, of course, the show must go on and all that, but we've prerecorded the introductory packages for each of our ever-so-stunning contestants, so that gives her just a little bit of breathing room so that she can knock your socks off—oh!"

The redhead turned to Kreios as he exited the limo, her smile, if possible, going even wider. "And she is going to be completely thrilled to see you looking so fine tonight, if I do say so myself. You ever decide you want to bring more than one friend to the party, honey, let me give you my card."

Kreios's chuckle was a deep rumble of desire as he took the bombshell's hand in his, lifting her lacquered fingertips to his lips.

"I can't remember the last time I got such an appealing invitation," he said, meeting the green-eyed vixen's gaze long and meaningfully as her heavily painted lips parted in a completely unfeigned gasp. "But you don't need to give me your card, Barbarella. I've had my eye on you for quite some time."

Barbarella's brows climbed up her forehead, until they almost grazed the deep cherry-hued bangs artfully curled around her face. Her inch-long false eyelashes fluttered, and a rush of color that had nothing to do with her expertly applied blush flooded her face. She drew in a strangled breath, breasts heaving beneath the green sequined gown that would've put Princess Ariel to shame, and she took a quick step back on her teetering white platform heels. "Nikki told me what to expect when I met you, but I never— I mean I simply *never*..."

Kreios gave her hand a gentle squeeze. "Well then, I look forward to being your first," he assured her.

We moved on before the poor woman stroked out, and I gave the Devil a sidelong glance. "Was all that really necessary?"

A surprisingly soft smile curved the edges of his mouth. "I assure you, it was not only necessary, it was long overdue. Barbarella James has only been in Las Vegas for a little under a year. Before that, she lived in a Deep South town that shall forever remain nameless, where she faced an upbringing I wouldn't wish on my worst enemy. And I certainly have some enemies who would deserve it. Anything I can do to help her express the beauty deep in her soul that has been yearning to shine, right along with her true identity since she was very young, it's my honor and privilege to do."

I pursed my lips as I looked away. It was such a simple expression of solidarity, yet it stole my breath. Say what you would about the Devil, he'd seen the worst and best of what humankind had to offer. He understood.

"Well, alrighty, then," I managed, and we stepped inside the Flamingo Casino.

It was easy to know where to go from there. For the first-ever Las Vegas Princess Drag Queen competition, Kreios had pulled out all the stops. A glittery archway that was the stuff of prom girl dreams snaked away from the main doors of the Flamingo, leading to one of the casino's performance venues. The archway was covered in millions of twinkling fairy lights, with several alcoves open for contestants and guests to have their photos taken. The casino itself was jam-packed with tourists and regulars alike—gambling, playing slots, and ogling the statuesque beauties circulating through the crowd prior to the competition. This was Vegas, so the concept of drag queens was nothing new, but the combination of glitz and glamour that attended this particular competition put even the most dyed-in-the-wool Midwestern-looking tourists completely at ease. There were several knots of them conversing with the contestants, both sides wide-eyed with excitement. Kreios might not be able to change minds, but he could at least give people new options to consider.

We bypassed the glittery Habitrail and made directly for the theater, Kreios signaling discreetly to a number of security personnel on the way. The crowd at the Flamingo was practically pulsating with energy, and that could go in a couple of different directions if he wasn't careful. Fortunately, his crew looked to have everything well in hand, and a few moments later, we were in the main theater.

The second we reached the doorways, I was nearly tackled by a flying blonde dervish.

"Dollface!" Nikki crowed, whirling me around and then holding me at arm's length to get the full experience of my outfit. It *was* a pretty impressive outfit, especially for me, and I struck my best runway pose.

"Sweet baby Jesus on a tricycle, will you take a look at you," she exclaimed. "Silver lamé?" She shot an awed look at the Devil. "You got her to wear silver lamé? And platform heels? I think I may faint." She swooped in for another hug, and I threw up my hands in alarm.

"You're going to mess up your makeup," I warned, but Nikki cackled as she tossed her head, piles of gorgeous blonde curls bouncing in echoed delight.

"Honey, there ain't nothing going to move this makeup short of a nuclear explosion. The Devil gave me the best of the best, and I surely do owe you for it, sugar face."

She said this last to Kreios, and he didn't hesitate. Unlike me, he had no concerns for Nikki's appearance and swept her into a knee-knocking embrace, tilting her all the way back as he planted a deep and searching kiss on her lips. All around us, photographers' cameras flashed, adding a brilliant starburst feel to the moment, but one that was entirely unnecessary. No matter where they were, Nikki and the Devil always stole the show.

A moment later, he righted her, twirling her out so that I could see more of her stunning ensemble. The white sequined gown flared wide, its shimmering silhouette hugging Nikki's ample curves and its twin thigh-high slits ensuring that she would have no problem gliding across the stage as she introduced the collection of hopefuls for the beauty pageant.

"We should do this every week," she said breathlessly, and I laughed as the Devil grinned. She couldn't stay with us long, of course, but she squeezed my hand.

"You've been to the office, right?" she asked. I looked at her, surprised.

"No, why?"

"Oh!" She flapped her hands at me, white fingernail polish gleaming bright. "No worries, no worries, Mrs. French is holding down the fort, so it's all good. Gotta fly!"

She hurried off, her long stride eating up the carpeted runway, and two tuxedoed ushers greeted her partway, then whisked her toward the main stage. The Devil and I followed right behind, until we found ourselves, as promised, ensconced at a table near the front.

I turned to him, immediately suspicious. "What's happened? I was only gone a couple of days, and I didn't have time to hit the office today. What was Nikki talking about? Have there been more calls for Justice?"

He shrugged. "There will always be new calls for your assistance. Mrs. French and Nikki have been working quite closely of late, so if she says it's handled, it's handled."

"Um...they've been what?" It wasn't that Nikki and Mrs. French had a bad relationship, but they weren't natural friends. Nikki was wild, flamboyant, and outspoken and Mrs. French looked exactly like what you'd expect from a Victorian-era librarian. Granted, they did work well together, so...

I felt a shiver of unease about what might be waiting for me back at Justice Hall, coupled with the all too familiar surge of dread that had been hanging around since Pompeii. I didn't have much time to think about it, however, as the party got underway in earnest. Just as Nikki took the stage, two other figures arrived beside us. I looked up, then jolted with recognition.

"Sariah?"

"*Sara?*" If anything, my alter ego, worse half...whatever you wanted to call her...stared back at me with equal surprise, scanning my gown with something approaching shock. Once upon a time, Sariah and I had occupied the same body, as the same person, until a teenage trauma had created a schism in my psyche so profound, it had generated two separate, thinking, wholly irrational beings. The ultimate in unblended families. I liked to think I'd gotten the better end of the deal, but there was something about Sariah...

Now she grinned, looking over at the Devil. "You dressed her, didn't you?" she accused. "There's no way she would've picked silver sequins out on her own."

"Hey," I protested as my look-alike twisted sister slid into the chair next to me, her date on the other side. Her date who was smirking. I scowled at him. "You know, just because you decided to run a brush through your hair, you don't actually deserve a medal."

"I do what I can." Detective Brody Rooks of the Las

Vegas Metropolitan Police Department leaned back in his chair, accepting the beer handed to him by a server who seemed to materialize out of nowhere. While Brody was wearing a suit, it was only a notch or two above his usual beat-up big-box-store model, this one in an indeterminate shade of gray. Granted, it was far nicer than his usual outfits of indeterminate brown, so I glanced with more than a little interest between him and Sariah. The two of them had dated for a short while not all that long ago, but then their relationship had cooled. Had something happened to rekindle it?

Sariah narrowed her eyes at me. "You might as well come right out and ask it. It's written all over your face," she said, twisting in her own chair as a glass of scotch was set down in front of her. I blinked in surprise at the drink. I didn't really know what Sariah favored on a regular basis, but today, it was almost as if she was going out of her way to be my doppelgänger. Instead of her usual somewhat goth attire—she favored a lot of black, a lot of leather, and a lot of silver jewelry—today she wore a slightly dressier version of my usual hoodie, the sleek black satin material somehow managing to work with her jet-black jeans and dark leather boots. She had on a slinky silver tank top and no jewelry except for a shot of silver at each of her ears. Her hair was styled back in a low ponytail, and I suddenly found myself wishing that I wasn't the one in the glitter-ball dress. I didn't know what to say exactly, because the questions crowding my mind were all completely inappropriate—first and foremost, *why are you dressed like me if you're out on a date with Brody?*

Instead, I managed something equally awkward. Because I have a gift.

"So have you guys been dating long? And since when, exactly?"

Sariah grinned as Brody choked on his beer.

"Well, you could just cut right to the chase," he muttered, but Sariah leaned forward, apparently happy to field the question. "Very recently, and we're doing quite well, thank you. We're not even gonna be staying forever at this place, but we wanted to put in an appearance to support Nikki. Then there's the fact that *she* said you were going to wear a dress, which, frankly, I had to see. And maybe make fun of you a little bit."

Despite myself, I reached out and touched the edge of her slinky jacket. "I don't suppose you'd mind switching clothes?"

"I think I should be offended," the Devil protested. "I happen to think you're extremely well-dressed for your position at this gathering. And given that the detective and Ms. Pelter plan on leaving this establishment on a motorcycle, she should be commended as well. You, however, have certain standards to uphold."

I frowned at him. "I do?"

"You're here as the special guest of the emcee of events, and there's the small matter of your official date for this evening, a former head of the Arcana Council, who rarely gets to see you in a dress."

"Yes, but he's not here. He's up there helping her, and—"

"Trust me, I see you."

The words sounded in my mind, but it was the sudden hushed expression of wonder that slid across the audience that clued me in that the Magician was somewhere close. As Kreios chuckled and turned to the front of the room, I did the same.

Armaeus stood by Nikki's side, resplendent in a custom

black tuxedo with long tails, his perfectly tied cravat adding an air of Old World grace to the ensemble. And he'd come to the party with favors as well. A gentle glow surrounded him and Nikki, then shot out to the left and right to illuminate torches ringing the center stage.

To the casual observer, it looked like an impressive act of pyrotechnics, but I knew differently. This was pure Armaeus, putting on a show to make Nikki look good. He succeeded too. Nikki began the introductions of the night's event, and with the arrival of each new contestant on the stage, dressed to kill in stunning evening wear, the special effects continued. Birds fluttered, fire danced, butterflies swarmed, and starry lights flickered throughout the room, depending on the theme of each of the new contestants.

"Why are they starting out with evening wear?" Brody asked, taking another pull on his beer. "Isn't that the final category?"

"Not at this competition," the Devil explained. "Evening wear is where this party gets started. The contestants will cycle through to athletic and casual wear, then finish the night with ballroom formals. If you think their dresses now are something to see, you'll need to stick around for that."

To my surprise, Sariah reached out and laid a hand on Brody's forearm. He jumped as well, which also intrigued me. "I suspect we may be on our way by then," she said, her voice low and a little dangerous. "See what trouble we can get into."

Okay...

At that moment, the prerecorded packages for each of the contestants kicked in, and sound filled the space. Sound and increasing levels of applause as each new contestant was able to share a little bit more about the circumstances that brought them to the stage this night.

While that went on, a blushing, dazzling Nikki was escorted off the stage by Armaeus and returned to us.

"Please tell me you have booze," she declared when she reached our table and slid into the chair opposite me. Armaeus took the seat next to her, his eyes glittering as he regarded me. We all leaned forward, and for the next five minutes, Nikki chattered as happily as I had ever seen her, regaling us with every detail of the event, every new surprise that the Magician had been able to conjure—quite literally —on her behalf. When she paused to take a breath, Sariah leaned forward.

"So we're headed out probably between athletic wear and the gala categories," Sariah said, her voice carrying a slight edge. "You guys got any good recommendations of where we should go?"

"On the Strip or off it?" Nikki asked immediately, but Brody raised his hands.

"Yo, I'm not in the mood to have my every action recorded for Las Vegas's finest, thanks. I was thinking we could hit the road, head out of town a ways." He shrugged, suddenly looking embarrassed. "Something."

Sariah grinned at him, then slanted a glance back to me. "Wasn't there a new casino up on the lake near Henderson?" she asked. "You've been up there, right?"

The Devil leaned forward a fraction, focusing on her face, but I frowned. "Yeah, there was a case last—whatever, it doesn't matter. But why go out of your way just to hit a casino?" I asked. "You've got like a billion of them within a five-minute drive."

Sariah snorted, but I could see her mind was made up. They were headed out of town—somewhere. Anywhere. And maybe that was for the best. She deserved to feel the wind in her hair. She, more than most, deserved to be free.

Either way, within a few short minutes, I found myself once more tucked between the Devil and the Magician. Talk about being caught between a rock and a hard place.

"An apt description, I would agree." The Devil smiled.

I rolled my eyes. It was going to be a long night.

6

The pageant was an unqualified success. To my surprise, a remarkable number of tourists had joined the audience and now jammed the tables, surprised and delighted with each new performance. The winner received her trophy, local modeling contract, and cash prize shortly before midnight, while wearing an extravagant gown of feathers lifted by an unseen breeze, a true angel walking amid the crowd. So overcome with her success, she belted out an a capella version of *Hallelujah* that brought the house down.

Kreios disappeared sometime during the final act to address issues only the Devil could be bothered with at midnight in Las Vegas, which left me alone with Armaeus, basking in the reflected joy of Nikki on stage.

"If it were any other person, I would say she's wasted in her supporting role with the Council," he said, his dark eyes tracking her across the stage. "But I couldn't imagine life without her."

I glanced at him, surprised to hear him echo my own unformed thoughts. My heart tugged a little, and he turned toward me, a gentle smile softening his lips. "You could say arguably that I've known Nikki Dawes longer than I've known you, even before my memories of you were taken from me. She's one of the reasons the fight to keep humanity protected from the Shadow Court weighs so heavily on my heart. She's a masterpiece."

"She's certainly that," I agreed. He reached for my hand, then stood and drew me away from the table. "I understand you need to return to Justice Hall. It's a fine night for a walk."

I stopped short of agreeing with him on that score, but I didn't mind the walk. My nerves were winding tighter and tighter, and I didn't know why. A walk would relax me—and refocus me too.

We exited into the cool desert night, the Strip lit up for our pleasure, the rush of crowds and traffic and noise a soothing balm. As we hit the pavement, Armaeus's grasp on my hand grew tighter, and he tucked me up close beside him, as if he didn't want even the slightest whisper of separation between us.

"The Devil chose well in your attire tonight, Miss Wilde, but you should know there's never once been a moment when I've looked at you and not been utterly destroyed by your beauty, your power, and your truth. Decorate the window however it pleases you, I wish only that I should be allowed a glimpse inside."

"Ah...what?" The statement was so unexpected and fraught with emotion that I blinked rapidly, glancing sharply up to search Armaeus's face. "Is something wrong? Did something happen?"

The Magician smiled—a little grimly, I thought—but he didn't meet my gaze. "We are so quick to assume the worst, aren't we? But no, or should I say, nothing more than what we already know. There is a pressure building. I can feel it in my bones. I can sense it in the air around us. The battle presses down, eager to be begun."

My heart tugged again, this time with fear. That didn't sound good, but it was exactly the same thing I was feeling. An apprehension— almost anxiety. Like a bullet had just been snapped into a chamber, only I didn't know where the gun was. "What kind of battle?" I asked warily.

"You asked what messages had come in through Justice Hall. I had the opportunity to query Nikki on the matter during our time together tonight."

Something about his voice made me quirk my brow. "Query?" I asked skeptically.

His soft laugh was whisked away on the shifting breeze. "Perhaps query is a looser interpretation than some might give it. But her thoughts were clear on the matter. The cries of the Connected are growing. Not just those involved in the demonstration in Pompeii. There are agents of the Shadow Court appearing throughout the world, identifiable only insofar as they are ghosts. They appear long enough to be remembered as a stranger in the midst of the communities they damage, then vanish just as quickly. Wherever they walk, destruction follows. Not always death, though certainly there's that, but fires set to homes, communities plagued with sickness. An instability is growing in the Connected world, and with it, fear. Worry. Panic. The pattern of disruption is so exquisitely woven as to seem almost random, but it's not. It's more like a spider's web that has been strung round and round, built from the outside in.

"Then we should torch that net," I said, my voice harder than I intended.

"It's perhaps not quite as easy as that," he countered. "Where there is fire, there is smoke and light. We will be seen. That is the nature of the trap the Shadow Court is setting, I suspect."

I understood in a flash what he meant. The Shadow Court was upping its game by striking hidden-away communities of Connected where no one was looking. Even if we had the best of intentions, if we were to go after them, rout them, we would be noticed. A violent accident in the heart of New York City might be something easily missed, but a conflagration on the open plains would be noticed for miles around.

Who was actually behind the Shadow Court? How had they managed to operate in secrecy for so long? They'd have to have powers almost equal to the Council's...but how could they, without the Council knowing about it?

I mulled over Armaeus's words as we continued up the Strip, passing through a sea of freshly updated casinos until we reached the mainstays that anchored the north end: Treasure Island, the Venetian, and the Palazzo. Only then did I glance up to see what so few of the travelers in the city ever could. The shadow residences that soared above the flashy casinos, viewable only by the strongest of Connected. The huge white tower over Treasure Island had been my first introduction to the Arcana Council when I first arrived in Las Vegas. It now was home to the Hierophant, the Archangel Michael—his very own ivory tower. As I turned and scanned back down the Strip, I could see the other domains as well. The glittering peaks of Simon's home above the Bellagio, the swirling lava-lamp skyscraper that the Devil called his home above the Flamingo. Even the black monolithic tower of the Emperor that shot sky-high above the Paris casino.

And then far at the end, the fairy-tale home of the Hermit, a tiny cabin perched atop a slender column, floating in the sky above Excalibur. It was dwarfed by the immense edifice behind it, Prime Luxe, the Magician's stronghold. A million turrets of glass, stone, and steel, each time grander than the last I'd looked at it. Now it flared brightly under my scrutiny, and I slid Armaeus a glance. "Have you done some remodeling?"

He lifted a brow. "Do you know how rare it is for me to get the High Priestess to leave Prime Luxe?"

I burst out laughing and turned back toward the Palazzo, where my own residence stretched high above the penthouse apartments I held there. Justice Hall. All marble archways and long columns, like its cartoon counterpart, because I really hadn't had the time or energy to care how it appeared to anyone else. I didn't know when I would.

Armaeus took my hand and drew it to his mouth, brushing a soft kiss across the fingertips. Once again, I couldn't shake the almost melancholy air to the gesture.

"You okay?" I asked, peering at him.

He didn't meet my gaze exactly, lifting his eyes instead to the wonder of the Strip. "I feel that we need another lifetime to learn all there is to know about each other to my satisfaction," he murmured, almost as if he were talking to himself. "I worry we will not be given that lifetime."

Another sliver of doubt twisted through me.

"You know, *worry* is kind of a strong word coming from you. Just FYI," I informed him, but Armaeus didn't respond to that. Instead, he walked with me up the stairs to the entrance of the Palazzo, nodding at the doorman, who straightened immediately. A definite flash of recognition flared across the man's face, and I thought about that too. Everyone knew Armaeus in this place. I suppose they knew me as well, but as what, exactly? Who was I to them? Someone with power, ability? Could they sense that? Or was

I simply another eccentric resident, the crazy lady in the penthouse?

"You feel it, too," Armaeus said as we moved past the elegant registration area and toward the glittering casino. "A building pressure. It will grow stronger yet as you review the requests for assistance that have come into Justice Hall, or that is what Nikki believes. Consider carefully what you decide to do."

I squinted at him. "Don't you mean what we *all* decide to do? As the Council?"

He continued as if I hadn't spoken, once more glancing away. "Or perhaps better stated, what you and I do together. Yes, yes, certainly that." He sighed. "I have much still to learn of the challenges that await us. Much I need to study."

We turned toward the elevators that led to Justice Hall. "No, seriously," I said again, reaching out to punch the button to take me to the top floor of the casino. "Don't you mean the Council as a whole?"

There was no response beside me, and I glanced back. Armaeus was gone.

"Goddammit," I muttered. "I hate when you do that."

"I am never truly far from you, Miss Wilde," Armaeus murmured in my mind. *"Know that above all other things."*

"Yeah, yeah." I sighed as I stepped into the elevator. The doors slid shut, and I could no longer feel the Magician's presence in my mind. So much for him never being far away.

"What is this thing lined with, kryptonite?" I muttered as the elevator whisked me upward. There was no one waiting for me on the top floor, and I picked up the thick silver cloth of my dress with some irritation, the garment seeming way too heavy all of a sudden. I moved down the hallway, aiming for the door at the far end of the corridor, the entryway to Justice Hall.

I'd only gotten a few feet down the hallway when a door far up and to the right opened. A well-dressed man and woman stepped out, quiet money oozing from their pores. I slowed my pace, my nerves pricking to full alert. I had never asked for the top floor of the Palazzo to remain empty. It had just always worked out that way. But who were these people? Why were they here? They were heading directly toward me, then looked up as if surprised they weren't alone in the corridor. Then they stopped cold at the sight of me, the man clapping his hands together in apparent relief.

"Justice *Wilde*," he said, his voice sounding familiar, but too high, too excited. The woman beside him went pale with what seemed to be shock.

"Ahh..." I said helpfully.

"Justice Wilde," the man said again, his words picking up speed. Now he was practically wringing his hands. "You must help us. I never thought—I couldn't have *dreamed* to be able to see you in person, but we are being *overrun*. Our people are dying, slaughtered at the hands of the Shadow Court. You must help us."

"Who are you?" I countered, trying to place him. "Who's hurting you? Have you been to see Mrs.—"

I gestured farther up the corridor, then glanced back to the couple, and that was when I saw it. The man's eyes suddenly turned black and then red, the woman's beside him as well. They weren't human, not even Possessed humans. They were demons. And they were blocking my way to Justice Hall.

This time, I didn't screw around.

"*Warrick!*" I shouted, as my hands went wide, and the human face stretched into a horrible grimace as the demon impersonating the man realized the game was up. A second later, four other doors along the corridor flew open, and a dozen creatures rushed out, each more hideous than the last —these weren't Possessed, these were full-on demons. Long, scaly arms that ended in paws tipped with bloody talons, pale skin covered in lesions, animalistic faces that I would *never* be able to unsee.

"Warrick!" I roared again, summoning the head of the demon enforcers, the elite fighting unit directed by the Hierophant. Demons themselves, the Syx had agreed to work for Michael the Archangel to atone for their sins, though they certainly had found themselves in other types of trouble during their six millennia of existence. Recently, with the new onslaught of demons overrunning Earth, their work had stepped up tenfold, and the archangel had given each of them a path to true and final redemption. None of that changed the fact that they were primarily a kick-ass demon-killing squad. One that was being decidedly slow at the moment. "*Now* would be good."

Beside me, the air went tight and a second later, the body of an immense man appeared, tall and burly, with rough, weathered skin, dark hair, and golden eyes. He looked around and cursed in a language so ancient, even I couldn't interpret it at first. Then it was his turn to shout out.

"Stefan," he snapped. "Finn."

Two more figures appeared at either end of the corridor, but I barely registered them as the creatures nearest me struck.

The first demon lurched forward and ripped my dress below the waist, shredding the material. If he hadn't already been covered in thick black goop, I would've kissed him for giving me more freedom to move in my party gown. As it was, I simply sent him hurtling to one side with a fireball to the chest, right into Warrick's waiting arms, where he happily dispatched the creature back beyond the veil.

And then the fight was on—brief, but strangely gratifying. Fortunately, the first two humans who'd stopped me in the hallway hadn't been humans at all—not even Possessed—and Warrick was able to knock them to oblivion with two powerful roundhouse punches. Since humans couldn't kill demons, even humans as powerful as me, I focused on being the least amount of nuisance I could be, serving as an occasional redirect with a well-placed kick or fireball. The demons went down with howls of fury and dismay, but they fought mindlessly, as if they were cannon fodder and not thinking, rational creatures. Granted, they were demons, but most had at least a semblance of coherence to them. Not these. Within a matter of a few minutes, only four figures remained standing. Myself and the demon enforcers.

Warrick, straightening and shaking the last bit of gore from his arms, grinned at me, though his eyes held a gleam of worry.

"They had to know they would fail," he said.

I grimaced. "Something was off, yeah."

He wiped a broad hand over his chin. "There has been a great disruption with the demons of the Middle East. Whispers of the djinn."

"The what?" I asked. The way he spoke the word, images of *A Thousand and One Arabian Nights* sprang to mind, Aladdin and his magic lamp. All very picturesque, except with the Shadow Court supposedly setting up shop in Dubai, I wasn't feeling too good about the idea. Besides, I knew that djinn weren't really a thing, at least not a different thing. "I thought you guys were djinn."

Warrick curled his lip. "Not hardly."

"But—" I frowned, struggling to remember back to

when I'd first met the Syx, and how. The Emperor of the Arcana Council had co-opted them as his own personal band of bad guys, and the results...weren't pretty. "Several members of the Council called you that, I'm almost sure of it. You know, back...before."

He snorted. "Back before, when we were temporarily trapped by the Emperor's hand in a bolt-hole of his making, along with the children he'd stolen away from this world? Very convenient of the Hierophant to remain silent during all that. But whatever the Council believes we were—or are —has little to do with fact. We definitely aren't djinn, and neither are these creatures. Djinn were not formed of sin and malice, but of the darkness between night and day."

"Oh. Sure." I sighed. "I suppose they're also super powerful?"

"They can be. What's more, the creatures we just dispatched stank of a compulsion spell I'm not familiar with. That, combined with murmurs of the ancient ones, doesn't bode well. Demons throughout the Middle East and into Africa are stirring with a call to arms we can't ignore. War is coming faster than we might want."

I made a face, then sent more of the demon gore flying with an angry flick of my fingers, fire sizzling down the long, ropey lines. "What *is* it with all the war talk? The last time we had a war, we ended up with a whole bunch more of you guys than we could handle. I'm not really in the mood for another demon orgy."

Finn chuckled as he gazed down the hall, staring at the river of black goop. "You'll have a hell of a cleaning bill if this keeps up," he agreed.

"Well, what we want and what is are rarely the same," Warrick said. "You know where to find us."

I nodded, and the three demons disappeared.

Picking my way around the remaining puddles of gore, I'd almost made it to the doorway of Justice Hall when the elevator opened at the far end of the corridor.

I whirled around, bracing myself—then froze.

"Sweet baby Jesus on a biscuit," Nikki wailed. "Why do I always miss all the *fun*?"

7

Rather than sacrifice her platform boots, Nikki shed her footwear and picked her way along the corridor, mostly avoiding the worst stretches of black goop. Her blonde hair bounced in perfect ringlets over her shoulders, and she couldn't stop grinning. Not even slogging her way through demon blood could dim her good mood.

"Was it fantastic? Did you love it? Was it everything that you expected?" she demanded, and I had to laugh.

"It was extraordinary, and you were extraordinary. It was impossible not to love it."

"I think so, too." She reached me as I paused in front of the door to Justice Hall. "They're already talking about doing it again next year, and begged me to be a part of it. I told them I was flattered, natch, but I couldn't commit. There was no *end* of VIP producers in the audience, though. And there's no telling how high my profile soared." She drew in a long, satisfied breath, then grinned at me. "Not that I plan on going anywhere, dollface. I leave you alone for twenty minutes, and you're covered in demon goop."

"I try."

I reached for the door, but it swung open before I had a chance to touch the panel. A stern-faced Mrs. French peered at us with a decidedly impatient scowl.

"Well, come in, then, come in! You can't expect a body to wait here all day for you. It was bad enough that I thought it prudent not to come out during the little hallway party you arranged, Justice Wilde, but I can't ignore you both talking right outside the door." She peered beyond us to the corridor. "I'll thank the Council for cleaning that up right quick as well. Who do I need to call?"

I glanced back, flicking open my third eye. A shimmering, radiant energy was already crackling through the blood and gore left behind by the demons. Sometimes that gore lingered in a place, a testament to the battle fought. But it wouldn't last long here or I'd be having words with the archangel, and he well knew it. Fortunately, Michael was nothing if not tidy.

"It's handled," I said. "Give it a half hour, maybe."

"Good. Come on, then." Mrs. French drew herself up to her full height, which was still considerably petite, her hair swept up into a bun on top of her head and her black buckled boots adding a half dozen inches to her frame. She needed every one of them.

What she lacked in size, though, she made up for in presence. Today's outfit was in line with most of her Victorian-era garb, a button-down dress with a frowsy ruffle of lace at the collar and hem, and heavy skirts in a deep charcoal gray, the line of pewter buttons down her bodice gleaming as she ushered us inside. The dress had a modest bustle and skirts that swished when she walked, which, along with the clicking of her bootheels, made for a surprisingly relaxing cadence as she stepped briskly through the outer office. She gestured us to the couch and chairs set up with a light tea service.

Nikki looked at the setup with marked alarm. "You don't actually expect me to drink *tea*, do you? It's one o'clock in the morning."

"I can think of no better time to drink tea than in the middle of the night, after all the excitement and exertion you've experienced," Mrs. French said tartly. Then her mouth slipped into a smile. "But you'll find the tea set is just for show. There are cut crystal glasses and a flagon just behind the pot and bourbon by the table. I just wanted to have a bit of fun, is all. I'll be right back."

"You're good people, French Tart, I don't care what they say." Nikki tossed her boots down on the couch and sat, reaching down for the bourbon.

I hesitated, my gaze sweeping the room, unease bubbling up again. The office looked much the way it usually did, with its conversational arrangement of chairs and couch in addition to Mrs. French's reception desk. But the two doorways at each end of the back wall were both standing open, which was unusual. One door led to my office and its innumerable canisters, each containing messages I needed to respond to, complaints issued by Connecteds about other psychics behaving badly. That door generally remained open unless we had guests in the outer office, since my inner sanctum remained in a near-constant state of disarray.

But the library door rarely stood open, even when it was just me and Mrs. French in the office. As the repository of all the unresolved cases lobbied by Connecteds since the office of Justice was formed, it arguably should be a relatively small room.

It wasn't. Rows upon rows of shelves, all lined with cases,

boxes, books, and scrolls, filled the many chambers of the Justice Hall library, a building that seemed to go on to infinity. I'd never actually seen a back wall to the place, though I was sure there was one. Somewhere.

When I first ascended to the position of Justice, I'd pledged to start sorting through all those unresolved cases, at least a few at a time, but the events of recent months had made that nearly impossible. The library still served a purpose, providing background research as needed, but I couldn't deny experiencing a sinking feeling as I glanced its way. So many calls for Justice had gone unanswered over the centuries. How well was I using the power of my position? Not very well, I feared.

Mrs. French hurried back into the room a moment later, her arms overflowing with canisters, and I grimaced. At least it wasn't for lack of trying to keep on top of the workload. I could only do so much.

"Told you it's been busy," Nikki said, toasting the stack of canisters with her glass of bourbon. "Mrs. French here has been taking a new approach to sorting them, though. Which is why you're going to see the process from start to finish."

"I can explain my process myself, thank you very much." Mrs. French sniffed. She squared her shoulders as if preparing to do battle and turned to me.

I pursed my lips. "You came up with a new organizational strategy? Why?"

"It wasn't even so much my idea," she confessed, a faint blush scoring her cheeks. "It was the boys'. They'd been taking down one of the old shelves that'd inexplicably caved under the weight of its contents. In the midst of transferring the old cases to a more stable home, they discovered something quite curious. There are *several* shelves that have recently broken."

"Several?" I frowned. "Why? How?"

"As to why, I consulted with the Magician, and he contends that it has much to do with your advancing abilities and responsibilities as Justice. As you have taken on a greater sense of direction regarding the duties of your office, the contents of Justice Hall have shifted. Almost like it's trying to catch your attention."

"Okay," I allowed, rolling that idea around in my head. It wasn't unreasonable. It was a room filled with requests from unhappy psychics. Some of those psychics were undoubtedly stronger than others and could be willing to throw their weight around to get noticed. "So what cases are making a fuss? Are there any similarities?"

I eyed the canisters she was stacking on the table. I picked up nothing unique or interesting about them, only the vague sense of power that attended anything imbued with Connected energy. I flicked open my third eye and saw a slight change, a leap in energy, but only slight.

"You're looking at these canisters with some level of concern," Mrs. French said. "And rightly so. It's not that the problems contained within don't merit our consideration. They most assuredly do. But I've brought them out to set the baseline. Because then we've got canisters like these."

She pulled a new canister out from the folds of her gown, and all three of my eyes blinked. This one not only glowed, it pulsed with an erratic, frantic rhythm, a schizophrenic rat-a-tat-tat so bright, I almost imagined it making a sound. "What is that, Morse code?"

Beside me, Nikki snorted. "That was my first thought, too. We tested it out. But no go. The thing just has a serious case of the shakes."

I looked back with some trepidation at the open door to

Justice Hall's library. "And there are more in there like that? How many more?"

"At last count, there were a good three dozen cases, canisters, and scrolls that generated their own unique activity, some more violently than others."

I finally caught up to her words. In addition to Mrs. French, the library was staffed by a team of misplaced youths who'd been subject to a Connected experiment conducted in the mid-1800s. As a result, up until quite recently, they hadn't aged—our very own staff of lost boys. I thought of their bright, eager faces, their mischievous smiles and laughing eyes, and my stomach tightened. "You said they shook so hard that they knocked down their shelves? Was anybody hurt?"

Mrs. French laughed. "Oh no. If anything, the boys found it the height of hilarity to determine which of them could recognize a case about to go so they could wrangle the beast to the ground. Some of the cases continued to shake, mind you. Quite energetically, even after we had them all corralled. But the majority of them actually seemed to become somewhat mollified once they were joined with their fellows. As if they had been waiting all this time to be sorted, and now they could rest."

"Except for the fact that they hadn't been gyrating up to this point, that would make for a really neat explanation," Nikki put in. "Regardless, what we found going through both the cold cases from Justice Hall plus these new requests is a surprising through line. They all deal with demon attacks."

My brows went up. "Demons? Have you notified the Council? Does the Hierophant know?"

"Not yet," Mrs. French said primly. "I didn't feel that we had sufficient information to get the Council involved, and I certainly didn't want them looking around when you weren't here to keep an eye on them. I don't trust any of that lot, not at all."

She said this last with a huff, and I bit my lip, casting a surreptitious glance at her. Mrs. French had been serving the office of Justice for more than a hundred and fifty years, with her first charge, Abigail Strand, having ascended to the position in quite challenging circumstances. To make matters worse, Abigail didn't survive the position long. As in, she didn't survive at all. The young woman had proven an easy target for agents of the Shadow Court, and the other members of the Council—including Armaeus—hadn't understood the danger she was in until it was too late. Mrs. French had a long and justified distrust of the Council.

"Fair enough," I allowed. "So you've identified that they're all related to demon attacks. Anything else?"

"Not just demons," she said proudly. "Specifically, djinn."

"Oh, really." I straightened. "That's the second time I've heard that term in the last half hour. I'm not exactly up on my djinn history. Apparently, I should be."

"I believe you should, indeed," Mrs. French said, lifting her chin like a schoolmarm, complete with a shake of her skirts. "You'll be happy to know, then, that I've done my research. The djinn are demons, no question, but they are specific to Arabian and later Islamic mythology. They can take many forms, including human. You don't hear about them much in the Western world. They also have a slightly different approach to their beliefs. They accept the existence of God, and they are not innately evil or good. Many believe they are simply unmoored spirits, but that's too narrow a definition. There's some suggestion that they were grandfathered into Islamic beliefs, as opposed to being a direct creation of Islam, but basically the term 'djinn' serves as an umbrella designation for any supernatural creature that is generally held responsible for misfortune, possession, or disease. There are some djinn that are good, but the majority are meant to cause humanity chaos and distress."

I thought about the curtain of smoke that had blown up over the parapet at the amphitheater of Pompeii, and the bird bats that had followed. Then there'd been the demon Rockettes that had tried to keep me from the stage, also curtained in smoke. But none of those creatures had seemed cool enough to be djinn. I remembered the sentience I'd felt, the formless watcher... Could that have been a djinn? "Are they invisible?"

"Oh my, no." Mrs. French shook her head. "Though, to be fair, they almost always work in mist and smoke. It's where the whole mythology of Aladdin's lamp came from. Genie, djinn. Same thing."

Nikki turned to me, her eyes wide over her glass. "You fought straight-up genies? Were they large and blue and funnier than they had any reason to be?"

I shook my head. "No, and if they were there, they didn't talk much. I got the sense of something in the smoke, but then I got a little bit distracted by the fact their...uh... mascots or whatever were chomping on me as I tried to reach Eshe." I winced at the memory. "Not a good experience."

"Mascots? I'll have to check on that, but it's entirely possible they employ subservient creatures," Mrs. French said. "Another attribute of the djinn is that they are considered to be guardians. The guardians of what, it's uncertain."

Nikki drained her glass. "Well, I've played enough video games to know that djinn are bad news, and they also can be compelled, much like a regular demon, to perform on behalf of powerful sorcerers. Nobody would accuse ol' Jarvis of being all that magical, but the dude definitely has connections." She looked at me. "You think the Shadow Court has got their own djinn?"

"I think they may well want us to believe that. But now you're telling me we've got an entire subgroup of past and present cases that are doing the jig related to demons from the Arabian Peninsula, maybe these djinn things. I don't have a good feeling about this."

"I don't either, especially since the more recent concerns regarding these attacks also had another line of connection, which I'm afraid I haven't been able to share with you yet either, Ms. Dawes..." Mrs. French sighed.

Nikki snorted. "It's okay, sugar plum, I've been a little distracted over the past few days. But you've got me liquored up now, so hit me."

Mrs. French smiled a little tightly. "There is a member of the Council who has been involved in some of these complaints. I know it is not our protocol to prosecute members of the Council, or even hold them accountable for transgressions against the Connected, though I'm aware that it happens, of course."

I grimaced. Council transgressions against innocent Connecteds had been directly responsible for Abigail's involvement with the Shadow Court a hundred and fifty years ago. I was starting to get a headache.

Apparently, Nikki was too, or could sense my growing tension.

"Well, go ahead and spit it out," she said. "Was it the Magician? And do you know if he remembers it?"

"Oh no," Mrs. French said, her eyes going wide. "No, no, it's not the Magician, or the Devil, though you would ordinarily think that, given the connection to the demons. Or, arguably, the Hierophant would make sense as he is in control of the Syx and therefore would have—"

"Mrs. French," I interrupted as gently as I could. "You don't need to tell us everyone it doesn't involve. Who *does* it involve?"

"Me."

The voice was harsh and direct, autocratic without being sophisticated, and it was quite definitely feminine. It preceded its owner through the door from Justice Library, and Mrs. French burst to her feet.

"You're not allowed in there! No member of the Council is."

Judgment of the Arcana Council stepped through the door, dressed in her usual garb of a vaguely military-esque long-sleeved shirt and heavy pants, heavy boots, and heavy attitude. Her black hair was pulled back in a thick braid, and her lean, weathered face, with its hint of Israeli heritage in her eyes and skin, evinced not even a shred of dismay at her trespass.

She gave Mrs. French a thin smile. "Yes, well, those rules were made before I was on the Council. And I would like to believe that Abigail Strand doesn't have as many tricks up her sleeve as I do, and also quite a bit fewer balls in the air. In short—"

I finished for her. "You do what you want."

She nodded at me, her expression becoming a shade grimmer. "Exactly. If you don't use the power that you have in this world, you lose it."

A snatch of an old song played through my mind, the tune hauntingly soft, but my attention refocused abruptly as Mrs. French turned sharply on Gamon. "Well, that's all well and good, but how do you explain the complaints leveled against your house?"

"Ex-house," Gamon pointed out. "And I'm aware of them. They've stepped out of bounds, running roughshod over the arcane black market supply chain, and harming innocents in the process. It happens."

"It happens," Mrs. French steamed. "It *happens*? And I suppose it also happens that long before you ever ascended to the Council, you yourself summoned a *demon* to suppress the people of southern India and the Indonesian islands to get what you want?"

"You what?" I asked, genuinely surprised as Nikki reached for more bourbon. "When?"

Gamon shrugged. "A long time ago. But sure. I did use those things. I contracted with a midlevel witch to summon a demon, a very convincing one, I might add, to scare the shit out of the local population. They were mining a particular brand of deep green jade that sold for astronomical prices on the arcane black market. Jade that I needed more than they did."

She slanted a glance at me. "If you'd been in the game at the time, it's exactly the kind of thing you would've gotten word of, and you would've been a real pain in the ass. Fortunately, you were still a baby, so it was a lot easier for me to get things done. And Justice was still MIA, so I didn't have to deal with any oversight. Win-win."

Mrs. French huffed, but I merely studied Gamon. "So why are you here now?"

"For two reasons. The first, you sent six dozen or so flapping, squalling creatures to my front doorstep earlier this week, and I wanted to thank you for that inconvenience in person. They're screeching lunatics with brains the size of pebbles. What exactly did you expect me to do with them?"

I couldn't help it, I smiled. "What *did* you do with them?"

"Let's just say I found them a good home that wasn't

mine. Secondly, there's been enough swell of chatter in a few of my old stomping grounds that it makes me nervous. Old magic stirring. Really old magic, the kind that people don't fully understand. The kind that was created when life was a lot cheaper than it is now. I thought you should know, and beyond that, I decided to poke around."

"In my library. Uninvited."

"Which shouldn't even be allowed," Mrs. French added darkly.

"Yeah, well, be glad I did. I found a few things I wasn't expecting. Namely, these djinn sightings aren't new. They've been on the rise for a while, but suppressed."

"Suppressed by whom—or what?" I asked. "The Council?"

"Nope." She flashed me a hard look. "The houses."

"What?" That stopped me in my tracks. The houses of magic had a long and twisted relationship with the Council, but they generally spent more time skimming money off magic, not meddling in the true depths of the arcane. I'd had a passing experience with house management, and nothing I'd seen during my time in the trenches had changed my mind about that. "We didn't have anything to do with the djinn at the House of Swords," I said.

She shrugged. "When I took over Cups, they already had an ongoing relationship with them. I kept it in place. Any complaints arising from that—and there were some—I quashed before they became a problem."

"Yes, well." Mrs. French sniffed. "Quashing was rather one of your specialties."

Gamon grinned at her. "You're not wrong. Apparently, I wasn't the only one. But I did tangle with some bad mojo once, well before my time with the Cups. Armaeus was the one who helped me out of that jam. He'll know more than anyone how you should proceed now."

"Really?" I scowled. Armaeus had said he was going to do research, and I assumed it was research on the Shadow Court. But now I got the distinct impression he was holding out on me. What was going on?

"So explain to me about the houses," I said to Gamon. "Why are they suppressing djinn reports?"

"In a word? Access. Djinn magic isn't tracked by the Council, especially the Hierophant and his merry troop of Syx, and it's far less challenging than trying to force demons to heel. That makes it very appealing."

"But I was there—"

"The Swords weren't much for it, at least during your time. Your predecessor at the House of Swords, a different story. The Cups, though—yes. The House of Pentacles too."

I thought of the jittery, avaricious Frenchman who headed the House of Pentacles as Gamon continued.

"Wands were kind of out of it, because they didn't exist for a hella long time," Gamon continued. "But now they're back. And they'll use whatever they can get ahold of."

"Well, that's just great." I looked to Mrs. French. "Are we getting a lot of complaints about the djinn, then? From the Arabian Peninsula, anyway?"

"Yes...but that's not all we're getting." She pulled one of the canisters free and handed it to me, the curved glass door hanging open. Nestled inside was an envelope of creamy paper, embossed with a symbol I didn't recognize, an Arabic-looking fiery sun, with Arabic lettering in the center. I took the card out, turning it over in my hand. There was no writing on it.

"What's this?" I asked.

"That would apparently be an invitation," Nikki said. "From one Sheikh Alsain Ahmad. You remember him?"

My brows shot up, the image of a primly dressed American woman I'd recently met in New Orleans flashing into my mind. We'd been trying desperately to stop the Shadow Court from targeting unsuspecting Connecteds with poisoned disaster relief materials, and she'd sought me out after the dust had cleared. She'd told me she was the representative of a sheikh who'd wanted to make my acquaintance—and then I'd never heard from her again. That had been weeks ago. "He's Connected."

"In more ways than one," Nikki said. "He's not only got a shack in Bahrain, but outside Dubai too. And in Qatar. The guy is loaded, and he apparently wants to chat with you."

Gamon scowled at me. "You should be careful. I know Sheikh Ahmad by reputation only. He's extremely reclusive and extremely powerful—even I wasn't able to penetrate his security. If he wishes to see you, he's likely playing a very complicated game."

"With the Shadow Court? Or against them?"

She shrugged. "It could be both. Or neither. I'm willing to tell you what I know, but my information on the man is old. Potentially useless."

"Oh, I wouldn't be so sure," Nikki drawled. "We could prolly learn a few things, if you're game to be interviewed."

"I'm afraid there's something else, Justice Wilde," Mrs. French said, speaking over Nikki. "Something we found in the stacks. A reference, you could say, to an associate of the Council who doesn't seem to still be, ah, active."

We all turned and looked at Mrs. French. "What do you mean?" I didn't know all the Council members, but there were only about half of them currently seated.

"Who do we have left?" Nikki put in. "We never did

properly seat the Empress again, and then there's Strength, the Chariot—"

"No, no, no," Mrs. French said. "This person isn't a Council member, exactly. She supposedly works with Justice, but not, ah, officially. There were several references to her in the archives, well before Justice Abigail's time. They called her the night witch."

A hissing burst of air blasted from the library, and the door to the stacks slammed shut, making us all jump. I glared at Gamon, but she lifted her hands in disavowal.

"First I've heard of her," she said, her expression intrigued, but guileless. "Who is she?"

"I'm not sure. It sounds like I need to make her acquaintance, though." I thought of Eshe and her milk-white eyes. She'd uttered that title to me right before she disappeared. But what did it mean?

"What have you uncovered so far?" I asked Mrs. French, but she only twisted her fingers together and sighed.

"Not very much at all, I'm afraid. There are several requests for her aid, in lieu of Justice's response—pleading requests, really. Begging. But no record of who she actually was, or what she did, other than an indication that wherever she went, death and destruction followed."

"Sounds like my kind of woman," Gamon put in, and I passed a hand over my brow. This was just getting better and better.

"Well, keep digging," I said. "I want every reference you can find, no matter how small. What she did, how she got her abilities, what her job description was—anything."

"I have looked, Justice Wilde—"

"I know. But look again." I couldn't shake the sense of foreboding the idea of a mysterious vigilante on Justice's payroll stirred up in me. Was she actually Justice in disguise, or simply a trusted enforcer? And if so...how far had she gone to protect the Connected?

Before I could parse those thoughts further, I felt a new pressure, light and unnerving, skate across my mind.

"Miss Wilde," the Magician murmured, his words sliding through my thoughts like a silken thread. *"My apologies for not sharing more earlier. Timing, as you'll see, is everything. And now—it's finally time. I would see you, if you can break free."*

"Perfect timing," I said, as I met Gamon's gaze, then Mrs. French's again. "Thanks for the heads-up, both of you. Keep looking for the night witch."

8

I exited back into the corridor outside Justice Hall, not quite ready to catch myself on fire, though I knew that was the fastest way to get to Armaeus. As expected, demon gore no longer stained the floors and walls of the Palazzo Hotel's top floor, but my mind still churned as I stalked down the hushed, luxuriously appointed hallway.

We needed information, stat. Fortunately, Gamon was a willing informant in this situation, and Nikki was an epic interrogator, even without her Connected skills. I suspected there was far more that Gamon knew than she even realized. The more details we could get about the djinn and this Sheikh Ahmad, the better.

Then there was the issue of this night witch character. Eshe's words had gone clean out of my head in the midst of my battle with the bat-winged creatures in Pompeii, and now I struggled to remember exactly what she'd said. Something about darkness and light?

And where was Eshe, anyway? Was she really hanging out in Dubai, living large with the Shadow Court? I didn't know much about the Arabian Peninsula, either Ahmad's home island of Bahrain or the UAE, where the Court was apparently headed. I'd only been to Thaj once, which was north of Bahrain on the Saudi Arabian mainland, to pick up some overlooked stones inscribed with arcane spells for a client interested in the architectural dig there. Another client had insisted I go—twice!—to the coast of Oman during its flash rainforest season, insisting the rainy season phenomenon was the result of an ancient promise between a god and his beloved human. The client believed there was treasure detectable only beneath certain flowers that grew during the rainforest period. As it turned out, he'd been right.

All three excursions to the peninsula had ended quite successfully, but I hadn't taken the time to appreciate the local color. Now I wondered if that was about to change.

I reached the end of the hallway and lifted my hand to punch the elevator button, then sighed. Like it or not, I didn't have time for another stroll down the Strip. Because I knew Armaeus's fortress better than any place in Vegas, I could return there without collecting too much char on my extremities.

"Stop being such a sissy," I muttered.

Focusing on his office, I lit up with a bare minimum of pain as my body incinerated into nothingness. I seriously needed to come up with a better transpo system.

I rematerialized in Armaeus's chambers. The sumptuous office had been redecorated to match the theme of our newest challenge, with Persian rugs stretching nearly the length of the room. The Magician's desk and the small seating arrangement that normally dominated the space had been replaced by low cushions draped in rich, jewel-toned fabrics, while the walls were now hung with a shimmery material parted to reveal the glittering skyline of the

Las Vegas Strip. It was going on three in the morning at this point, but Vegas did its best work at night. The Magician stood with his back to me, staring out over the grand expanse.

"The city at night serves much the same purpose as an oasis in the desert, and was, in fact, built around that premise back in the 1930s," he said as I approached. "A lure to those who needed a respite in the night, a place to relax and spend their money."

"Spend it or lose it, either way," I countered. I took the opportunity of Armaeus's attention being on the glittering expanse to study him more closely. He remained dressed in his dark tuxedo from earlier in the evening, his sleek ebony hair brushed back to curl over his collar. He didn't look over to me, though his mouth quirked as my gaze roamed the elegant planes of his face, the features holding a hint of mystery and danger, as well as the exotic lure of his heritage. What would it have been like to have been born during the Crusades to a soldier and...

Armaeus chuckled softly. "A soldier and a witch," he filled in for me. "A priestess, more exactly, who served an ancient goddess. Much has changed since that time, but one thing has remained constant. Man has an endless appetite for knowledge of the arcane and for learning the mysteries that exist beyond the realm of mortal understanding."

Well, there it was, my opening. As much as I would rather have remained focused on Armaeus's sensual gorgeousness, I saw no point in avoiding the reason I was here. He was the one who'd sent for me, after all. "And that's what is happening here? With these demons or djinn or whatever they are?"

He folded his arms over his chest, looking like the world's hottest lawyer as he considered the question.

"Demons do not rise up of their own accord. They are summoned. They are tools and levers, called into the night, then banished back into their holes as quickly as possible. With the distinct exception of the Syx, they are in almost all cases beyond redemption, good only to serve the needs of those sorcerers stronger than they are."

"Okay..." All super interesting, yet not super helpful. I tried again, this time leaving the subject of the djinn to cool its heels. "So...someone is calling up a mess of demons for reasons of their own?"

"Yes. I had sensed a shift in the play of magic, but that play had not originally been pinpointed to a specific location, or I would have been better prepared for the adventures you encountered in Italy. That has changed over the last twenty-four hours, since Eshe disappeared after the Pompeii Stratosfaire. While the cries of the afflicted have increased only slightly, the use of magic on the Arabian Peninsula has expanded tenfold. If this is the Shadow Court's work, it is a new gambit for them. Since I first ran afoul of the organization in the mid-1500s, they have always been largely a European syndicate. Old World money that used the rest of the world to fund their exploits, without deigning to mix with any societies outside their own. For them to be establishing a base in the Arabian Peninsula, if that is what they are doing, is...concerning."

I lifted my brows. "Why? Why would it be any more concerning there than it would if they were holing up in the US or South America?"

Armaeus's jaw tightened. "To answer that would require us to go back through centuries of racism and treachery, colonialism and murder. The Shadow Court used the Connecteds of the Arabian Peninsula ruthlessly in the past, taking their treasure and plundering their arcane secrets, but they consider them far substandard to any of their contemporaries. You can be certain that, if they have struck up relationships there now, it is not with the oldest families who were the victims of their treachery, but with those that have made their fortune in oil, who perhaps do not have memories quite so long. Even then..."

He shook his head. "It is a concerning development. There is great power, without question, but it comes at a tremendous risk. The magic of the Arabian Peninsula is darker, deeper than most mortals fully understand. For the Shadow Court to be willing to engage with it implies that great swaths of the world are in danger."

I flapped my hand in a "get on with it, already" gesture. "English, maybe?"

His mouth twitched with amusement as he continued. "Put more succinctly, the Shadow Court likely no longer cares who remains standing when the dust clears after this latest power grab. Only that they and their allies are left with a world they can rule without restriction." He said this last with a distant resonance to his voice, almost as if he was repeating it from something he'd read long ago.

I sighed. None of that sounded like a lot of fun, but I couldn't say I was surprised. The Shadow Court clearly was escalating their game. "Okay, so what do we do now? There has to be some way to stop them for good, right? We can't just keep cutting the head off the hydra and waiting for it to regrow somewhere else. Too many people will die."

"Agreed, but they have been very careful. They have not acted yet other than to incite the locals, causing harm in a way that we cannot truly address as a full Council. We need more. And so tomorrow you will go visit this Sheikh Ahmad and attempt once more to blunt the edge of the Shadow Court's swords."

I made a face. "Can't we do more than that? Can't we blast them off the face of the planet and be done with it? These are really bad guys, Armaeus. Like, they seriously suck."

"That isn't the purpose of Council," he reminded me, but there was a new edge to his voice as he turned to regard me with his dark eyes.

"And yet, you're not the head of the Council anymore," I pointed out, holding his gaze. "Maybe we should ask the new guy and see if he has a better answer."

Armaeus only shook his head. "Kreios, for all his personal preferences, is well aware of the purpose and position of the Council in this world. He is not quite the rogue you suppose him to be."

"Uh-huh." I had a sinking suspicion Armaeus was right, but still, a girl could dream. I mean, the guy was the Devil. If anyone would make a snap decision not to play by the rules, it would be him. Armaeus, after all, had decided not to play by the rules. He'd stepped away from leading the Council and now...now he was closer to being a rogue than any of them. That said, I didn't want to put Armaeus at risk. He'd done enough to keep me safe, at great personal harm to himself. It was time the Council stepped up and started being the Big Swinging Deities they always acted like they were.

Armaeus had turned more fully to study me, and I sensed the shift in his intensity, a gleam in his eye that wasn't there before. Had he just read my mind? I needed to be more careful about protecting my thoughts around him, and yet—I didn't necessarily want to anymore. Did that mean I trusted him more? Or mistrusted myself less?

"A curious question, Miss Wilde," Armaeus murmured, his dark eyes now glittering as I felt his gentle touch slide across my mind, rippling through my thoughts like a breeze over still water. At the last second, I tucked away Mrs. French's information about the night witch. That issue was the province of Justice, not the Magician. I needed to track it down myself.

Armaeus lifted his brows, but if he noticed my subterfuge, he didn't seem too bothered by it. "And in all truth, there is nothing we can do at this exact moment. Except, perhaps, enjoy the time that we have been given this night."

He turned toward me more fully, his gaze never leaving mine. The energy between us crackled as he took me into his arms—but there was more than simple sensual interest fueling his movements, I thought. I couldn't shake my suspicion that something was off.

I narrowed my eyes at him. "You know...you've been acting a little weird tonight."

"Weird?" he murmured as he gazed down at me. "That's an interesting word."

I edged back, searching his face. "Yeah, like the kind of weird where someone really wants me to figure something out, but doesn't know how to tell me. If you were any other guy, I'd say you were trying to dump me."

He chuckled. "Never that." He tilted forward to brush his lips over my brow. There was no denying the surge of pleasure that leapt within me, quick and hot, and I somehow didn't care so much anymore about his motivations. It was enough that he was here, and I was here, and that—for once—we had time.

"Well, good," I muttered, my breath catching a little as Armaeus's mouth drifted down my temple, his lips trailing kisses to my ear, and then along my neck. I shifted back farther, giving him more access, not missing how my heart shivered at the soft touch, or quailed at the mere idea of the Magician no longer being the central focus of my world. He had come to fill my every moment. As constant as the stars hanging in the sky, whether or not I could see them, there would always be the Magician there. I couldn't imagine a world without him, not anymore.

"So what is it you're not telling me?" I managed, as Armaeus edged closer, his mouth drifting across my collarbone.

"Do you really think conversation is what I am most interested in right now?" he asked, his tone only slightly exasperated as he lifted his head until his mouth was even with mine. "In the slightest?"

I sighed and pressed against him. "No," I whispered. I touched my lips to his. "You just need to never die. That's not going to be too much of a problem, is it?"

"I won't," he said immediately, then he stiffened, his eyes flaring slightly before he tilted his head, studying me with surprise. "For anyone else, that would be a promise I could never make. What you do to me, Miss Wilde..."

He leaned forward and kissed me in earnest, then, the pressure of his mouth stirring the excitement in the pit of my belly. My blood rushed through my veins, and my heart started to pound. There was something about the Magician that, no matter how long we'd been apart from each other, no matter the fact he couldn't even remember anything that had happened between us before a few months earlier, it all fell away when our lips touched, when our bodies twined together like two branches of the same tree.

Armaeus turned me. A breeze whispered through the completely enclosed room, setting the curtains to fluttering, making the walls of his skylit aerie look like flowing water. With a murmured spell, stars appeared inside the room, spinning as we turned. The effect should have been disorienting, but instead, it seemed to contribute to the haze of surreal joy that billowed through me. I reached for his shirt, pulling it free from his pants, knowing he could whisk both our clothes away with the barest spell.

He didn't, though. Instead, he watched me with heavy eyes as I unbuttoned the luxurious, silky cloth of his shirt, spreading the material wide to reveal the hard swells of his chest and abs. I flattened my fingers on his warm skin, feeling the whoosh of his blood beneath my palms, the thud of his heart. His breath hissed out, warm and eager, and I skimmed my hands over him, sliding them down to his waistband.

"My God, you have got to be one of the most beautifully made men who ever walked the earth," I murmured, my gaze following the greedy trail of my fingertips as I twisted them into his belt loop, tugging it free.

"And I will never tire of—ah!"

Armaeus's head snapped back as if he'd been struck, and then again, his chin jerking sharply to the side this time, his arms dropping mine to spread wide, as if to steady himself.

"What is it?" I gasped as I pushed back from him. My heart kicked up with a flare of panicked beats as he grimaced with real pain.

"No," he breathed. "Not that, *no*."

His eyes were wide, unfocused, and when he jerked his head back to me, I could tell he wasn't really seeing me. His eyes focused on something far darker, something that made his gorgeous bronzed skin go pale, his expression turn haggard. The stars winked out around us, and the fluttering curtains went still.

"What *is* it?" I demanded again. He shook himself hard,

refocusing on me. His face looked positively gray, real fear tightening his jaw. "Armaeus, tell me. What happened, who—"

"*Sariah*," he managed. "She's—no!"

Then he yanked me close against him and whisked us both away in a rush of smoke.

———

9

We rematerialized in front of a boutique hotel and casino on the shores of Lake Mead that would have made a stunning silhouette against the night sky on any day, but this night it most especially did, given the raging fire that had exploded one side of the building.

I looked from the casino to the lake stretching behind it, its smooth surface reflecting the dancing flames, and suddenly, it came together for me. An attack. There'd been an attack.

"This is where Sariah and Brody were," Armaeus said tightly, his words low and fast. "There was a rush of magic —ancient magic. I couldn't trace the source, sensed only that it was building in the distance, then it shot straight up like a dust devil and struck. I braced the wards of Prime Luxe, but it wasn't attacking us—it never even angled toward Vegas, but beyond it. Here. I felt the impact, but it was—"

At that moment, the doors of the building burst open and firefighters rushed out with multiple gurneys and spinal boards, hauling people free of the still-burning building. I heard a familiar but raspy voice, and I surged forward.

"*Brody.*"

The man in the scorched gray suit wheeled around toward me, and his eyes welled.

"Sara!" he gasped. "They came for her. They thought she was you, I think that—that had to be it. There was nothing —less than nothing. A slight breeze over the water, an almost warm, smoky smell. Campfire. Like a campfire, that's it. Nothing more than that. A fucking *campfire.*"

He was shaking now, and I clamped his upper arms with my hands, so shocked, I couldn't at first form words. Brody looked like absolute hell, his face blackened with smoke, his light blue eyes now a watery gray and wide—too wide. They stared at me like I was a ghost. He shuddered, swaying toward me.

"What happened after you smelled the fire, Brody?" I asked, keeping my words low, easy. Around us, more fire-fighters swarmed, but the fire was already out, and Armaeus had left my side. I was sure the two were connected, but I kept my gaze steady on Brody. Armaeus would find Sariah, but I needed answers. "What happ—"

"There were so many of them," he whispered, refocusing on me with his wide, watering eyes. "Birds—bats. I don't know what they were. Demons—but not demons. Not like..." He shook his head, shuddering. "Not like that. These were more like a swarm of some kind. They rushed us from the lake and came at us, wings and claws and beaks. People went down screaming, but they didn't stop. They didn't stop..."

He blinked again. His mouth kept moving, but no sound came out. He suddenly stopped shaking, went stone-cold still, his arms icy beneath my hands.

"What happened after that, Brody?" I asked again, more softly this time.

He was staring now, but no longer at me. "I pulled my gun. I did. But it was too late. They took her even before the fire. The fire—the explosion. It was too late."

Wait, what? A darkness slid through me. "What do you mean they took her? Who? The bat creatures?" I could picture them, squalling in the night. Were they the same ones I'd sent to Gamon, coming for revenge? Was that possible?

"I don't know," Brody whispered, and it was a testament to his shock that he kept shaking his head, his mouth working for several seconds before more words would come out. When they did, they were barely a whisper. "She wasn't surprised, Sara. She wasn't *surprised*. She was expecting them."

The darkness expanded, leaching out from my spine to flood my torso, my legs. "What are you talking about?"

A flare of irritation spiked across Brody's face, and with it, some color. "Oh, come *on*, Sara," he snapped, sounding almost normal. "She was dressed like you, she looked like you. I thought it was weird, but she just laughed it off. Assured me she wasn't trying to fuck with me, and she sure as hell wasn't hero-worshiping you, but she had a theory...a theory. That's what she said." He shifted a little, glancing out over the water. "We laughed, we talked. About nothing. Stupid shit. Then she smelled the fire, and everything shifted. She...fuck me, Sara. She was *scared*. She *knew* what those fuckers were."

He started trembling again, and I clamped my fingers down harder over his arms. Where was Armaeus? He should be out of the firebombed hotel by now, carrying Sariah. Healing her. I needed Brody to hold it together long enough to understand what had happened here. "And what—"

"They called her *Sariah*. Oh my God," Brody whispered. "They said they were taking her *home*. Her true home, her only home."

He was back to rocking again.

"Home?" I stared at him, noting the sweat beading on his pale skin, his glazed, unfocused eyes. "Brody, what are you talking about?"

Armaeus chose that moment to rematerialize beside me, and I turned on him. No Sariah. "What the fuck is going on here?" I demanded. "Where is Sariah?"

Armaeus merely turned in a tight circle, lifting his hands as if he were taking a sample of the air around him. When he spoke, his voice was cold and toneless. "Hellspawn, called from the pits of that dark place specifically because they know the path back. They've taken Sariah with them."

His cold eyes settled on me. "She won't survive there. As strong as she is, she cannot survive a return to Hell."

"Well, fuck that," I shoved Brody toward Armaeus, the darkness now blanketing me from forehead to toes. "I'm going after her."

"No." Armaeus's eyes flared. "You can't. You're immortal. You're not allowed to enter Hell."

He was right. I knew he was right. That didn't change the facts. "They *took* her there."

"I *know* they took her. We cannot choose this path to get her back, however. There are some doorways you cannot go through and expect to emerge unscathed, Miss Wilde. This is one of them."

"*Watch* me," I shot back, a burst of fury erupting inside me. "Those rules were made before I was ever born."

Squeezing my eyes tight, I burst into flame.

It'd been well over a year since I'd gone to Hell and back, but I remembered well the place where I'd found Sariah, the dark and twisting corridors filled with false hope and deception. I remembered even more the worst and best moments of those deceptions, when I'd thought Armaeus and I had found a place to live and grow old together, time out of time. The visceral horror of that moment washed over and through me, and I *saw*—saw it like it was my own bedroom. Felt the walls around me, lived the aching betrayal as Sariah had laughed with rich, delicious satisfaction—

When I crackled back into existence, I couldn't breathe. The smoke and flames were so thick all around me, it was as if I'd been cast into the heart of an inferno. While I may have remembered this place from another time, the decor had definitely changed. Hell was no longer quite so eager to receive me. Was that because I'd become immortal? I didn't know.

But Sariah was my sister. She was more than that—she was *me*. For better, for worse, forever. She was my beginning, and I was her end, and round and round we would forever go. I *would* find her.

With a roar of pain, I flailed out, immediately coming into contact with a stone wall. I bounced off that and into another one, this one giving way in a rush of liquid fire. I screamed and crashed through it, landing hard on a pile of sticks scattered over a stone floor. Not sticks, I saw immediately—bones. Were there bones in Hell? Why?

My thoughts flying wild, I scrambled off the pile, trying to get my bearings. I had first met Sariah in a series of interconnecting corridors in Hell, and sure enough, there were several exits from this central room, each one blazing with fire.

"Sariah!" I shouted, dashing toward the first exit, but as I passed beneath its archway, an unseen force pushed me back. I shifted directions and tried another doorway, with the same result.

"What the fuck is this?" I demanded. I didn't have time to screw around here. I didn't have—

"*Sara...*" The word was a barely fractured whisper. I couldn't place its location, but—

"Sara," Another voice cut in, loud and authoritative, the same voice that the demon from the hall of the Palazzo Hotel had used. This time, the connection apparently was stronger, and I recognized it immediately. Jarvis Fuggeren, the head of the Shadow Court, his heavy European accent overlaying centuries of entitlement. He laughed, the sound rich with deep, rolling satisfaction. Then he kept going.

"Who would've thought you could break into Hell? Are you a god, Sara, not merely immortal? Not a human at all, anymore? Here we've set the trap for the High Priestess...but was it you we should have caught?"

I looked around frantically, but there was no way Jarvis could see me, no way he could be here. There was no amount of magic that could make him that strong, right?

Right?

"Illusions," I muttered to myself. This had happened the last time I was in Hell. I'd gotten sucked into a stage play of my own fever dreams, believing what was in front of my eyes, only to have it ripped away at the last second. But I hadn't been looking for Sariah, then. I didn't have time for this. These passages were closed for me, so I needed to try—

With Jarvis's laughter echoing around the chamber, I turned back to the pile of bones, only the pile wasn't there anymore. Instead, there was a black pit with something dark and unctuous roiling far beneath it, sending smoke billowing up and over the edges. I'd seen a pit like this once before. Not in Hell, though. It has been in the Magician's chambers, a pit that had contained the base, primeval magic that Armaeus drew upon to feed his power. Was this where Sariah was? I dashed forward and crashed to my knees, shoving my fist into the open space. I met no resistance. Was this the way out? Was this the way through?

"There are some doorways you cannot go through and expect to emerge unscathed, Miss Wilde." Now, instead of Jarvis, it was Armaeus speaking to me. Or was he? The sound of his voice reverberated off the stones around me, echoing and turning on itself.

I edged my face deeper into the pit, trying not to gag on the stench of char and oil and death that rose up from it. Hell wasn't supposed to be an easy place to love, but this seemed like overkill. I glanced back up at the other exits. Surely there had to be more than one way out. Or was this pit yet another illusion, a trap to lure me away from Sariah?

A flash of light appeared in the churning pit beneath me, and a white hand stretched up. A woman's hand. A face emerged a second later, my own face staring back at me with wide eyes and a terrified grimace of pain stretching her mouth wide.

"Sara!" she gasped, sounding so much like me, so much like *Sariah*, that I lunged for her. Our fingertips seemed to barely touch, then she was sucked back down into the pit, gone.

Illusion or not, I didn't hesitate. I dove into the pit and hurtled downward, screwing my eyes shut as I plunged into the murk. The moment my outstretched hands pierced the sludge, everything erupted around me. I had dropped into a pit of oil and set it alight with my own smoldering body. The pain was excruciating, and the fuel in the pit dragged on me, simultaneously burning me alive and drowning me. The heat was so intense that I felt as if my bones were fusing together and I thrashed around wildly, kicking down deeper into the incendiary liquid, trying to force myself down, down—swimming, fighting, *forcing myself* through. And all the while, Sariah's voice filled my ears, screaming. Not my own screams either, but ones laden with rage and despair and, at the end, pure terror.

Sariah! I screamed back in my mind, hoping, *praying* she knew I was near. I struck out to the right and slammed into a wall, but even as I did so, I heard Sariah's scream leap with recognition—even hope. Bringing all my rage to bear on the wall, I brought my fists against it once, twice. Then I burst through.

As soon as I was on the other side of the wall, the oil congealed behind me and resolidified, a thick sludge of lava rock that somehow managed to keep the oil from filling up this chamber too.

I didn't have time to catch my breath, though.

A horde of creatures waited for me, the leathery bat-winged beasts that I had most recently encountered on the stage in Pompeii. What the fuck had Armaeus called these things? Hellspawn? Before a few days ago, I had never encountered them. My lexicon of mythological bestiary wasn't all that extensive, but it seemed like I should've at least *heard* of these things at some point.

As if determined to make up for lost time, they came at me in a rush. I grabbed the nearest one and used it as a mace to smack the others away, and as my eyes got used to the flickering fire around us, I could see still more of them all in a heap at the back of the chamber, scratching, fighting over pieces... Pieces of *what*? My stomach pitched, and I rushed forward.

I had to get away, had to act. I plunged deeper into the wall of bat birds, shooting fire, the Magician's chastising words once more filling my mind. Only this time, he had more to say. *"There are some doorways you cannot go through and expect to emerge unscathed, Miss Wilde. It is not the province of mortals or immortals. It is not the province of the living at all. It is the home of the dead, and death that profound can leach into your bones and remain, a spreading cancer."*

I didn't care. I could fight the leach of doom. I could heal myself. It was one of the things I did best. But I couldn't let Sariah stay here another minute. She was *not* going to die because of me.

One of the bat things grabbed hold of my shoulder, and I learned another important truth about their anatomy. Lining their pokey beaks were razor-sharp fangs. When this creature's teeth sank into my flesh, a new surge of rage kindled inside me, setting my insides on fire to match my outsides.

I lurched on, thrashing and flailing, but when I finally burst through the wall of creatures, Sariah was there...she was there!

Or what was left of her was.

"Sara?" she whispered.

I crashed forward, dimly aware that I was still on fire, dripping bat and bird parts. I must look like a monster to her, but Sariah recognized me. She welcomed me. Perhaps she was only hoping I could put her out of her final misery, but I wasn't willing to do that.

Her skin was blackened over two-thirds of her body, her face smashed beneath a fall of jagged rock. Her arms had been separated from her body, her legs amputated above the knee, shinbones and feet tossed beside her with wicked glee. Blood gushed from a long wound down the only stretch of her body that hadn't been burned black, and something had taken a huge chunk out of her neck. But her eyes were alive. Wild, crazed, and staring at me from her partially shattered skull. Her mouth remained wrenched open in a permanent grimace, her hair matted to her face.

"Oh my God," I groaned. "Sariah, what have they done to you?"

"So—there were so many of them," she managed. "I didn't expect...that."

I couldn't even fully understand how I was processing Sariah's words. Her mouth had been sheared away on one side, the skin stripped all the way to the bone. Blood bubbled up at her lips every time she took a breath.

"I've got you—I've got you," I said, not knowing what else to say. Only I didn't. She was still in pieces—so many pieces. As my stomach churned, I reached for the nearest limb and pulled it close, then grabbed more, when a new sound erupted from the shadows beyond Sariah.

A wave of darkness rolled up as a horde of creatures spilled out of the caverns and came racing toward us. Their faces were scarred over with thick ridges of tissue, their arms and hands misshapen, wings broken off, the horns jutting out from their foreheads also broken. But their eyes were the worst of it. Wide open, desperate, *needy*. So needy. The eyes of the condemned left without even the hope of death. The eyes of the forsaken, suddenly given another chance—at what? Redemption? Hope?

Why were they coming after me, though? What had Sariah and I ever done to them?

I knew the answer immediately. We had *escaped*. We had cheated. We had done what they could not do. And I had almost forgotten how to do it again.

I grabbed the last of Sariah's limbs and held her close,

managing to shove my chin into the tattoo that had been etched into my arm. It was the only thing I could focus on with Sariah's endless pain cascading through me in waves of horror and fire. Death herself had given me that tattoo when I'd been worried I'd lose my best friend to the life of danger I was exposing her to. Instead, it would be that friend who would be saving me.

Again.

"Nikki," I breathed, pressing down hard. "Nikki."

10

Nikki was no longer in Justice Hall.

    I crackled back into existence in the middle of a pulsing night club dance floor, only this time, I had far too much fire going on for it to simply whisper out. Screams erupted all around me as I collapsed on top of Sariah, desperately trying to hold her body together. I was a healer as skilled as Armaeus. But Sariah was all but dead and literally in pieces. I didn't know how to fix this.

"Sara!" Nikki dashed to my side as I bent over Sariah, then she whirled, her loud voice carrying over the room like a bullhorn. There was none of Nikki's trademark flash and flamboyance in her commands, just harried Chicago cop at a crime scene.

"Get back! Get back right now," she snapped. "Somebody go cut the fucking music off. I need this place cleared immediately. Call an ambulance. Nine-one-one. I don't give a fuck who you call. Just get the *fuck* back. *You!* Stand back, or I will rip your face off with my own bare hands, and trust me, this manicure is lethal."

Okay, there was some of the trademark Nikki in there.

The music cut out immediately, and then there was a flood of movement around us, hustling and hurried. I held all the pieces of Sariah together with my own body, not willing or able to move.

"Sara," she whispered, though I didn't know how. My face was pressed against hers, my smooth, tear-streaked cheek fusing into her charred skin. "I knew you would come. Knew it. Do you understand how important that is? Do—you?"

"Shut up, you freak," I whispered back, choking on a sob. "Shut up and focus on healing."

She sagged back, rasping an exhausted laugh, but didn't attempt to speak further. I tried to focus on healing her as well, but it was as if I was shorting out. All I could do was think of her body torn into pieces, charred to black. I gagged on the smell of burned skin and bones, and every attempt I made at healing sent my mind whirling like a fidget spinner tossed down a stairwell. Plinkety, plinkety—

"We're here, Miss Wilde." Armaeus's smooth, authoritative voice filled my mind, and suddenly, the unmistakable presence of both the Magician and the Devil occupied the space beside me. Beside us, though, thankfully, Sariah had finally passed out.

I tried to shift back, but couldn't peel myself from her body. Her skin had adhered to mine. She roused the moment I tried to pull away, her voice reduced to nothing but an animalistic whimper that froze me in place. Once again, I knew I needed to heal her—knew *how* to heal her—but I couldn't. I couldn't do anything more than simply exist in the same space she existed, connected in a way neither of us would ever have wanted or expected. Armaeus knelt beside me, while the Devil spoke over the still-gathered crowd, his voice at once soothing and hypnotic.

"Ladies and gentlemen, your solidarity at this terrible time is appreciated, but no longer necessary. This club has many dance floors, many other sights for you to see. You don't need to be here any longer. You can go. Go, and remember only the pulsing lights, the joyful music, the memory of a night that ended as happily as it had begun. Go, and go now. You will be safe."

Over the Devil's melodic drone, Armaeus spoke, still in my mind. *"We cannot take her from this place until she stabilizes. And we cannot move you either yet."*

I'm fine, I grated out.

"You are not fine," he corrected me. *"But we will address that shortly. First there is the issue of allowing me close enough to help you."*

"Are you kidding? Please," I practically groaned, speaking aloud. *"Please* help me. I give you my fullest permission."

There was the briefest pause. *"I cannot get near you, Miss Wilde. I need you to allow me to get close."*

"What?" I couldn't understand what he was saying, and I couldn't understand why he didn't *fix* this. He was the Magician of the Arcana Council. He was every bit as strong as I was, and he knew what the hell he was doing way more often than I did. What was taking him so long to get his act together? Did he need the Devil to hold his hand? Was that the problem?

"Miss Wilde," Armaeus said again. Irritation flared through me, and I jerked up my head, ignoring the sudden hiss of pain from Sariah as my skin peeled away from hers.

I gasped. A wall of crimson fire surrounded Sariah and me. Licking over our bodies, scorching the floor. Sending up plumes of smoke. Armaeus knelt directly beside me, yet it was as if he was trapped on the other side of a glass barrier.

His hands were up, fingers stretched wide, his entire body vibrating with energy. But it was energy that could not reach me.

"How?" I whispered.

Even through the fire, I could see him grimace. *"I confess, I do not know. I have never encountered a block such as the one you are enforcing. I also have never encountered a Council member who entered Hell the way you have and returned the way you did. It should not be possible. The pathways of Hell are created specifically to ensure that they are not used in such a way. I actually thought you would be turned back immediately. What you did...it should not be possible."*

One part of my mind vaguely understood what Armaeus was trying to do with his calm, soothing voice. He was trying to get me to relax, to unclench, to recognize him as a friend. He was thinking that perhaps he could get closer to me, that I would let my barriers drop. But I wasn't in charge of my barriers right now. I wanted nothing more than to welcome his help. I couldn't understand why I wasn't letting him get closer.

"Sara."

I looked down at the horrifying rasp, my eyes filling with stinging tears. Sariah's one working eye was open. The other was lost in a mass of blood and burned skin.

"Sariah?" I pleaded. "Are you doing this—keeping Armaeus out? We need to help you, honey. You've got to let him in."

"*You* can help me." She fixed me with her eye. "You *did* help me. I knew you would come, and you came."

I shook my head, a spurt of crazy laughter welling up. "But I can't finish the job. I'm stuck to you. I haven't gotten to the unsticking part yet. It's kind of an important step."

Sariah's lips stretched into a ghastly grin, one that made

her wince. "Not—just this," she said, her body shuddering involuntarily, allowing me to pull a bit farther away. "That's not what I mean. You *came*."

"Sariah, come on, work with me here," I begged. "Let down your walls."

"But they're your walls now, don't you see? Mine, yours. I take from you—you can take from me too. Everything I have is yours, like—" She coughed, and blood welled at her ruined lips. "Like sisters."

I clenched my eyes shut, trying to stem the tears. "Sariah..."

She sighed as I blinked the salt away, her one eye drifting closed. "I am going to go away for awhile, I think," she murmured. "There are things I need...to remember."

Her voice started to fade, and I stared at her in alarm.

"You're not going anywhere, Sariah," I said, my voice shrill. "You're going to get better, and you're going to heal and—"

"Just...shut up for a goddamned second." She sounded so fragile that I did, in fact, shut up. I leaned closer as she sucked in a shaky breath. "I thought I was being smart. That I could draw them out, make them screw up. I thought that...because I could pull from your magic, *become* who you were...with the magic of the Devil and Armaeus I borrowed as well, I thought that would be enough. It *was* almost enough. Tell Brody I'm sorry."

I stared at her, trying to make sense of what she was saying. Confusion washed through me, almost debilitating in its horror. "But why, Sariah? Why there—then? What were you trying to accomplish?"

She sagged on the floor, her breath rasping in her throat. "A win," she whispered. "They...they need a win. Just one."

"They *who*?"

Armaeus's voice cut across my mind. *"Miss Wilde, if you're going to save her, you need to do it. She's right. You do not need my help. But the trial is great and will take an enormous amount of strength from you. Strength I'm not sure you still have to spend."*

Sariah seemed to be tuning in to Magician radio, because she suddenly jerked. Her eyes flew wide.

"What? No," she said, her one working eye rolling wildly, as if she was trying to see all of me. I moved my head away just as quickly. I didn't want her to see the damage I'd sustained, couldn't let her see it. "You can't get hurt, Sara, not really. No. That wasn't the point of this."

"I'm trying to save you—"

"Well, *don't*. You have to let me *die* if it means—if it means—"

Panic surged through me, hot and sickening. *"What?"*

A new figure appeared in front of us, crouching down until he was eye level with me, and I wrenched my gaze away from Sariah—and froze.

"My dear Sara Wilde," the Devil said, and just like everyone else in the entire goddamn room, I couldn't resist him. I couldn't look away. "Show me your truth, Sara," he murmured, his voice heartbreaking in its tenderness. "Show me."

"She can't die, Kreios," I whispered. "She can't."

"For a moment—yes. She can, Sara. You have to soften your hold on her, for the barest second..."

Staring at him, my mind howling against the horror of his request, his demand, I drew in the slightest, shaky breath, and everything shifted.

In that moment, three figures moved around me—three, not two. The Magician, the Devil, and a slender, hard-eyed woman with timeless features, appearing like a young punk until you got a good look at her face. Close-cropped plat-inum-blonde hair spiked on one side, a sleeve of tattoos snaked down one long slender arm. Death.

All three of them pressed in on Sariah and myself, but it was Death's touch that reached me first. Her gentle hand on my arm, sending a rush of soothing chill through me. On the other side, Armaeus was speaking so low as to be indistinct, but the words were ancient and drew upon a deep magic I had barely glimpsed in the farthest reaches of his stone-and-glass fortress. Meanwhile, the Devil cradled Sariah's head beneath me, looking down into her one working eye and whispering something only she could hear.

"Sara," Death said, drawing my attention. "It was not her time. It was not your time. But you do not enter Hell without paying a terrible price. Surely you knew that."

As she spoke, she drew me slightly away from Sariah, and the Magician moved in, waves upon waves of healing magic sliding between us, through us, lighting up her poor shattered body and drawing her severed limbs closer to her blighted torso.

"I wasn't going to let her die." I don't know if I said the words aloud, but Death could hear me all the same.

"And you are more powerful than you should be," she agreed. "But with every use of power, there are consequences. Consequences we cannot fully understand, because nobody has done this before."

"Bullshit," I said, my heart racing as I watched Sariah's skin slowly return from a charred and bloody hulk to restitch together, stripes of healthy pink flesh appearing amidst all the ruin. "I'm not the first person to go into Hell and bring out somebody who shouldn't be there. There are stories about that going back to the dawn of time."

Death chuckled drily. "That may be, but most of those

stories end up as cautionary tales. I think maybe you forgot that part."

"There, yes. There," Armaeus whispered again.

Though I kept a line of communication open with Death and the Magician, I didn't forget the primary job at hand. I mentally traced over Armaeus's every touch, adding my strength to his. I watched with a strange disconnect as Sariah's body continued to heal. Her eyes remained locked on the Devil, but even when her skin had largely re-formed, she gasped and whimpered as I tried to edge away. I shot a concerned look to Armaeus, and he held my gaze, his voice filling my mind.

"You have become two people, but you were not always so. You once were one. The heart doesn't forget. But you must...you must take what you've taken and step away from her, Sara." His voice sounded strangely fraught, and I didn't miss that he used my first name. That...seemed odd. *"You must."*

I nodded, and Death's hand firmed on my arm, pulling me gently away. Beneath me, Sariah convulsed, and it was all I could do to keep going until I had pulled myself off her, my momentum sending me backward, hard, until I landed on my ass. Death still held me by the arm, which I thought was nice, but not necessary. And then I realized that my arm was bent at a seriously awkward angle.

I glanced down and jolted. My arm was no longer attached to my body.

"What the *hell*?" I whispered.

"Consequences," Death stated, her voice flat, matter-of-fact as my own hysteria grew. "In the extremity of your fear, Sariah's pain has become yours. Her injuries, yours. You must let go, Sara."

"Let go of what?" I bleated. "You have my hand."

I gasped in horror as I looked down at the rest of my

body, the pain only now hitting me. Though my face appeared to be intact—I could see with both eyes and speak —the rest of my body was now as charred and shattered as Sariah's had been. My legs sprawled out, no longer connected to my torso, and Nikki knelt beside me, holding my left arm tight to her body. Her beautiful neon-blue minidress was now stained with blood, and her eyes spilled over with tears that tracked down her face. I blinked at her, suddenly distracted.

"How come your mascara doesn't run?" I asked, my thoughts scattering and coming back again, a kaleidoscope of crazy.

"Dollface," she said, her voice cracking.

"Miss Wilde," Armaeus said at the same time, using his outside voice. I looked up. The Devil and Sariah were gone.

I stiffened automatically, but he lifted a hand. "She's safe. She could travel. You, however, still cannot. You must heal. You must let go."

I jerked my chin up, my gaze meeting his. Death had said the same thing, but I still didn't understand. "Let go?"

"Your need to protect Sariah was so great that you were able to pull her out of a death prescribed by the minions of hell. As long as you kept her in a cocoon of safety, connected with her, you were also protected. Now you have released her, and though she will heal, your body will only get worse."

"Consequences," Death murmured.

"But..." I said, or I started to say, but the words were garbled in my mouth. I moved to lift my hand, only I didn't have one. Yet I could feel the blood filling my mouth, pouring out over newly cracked lips. I looked at Armaeus and could only see him through one eye.

Fear jolted through me. He moved forward even as

Death barked a sharp rebuke, but Armaeus, for all that he could no longer remember me, *knew me* through and through, and some deep and primal center of me recognized him and welcomed him home. He blasted through the last of my defenses, and a shower of sparks erupted between us, my mind suddenly clear of the fog of pain as electrical currents raced through me, healing my body, dousing the unholy fire that burned within. Death and Nikki burst into action, bringing my limbs in close as the Magician placed his hands on my shoulders, his eyes hooded and dark, his lips moving in a constant stream of arcane spell craft.

The moment I regained feeling in my fingers, Nikki gripped my hand with both of hers. She trembled uncontrollably. Death, on my other side, held that arm down. She was also beset with tremors. Then I understood. Death and Nikki weren't the ones shaking. I was.

"Slowly, slowly," the Magician said, his voice finally reaching me. "Slow."

Suddenly a scream rocked through the room. Sariah's scream, and I jolted in Nikki's and Death's arms, my heart nearly surging out of my chest. They piled on, pressing me to the floor, as I looked around wildly.

"Where is she—what happened?" I demanded. "What's wrong with Sariah?"

Magician cocked his head, then shook it. "She's fine. She's resting peacefully. She hasn't regressed."

My lungs heaving, I sagged back. I hadn't imagined that scream. One long garbled sound, the words strung together incomprehensibly, but still clearly a command, a command I couldn't ignore, a command I wouldn't ignore, not anymore.

"She tried to draw them out," I whispered. "That's why she was dressed like me. That's why, at least in part, she was with Brody. They thought she was me. She wanted me—to act. To fight. To..."

I fell silent as the Magician shook his head. "You don't know that."

I grimaced, but he was wrong. I did know that. That was exactly what Sariah had done. Once again trying to act before she was prepared, willing to trade the temporary uptick in her abilities that she'd gotten through proximity to us, to leverage those borrowed powers to draw out the Shadow Court. Not because of any exalted desire for justice, or to protect the Connected community, or even to preserve magic for all...simply because she wanted to *fight.*

When would she learn?

Or was it me she was trying to teach the lesson to?

I let the Magician pull me to my feet, my legs like Jell-O. "I need to speak to the Council," I managed.

Then I collapsed again.

11

Apparently, dragging your better half out of Hell took a toll on a body, even a body as used to physical trauma as mine.

The first and most overriding sensation I had was of pain, a deep violating agony as I relived the sensation of having my limbs ripped from my body over and over again, then shoved back together, cauterized, the stench of smoking flesh and the squish of raw tissue combining into an endless loop of horror.

It wasn't a horror I could easily float above either. Because I wasn't alone in the shadows of my mind. The Magician was there, a far-off island of safety, ready and waiting for me to flail his way. But I could only swim during the brief moments that my body was all connected. When it wasn't, I was tossed on a churning sea of sickening sensation, thrown up, then plunged down. Dimly, I understood that I was assimilating something, learning it, but I couldn't quite figure out what that something was. Only that I would never willingly go out on a boat again.

Eventually the periods of time that my body hung together lengthened, and I was able to make more headway to the distant island of safety. Not only safety, *peace*, I decided. The peace of connection, of knowing. That was what the Magician represented to me. He was a person in this world who understood what I was, supported it, and was willing to defend it. Without him, I might as well be shark chum. Not because he was stronger than I was, but because we were infinitely stronger together than we were apart.

So I swam, and swam. Each time getting closer, before my body fell apart again and I began the journey all over again.

I slept for twenty-four hours straight. When I woke up, Armaeus was waiting for me. Waiting next to me, in fact, his dark eyes fixed on mine, his face taut and concentrated. He evinced no surprise when my eyelids fluttered open, but his gold-rimmed eyes gleamed with satisfaction.

"You will want to eat," he said.

"I need coffee," I muttered, pulling myself upright. My mouth felt like chalk, and I shook out my hands experimentally, beyond relieved when they remained attached. I manfully managed not to cry. "How's Sariah doing?"

"Her recovery was far less traumatic than yours, you'll be happy to know. She slept without seeming to dream, her body at rest. With the help of Dr. Sells, we dropped her into a deeper medical coma, but the connection she formed with the Devil allowed her to retain awareness and lack of fear throughout the process. She understood she needed to rest. Or she simply didn't fight it."

"Yeah?" I tried to settle myself against the pillow without getting swallowed by it. "That doesn't really sound like Sariah."

"She...is not the same Sariah, I would counsel you, Miss Wilde."

I looked at him sharply as the door to my room flew open and Nikki Dawes strode in, carrying a tray of coffee. My jaw dropped at the sight of her, but I didn't have enough energy to respond more vocally.

"Dollface! I know, I know. It's fantastic, isn't it? There were so many options, but I decided in the end that Armaeus could take only so much awesome at one time. So you get Florence Nightingale and not the French maid. You're welcome, love buns."

She said this last to Armaeus, but the description was apt. Nikki was dressed in a coyly conservative, high-necked white nurse's uniform, with sheer white stockings over white platform go-go boots. A jaunty red cape hung over her shoulders to her waist, and a white nurse's cap tilted smartly to one side of her dark 1930s-era bouffant. She even wore white gloves.

"First things first, because I know you're going to ask, but if Armaeus hasn't already told you, Sariah has improved. She was doing this thing where she'd flash in and out of consciousness, and sometimes in and out of existence, occasionally coming back a bit bloodied all over again—"

"*What?*" I demanded, but Nikki flapped her hands.

"Dr. Sells was right there, and said it wasn't surprising. The magic you all threw at Sariah was some heady stuff, you know. It was a lot for a body to take, especially given the amount of healing she required."

I winced, recalling the image of the broken, battered Sariah, barely visible through the smoke and flames. "Yeah," I muttered.

"Anyway, now she's back, apparently for good, and she's sleeping like a baby," Nikki said. "I think that's honestly for the best. She'll just get herself in more trouble if she starts up again. As it is, poor Detective Delish is beside himself with guilt. Not his fault, I kept telling him. That boy was practically blasted to bits, but he feels responsible for Sariah on the best days, and a little like an idiot right now. Add that I think he was developing actual feelings for her, permanent, meaningful feelings, so he's a few coeds shy of a pillow fight right now."

I blinked at her, trying to follow the avalanche of words. "What?"

"Never mind, dollface. What you need to focus on is that he's fine and Sariah's going to be fine, and you're going to get your shot in front of the Council, just as soon as you can stand without listing to the side."

I shoved myself higher on the pillows as she brought the coffee close. "I'm also fine," I informed her.

"That you are." She set the tray of coffee on the side table and gave me a mug, heavily laced with cream and something with quite a bit more kick.

My brows shot up. "Exactly where did you get your nursing degree?"

She grinned, pulling up a seat. "Sugar pie, for what I've got to tell you, you're going to need some ballast." She shot a look over to Armaeus. "You've confirmed it all?"

He nodded. "I have. Tell her. The information will not get any more palatable if we choose to wait."

Nikki snorted. "That is certainly true."

I narrowed my eyes, tracking their verbal volley only a couple of seconds behind. Still, those seconds were beginning to feel more crucial. "What?" I asked. "What have I missed?"

"So you were right. Our girl had a plan," Nikki launched in without further preamble. "A dumb plan, but a plan.

When she got put back together again after her Humpty Dumpty stand, I got a hand on her. I picked up a few things."

I stared at her over the rim of my coffee mug. "Like what?"

I didn't need her to explain how she'd learned what she'd learned, of course. Nikki's particular Connected abilities had come into focus more sharply of late, but she'd always had some level of the skill of reading people's memories. Not so much their mind or their thoughts, but what they'd seen, what they'd experienced. Even though it was inevitably filtered by their own biases—their fear, anger, hatred, and a whole host of other emotions—it was still an invaluable skill when she'd served as a cop. Now, it came in even more handy, as all too often, Connecteds were a little cagier than most people. If they wanted to keep their secrets, they generally could. Not with Nikki around, though. All she needed to do was touch the skin of her target, and their memories would come flooding through. Particularly those memories that were top of mind. Given what Sariah had just endured, her most relevant memories were definitely going to be top of mind.

"All right, so what are we talking about here?" I asked. "She tried to tell me something after we got back, but I couldn't make much sense of it." I couldn't remember much of it either, frankly. That entire conversation had been swept up in the haze of the Eternal Swim to Shore.

"Sariah had a theory," Nikki said. "She decided that you were being watched all the time, but not by the most important people. In her opinion, the Shadow Court was assigning minions to do the job. The reason being that if anybody got caught, they would be so far down the food chain that it would never get traced back to the Court itself.

Fortunately, you have enough enemies that this wasn't a completely unreasonable approach. Her attire last night was quite deliberate. So was her date."

I winced despite myself. I did remember this part, now that Nikki made a point of it. "So Sariah's not interested in Brody?" This wasn't a critical issue, but it still made me a little sad.

"Let's just say her feelings regarding Detective Love Donut are complicated. But she used him, no doubt about it. She figured they picked up a tail right outside the Flamingo, and she made sure that they took their time getting over to Lake Mead. It was only a matter of time, she thought, before they approached her."

"But what was the point? What was she going to do once she drew them out?" I'd asked Sariah the same question, I was pretty sure, but she'd devolved into talking about how she'd known I was going to save her. Which, while gratifying, wasn't super helpful.

Nikki blew out a long breath. "This is where things go a little sideways. Sariah also put the word out that she was amassing forces against the Shadow Court. Building an army, basically. People who were in that army were supposedly going to meet her at the casino."

By this time, I'd gone completely still. "Please tell me you're joking. Sariah isn't exactly the fearless commander type."

Nikki raised a finger. "She's not. She doesn't have to be. You do."

"I was nowhere near the casino last night. I couldn't have met those people if I wanted to. And who exactly are those people?"

Nikki waved off the last question. "You're missing the point. There were no people coming to meet you. Not yet, anyway. It was just Sariah and Brody. But she figured that this planned meeting would draw the attention of some of the higher-level minions of the Shadow Court. Since she had conveniently been sandwiched in among some high-level Connecteds courtesy of my fabulous shindig, she picked up some of their abilities temporarily, which she planned to use to full effect."

Beside Nikki, the Magician shifted.

"The Devil's ability to gain the truth, your ability to read memories, my ability to transport."

"Yeah," Nikki said. "She was pretty sure she'd be able to whisk her and Brody out of harm's way if anything went down. She was watching all exits, feeling pretty good about things, when the flight of a thousand dino bats happened. That was definitely not on her radar. Full-on demon attack, whisking her straight to Hell. She was so disoriented and damaged by the entry, she didn't get your healing mojo working in time, and they hit her with everything they had. It was clear, to her mind anyway, that they thought she was you. They went at her with teeth and claws, cutting her up, separating body parts, setting everything on fire, smashing and dragging away any bones they could reach. She finally got her healing process to work, but by then, it was a war of attrition. She could only hang on, knowing you would come and save her ass."

"She actually thought that?"

Nikki looked at me, her smile rueful.

"Yeah, she did. In her heart of hearts, she knew you would come." She slid a glance to Armaeus. "And she knew *you* would know if something really yanked her chain, Love Pooch. That she and Sara were that connected, like it or not."

"Jesus," I muttered, rubbing my hand over my face. How

had she known? I'd witnessed Armaeus's reaction when Sariah had been attacked, and I'd never seen him react so strongly—to anything. But how had Sariah been so certain? And more to the point, what about the aftermath of the demon attack? "So, who bombed the hotel? That wasn't the bat-bird things, right?"

"It was not," Armaeus put in. "Surveillance cameras show a delivery late in the evening to the kitchens, approximately twenty minutes before the attack of the hellspawn."

"The dino bats," Nikki put in helpfully. Armaeus continued.

"The explosion was intended to occur exactly when it did, and merely as a diversionary tactic. No sooner had the attack occurred than the casino and hotel guests would be disoriented by the explosion. Their accounts of 'dino bats,' as Miss Dawes would say, would easily be discounted."

"But were the hellspawn looking for me or Sariah?"

"That is unknown," Armaeus acknowledged. "Detective Rooks advised that they called Sariah out by name, but did they know it was her from the start, or..."

"Or did they recognize her," I finished for him. I shuddered. I'd never asked Sariah about her time in Hell. God only knew what kind of neighbors she'd had there. "Okay, so we now have a direct strike from the Shadow Court. How do we respond?"

"The Devil has assembled a quorum of the Council to speak to you when you're ready," Armaeus said, and I narrowed my eyes at him.

"What do you mean, a quorum? Why isn't the entire Council there?"

Something dark flashed across Armaeus's face but was gone before I could fully identify it. He turned his cool eyes to meet mine. "Because the Council has already voted," he said.

My eyes shot wide. "How could they vote? I wasn't there. Eshe is out of commission. That's two whole Council members who didn't get to raise their hands."

"And if the results had been close enough for two additional members' input to matter, the vote would have been postponed. It was not close. The majority ruled to take no action."

"*What?*"

I crackled out of existence before he could answer. I knew where I was going. I had spent more hours of my life in the Magician's conference room than I'd ever cared to admit. When I appeared, a few embers hissing into ash around me, nobody in the Council seemed surprised. I swept the room with a glance.

"*This* is what you call a quorum?"

The room was only half full. The Devil, once more in his Mediterranean cool groove of a long white linen shirt and well-draped, frayed khakis, stood at the head of the table, his face stony, which caught me up short. I'd never seen him with any expression on his face other than a laconic smile or some level of private amusement. Beside him was the Council's second-in-command, the Emperor. Tall, trim, and aristocratically blond, Viktor Dal stared at me with something approaching amusement, excitement lurking behind his pale blue eyes. He looked entirely too smug, but not in the cloying way he usually did. He was alert, eager. Ready for action, and yet I somehow didn't think it was the kind of action I was going to support.

"Hello, Viktor. Good to see you," I said.

"Justice Wilde," he replied, with such obvious relish that I knew something was up.

The High Priestess was conspicuously absent, of course. Ordinarily, she didn't miss a Council meeting, given that it was always right down the hall from her. But she was either tied up or kicking it Saudi-style with the Shadow Court, so unless she voted by text, her voice didn't count.

The other present members of the Council stood around the room like gloomy sentinels. The Hierophant, his skin once more paper white, his pale ice-blue eyes inscrutable, fixed his gaze out the window at the reflected glory of the late-night Strip. Nikola Tesla, the Hanged Man, sat with his lips pressed tightly together and would not meet my eyes. His tailored steel-blue suit was neat and crisp, his black hair slicked back from his gaunt face, and his elegant, long-fingered hands clasped in front of him. He and I weren't friends, exactly, but we'd come to have a certain grudging respect for each other. Nevertheless, I wasn't shocked he hadn't voted for action. He was the consummate analyst of the Arcana Council, more than ready to weigh all options and constantly tinkering with the solution based on new, incoming data. Fast action would deprive him of the sport of preparation.

Simon was there, of course, and he met my eyes fiercely, his face flushed, his hands gripped into fists as he balanced on his toes. In his orange knit cap covering his unruly hair, a red short-sleeved shirt over a white long-sleeved shirt, he looked like one very pissed-off Where's Waldo. I gave him a reassuring grimace, but his expression only turned darker. Simon was good people.

Far less so were the couple to his right, Hera and Zeus, late of the attack of the gods. Gorgeously Greek, from Zeus's curling white hair, chiseled features, and still-robust body to Hera's lush goddess-in-residence curves, they were constantly at each other's throats. Even now, they sat pointedly not looking at each other, lost in some private feud. I rolled my eyes.

And then, to my surprise, there was the Hermit. The guardian of the veil between the worlds, he stood at the farthest edge of the room as if eager to be the first to leave. Today, he was rocking the knock-off Gandalf look, all gray beard, gray robes, and scuffed, dusty boots. All he needed was a gnarled staff and a peaked hat. I didn't know whether I should be impressed or annoyed.

"Hey, Dad," I muttered. I could tell from the look on his face that he hadn't voted for action. The Hermit never did.

Gamon, notably, wasn't there. Neither was Death. At this point, I honestly didn't know how either of them would swing, and for the first time, I appreciated the complexity of this vote to act. The Council had a balance to keep in the world, whereas I wanted nothing more than to salt the earth wherever the Shadow Court stood.

"So which of you assholes was the deciding vote?" I started in. "And where is the rest of the team?" Just that quickly, I was back on Team Action. This was the Shadow Court we were talking about here. They legitimately were bad news!

Viktor spoke first. "The votes of the Arcana Council are private. Surely you know that."

"What I know is that there's something seriously wrong with the Council if you legit expect me to believe that more than half of you prefer to sit on your hands and do nothing as opposed to hold the Shadow Court responsible for attacking a member of the Council. Even one by proxy."

"The attack on Sariah is regrettable, but also highly instructive," Viktor countered. "And there is much we can learn by studying the Shadow Court's strategy. We will do well to watch and learn what they do next, not wage an all-out war."

"Who even are you?" I demanded. "Since when are you the watch-and-learn type?"

As soon as I'd spoken the words, of course, I knew the answer. Viktor had nothing to gain from action. This attack had been against me personally, more than the true Council. Hell, I'd barely been on the Council longer than a minute by their standards. Only Gamon was newer than I was, and then only by a hair's breadth. I suspected that the Emperor would not mind all that much if I proved to be the victim of an overeager rival council. Going to war might upset the careful balance he was trying to strike in the world, or could even run counter to some secret arrangement he had in place already with the Shadow Court. Before I could fully build up a head of steam about *that*, however, he lifted a lazy hand.

"You forget, we also had a member of the Arcana Council embedded in the heart of the Shadow Court. Do you really think it would have been advisable to do anything that might cause her harm?"

That stopped me. I didn't want to admit it, but of course, Viktor was right. Viktor was also speaking in the past tense. I shot a look at Simon.

"You've found her?" I asked, not missing the way he flinched at my tone. Well, too bad. I was in the mood to make them all flinch.

"We have," Simon said. He planted one knee on a chair and leaned toward the laptop screen open on the table in front of him, his gaze dropping to it as he typed. "She's in Dubai—and she's safe. Her communication with Kreios this morning was brief, coded, but definitely on the up and up.

She appears to be the honored guest of Sheikh Alsain Ahmad now."

I stared at him, my breath strangling in my throat. "*Ahmad* is with the Shadow Court?" Was that why he'd reached out to me, as some sort of very obvious trap?

"Not at all," Kreios broke in smoothly. "It would appear that Ahmad encountered Eshe while she was shopping in Dubai and promptly left the retail district with her. They weren't stopped. Her communication to me was that the Shadow Court operatives involved in Stratosfaire were all low level. The celebutantes were allowed to leave immediately, but the three virgins remained behind in Pompeii, ostensibly unharmed. Eshe remains linked to them mentally, but hasn't attempted to reach out to them because she's being constantly monitored. In fact, she believes that the young women are being held specifically to keep a link open to her, and she is loath to break that connection until their rescue is imminent."

"She's still being monitored? Even though she's with Ahmad?" I asked.

"She believes so," Kreios said. "I know nothing more than that. There's been no sighting of Jarvis Fuggeren, either. At this point, we don't know if he is involved in any of this."

"Oh, he's involved all right. He spoke to me in Hell. Explain how he was able to do *that* without the help of one of you guys—or Eshe?" I scowled. "He said he'd set a trap for the High Priestess—that he'd set the trap, not her. How convinced are we she's okay? Or that she even knows what they did to her?"

Kreios tilted his head, his cool eyes studying me. If he asked me to tell him my truth, he wasn't going to like what I had to say. "Eshe does not have the ability to serve as a conduit to Hell," he murmured. He glanced to the Hierophant, who had finally turned toward us, his interest apparently snagged with the mention of Hell.

"A strong enough demon could," the Hierophant said.

"Yeah? " I pressed. "What about a djinn? Because given where they're all hanging out now..."

"No," he said, surprising me. "Djinn are an entirely different type of creature, not linked to Hell. And they do not mix in the affairs of mortals willingly."

"Well, someone sure is," I snapped back. "And that someone handed their cell phone to Jarvis with a direct line to down under. He knew I was there, and he knew I shouldn't have been able to do that. So either he's got more power than we think he does, or there's someone big and bad leaning over his shoulder, calling the shots. Either way, we need to stop playing games here. We've got to figure out who's behind the Shadow Court. And while Eshe is on her shopping spree in Dubai and you guys are all sitting around smug in your little vote to once again do *nothing at all*, there are at least three young Connecteds who remain unaccounted for after the Pompeii throwdown *and* Sariah was nearly killed. You may not give a shit about that, but I do. Because believe me, the Shadow Court isn't going to stop with these opening shots. They'll only get cockier once we show our indifference. We need to act, and we need to act now."

"No." The voice that spoke was the last I would have expected, and everyone in the room swiveled again toward the Devil. His face had grown even darker, as if he was wrestling with his own internal demons, but his words were absolute. "The vote has been cast, Sara. The Council will not be acting at this time on the matter of the Shadow Court. We wait, we watch, and we remain in the shadows.

The decision is final. This is not war, and we will not fight. Not yet. Potentially, not ever."

"Even though people will die?"

The Devil's smile was barely a flicker, but his eyes remained curiously flat. "People die. That's what they do."

It was there again, the surge of unexpected white-hot fury from deep in my core, propelling me to action. I stared at Kreios, a thousand comebacks racing through my mind. I mostly wanted to punch him right in his beautiful face.

"Fine," I said instead. "Nice chat."

With that, I caught myself on fire. For the first time ever, I looked forward to the burn.

12

Mrs. French was alone in Justice Hall when I stalked back into the outer office, sipping tea at the reception desk like a proper library matron. I frowned at her. "You okay?"

"Quite," she said primly. "Yourself?"

"I've been better." I rubbed my hands through my hair, half pulling it out of its ponytail. I ruthlessly lashed it back into place.

"Nikki gave me the full accounting," Mrs. French said. "You should probably not be up and around at all, Justice Wilde. I understand that you must be, but...I do worry." She set her cup down carefully. It shook a little in the saucer. "The Council should provide you with more security."

I snorted. "Well, you can count that idea out. We've got no support from the Council. Zero. I don't know what I expected, but it wasn't that they'd turn into a bunch of weasels. They want to identify who's behind the Shadow Court, but they don't want to take direct action. *I* want to keep those assholes from taking pot shots at me, Sariah, and anyone else on the Council, let alone keep them from jacking up the entire Connected world, but I'm the only one with any sense of urgency about it."

"Surely they can't want the Shadow Court to—"

"They voted against me." There. It was out in the open, stark and unassailable, and I scowled at how frail my voice suddenly sounded.

Mrs. French raised her hands, as if in denial. "Oh, Justice Wilde, surely not. You have several staunch allies on the Council."

"You're right. It wasn't about me. They voted against the Connecteds. And that's way worse."

Anger lit along my nerves. I turned on my heel and walked the length of the room. As usual, the door to my office stood open, and I could see the cases piled up on my desk and stacked on the floor next to a scattered pile of silver cuffs. The cries of the Connecteds seeking Justice. And I wasn't giving them that. I wasn't giving them anything. "We have to do something, and now. The Shadow Court has been operating behind the smoke screen of Jarvis Fuggeren for way too long, and before that, some other patsy, another rich, entitled figurehead who was their mouth and their face, but not their heart. Not their mind. That goes deeper. It's got to go deeper."

I turned again, my gaze raking across the closed door at the other end of the room, the gateway to the library and its hundreds—thousands of years of cold cases. Cries that had long ago gone silent, unanswered. Another lick of fire bolstered my rage. "But Jarvis is the one pushing me now. He's getting greedy, stupid. He's going to make a mistake, I know he is. Hell, he already has."

I shot Mrs. French a hard look, freezing her midsip. "He sent a demon to Hell to taunt me. Did Nikki tell you that? I don't know how he got there. He doesn't have enough magic in him to bend a spoon, but it was definitely Jarvis's voice. Laughing at me while I was trying to find the pieces of Sariah after she'd been *ripped apart*."

"She did," murmured Mrs. French, but I was on a roll. Another turn, another shot of the canisters piled in my office.

"And I'm supposed to just sit around and wait for the Council to do something? They have all the magic in the world, all the resources, but they won't act. They won't do anything but watch and wait. Hell, they won't even go after Eshe."

"Nikki said she was no longer with the Shadow Court—"

"But she's still *there*," I said. "In Dubai. Why? She's still hanging out with whatever the hell his name is, Sheikh Ahmad. If she's safe, why doesn't she come back?"

I turned again to Mrs. French. "What'd Nikki and Gamon figure out about him, anyway?"

"That discussion was briefer than I would have expected," Mrs. French said. She'd abandoned the cup entirely now, her hands clasped tightly on her lap. "Gamon did not, in point of fact, remember much about the sheikh, other than he had been instrumental in stopping her establishment of a supply chain through Saudi Arabia for a drug syndicate early in her career, when she was working with a wholly unsavory organization Nikki didn't recognize. Gamon assured us that she had dismantled said organization herself a short while later, while working for another client, and I must say, I believe her. She's a...somewhat frightening individual."

"She has her moments," I agreed. "But that doesn't help us."

"It doesn't...but this might." She rapped her knuckles against a tall stack of books and papers sitting beside her on the desk. "I've found more information on the night witch—documents, cases. She apparently took on cases in situations of dire need when Justice was otherwise engaged, only she was far more brutal in resolving them. Quite a bit of bloodshed, I must say."

"Yeah?" I grimaced. The way I felt right now, I could see the allure of shedding a little blood for a good cause. "When was the last time she showed up?"

"Oh, not for a thousand years. Here—" Mrs. French lifted the topmost book, peeked beneath it, then frowned. "Well, bless me. It was right here earlier this morning, I swear it was. Those *boys*."

She said this last with a disgusted sniff, and I hid a smile. She loved her junior librarians with a stalwart affection, even when they did act like the children they still were. They'd had a hard life prior to coming into her employ, and she couldn't help but dote on them.

Now she turned back to me, lifting her chin. "Well, never mind the actual pages. I'll find those for you later, but this about sums it up—the night witch was a killer who went out to assist Justice when she was most needed, then she'd vanish like a wraith. She could kill anything, viciously and efficiently, with a set of blades she crafted from Justice's own silver cuffs. That's what gave her the power of a Council member, you see."

"Got it. And we're sure she wasn't actually Justice in disguise?"

Mrs. French pursed her lips, turning again to rummage through her papers. "Well, I suppose that's possible, but the notes seemed quite adamant that Justice was...somewhere else. That she and the night witch were operating at the same time, if you will, fighting the same battle from different directions—oh, I will *box* their *ears* if they hid that file from me..."

She sighed, shoving the papers back into a tidy square, then picking up a heavy note card beside the stack. "Enough of that for now. We've received another summons from Sheikh Ahmad this morning, this one a bit more forthcoming."

She stood, but I crossed the room before she could take the first step. I took the card from her. The note was written in English, a heavy, slashing script.

I understand you have a demon problem. Perhaps I can assist. Come to Dubai.

"What the hell is that supposed to mean?" I muttered. Was this what Jarvis had hinted at, by trapping me instead of Eshe? But the problem was...Ahmad still *had* Eshe. And between the demons that had shown up at Justice Hall and the ones who'd attempted to dismember Sariah, I definitely had a demon problem.

So what to do about it?

I tossed the heavy card stock back to the table, my hands going to my own pockets. Empty.

"Do we have a Tarot deck here?" I asked Mrs. French.

"Oh!" She hopped up from the desk, clearly happy to have something to do. "Well, of course we do, right here, just a moment." She hurried out of the room and disappeared into the office, and I winced as a stack of canisters went crashing to the ground.

"Ah—Mrs. French?"

"Be there in a jiff," she assured me, and, true to her word, she appeared a few moments later, holding up her find. My eyes widened. The deck she had was branded with the Flamingo Casino—where the Devil resided. The *Devil*, who was now the head of the Council and one of the trickiest

Connecteds I knew. If he'd somehow snuck a deck into Justice Hall to spy on me...

"Where did you get those?" I asked Mrs. French, as casually as I could.

"Well, I'm not sure I know. I assumed you brought them in? No?" She frowned down at the deck, clearly at a loss, then brightened. "Not a problem at all. There's another. One of the boys snuck it in from the gift shop, hold on a tick..."

This time, she reemerged without incident, but in her palm there was a bright pink plastic case about three inches square, attached to a carabiner hook. On the front of the case was a symbol that looked a lot like...Disney's Magic Kingdom?

"What is *that*?" I asked, while she popped the lid, then shook out brightly colored cards.

"Aren't they dear? An entire set of Disney-themed Tarot cards, with its own carrying case. An ingenious idea, really —here you go, then."

She dropped the cards out into my hand, and I scowled down at them as I tried to shuffle the perfect squares of coated plastic. The backs of the cards were magenta pink as well, again boasting the castle logo, while the fronts... I braced myself and drew three cards, placing them on the table, facedown. I turned the first one upright, and a cartoon version of Princess Jasmine stared back at me, her eyes wide and innocent as she peeked up demurely from her magic carpet.

"What in the..." I frowned, then saw the Roman numeral etched at the top of the card. "Chariot," I muttered. "you've got to be kidding me."

Mrs. French practically bounced on her toes. "Well, now, it's very pretty, I think. And that movie was always one of my favorites. It suits, wouldn't you say? If you're asking about a sheikh, to pull a magic carpet?"

"Yeah, it suits, all right." I turned over the next two cards in rapid order, like ripping a bandage off a wound. Better to get it over quickly. Then I blinked.

"Oh! How marvelous," Mrs. French cooed, leaning forward. "That's from *The Sword in the Stone*, isn't it? The boys' absolute favorite. Walt Disney was a genius."

"Ace of swords," I murmured before glancing at the last card. "And, um—the Sun." The card depicted a lion with a dark flowing mane, sitting next to his cub. They both watched a mighty sun rising in the distance.

"Simba and Mufasa," Mrs. French sighed. "So very sad, what happened to Mufasa. I...I honestly can't even think about it without tearing up. I mean, truly. Such a tragedy."

I shot her a questioning look, and she blinked at me, then put both her fists on her ample skirts in something approaching outrage. "Well! You cannot be serious. Surely you have seen *The Lion King*. You were only a child when it came out!"

"Of course I did," I agreed readily. "Many times. Super sad. But what's important is this reading points to a journey involving a sword or a new beginning—to, the Sun...wait a minute." The Sun card appeared unusually thick, and when I picked it up again, I realized why. A second card was stuck to the back. I peeled it away.

"Well, they really are going back to the beginning, now, aren't they," Mrs. French said, clearly pleased. "Chernabog. He *is* a fright."

"The Devil," I murmured, but just as in Pompeii, I didn't think it was Kreios who was indicated. Chernabog was the original incarnation of a Demon Most Foul in Disney's *Fantasia*, and he looked straight out of central casting—

large, midnight blue, glowing yellow eyes. "My demon problem, in the flesh. But how do I fight you, big boy?"

Almost absently, I drew another card—and burst out laughing.

"Oh my," Mrs. French said, biting her lip as she peered down. The woman depicted on the card was regal, haughty. She wore a bright gold crown and a murderous scowl. "Queen Grimhilde. She was a nasty one, make no mistake."

"Queen of Swords," I said, tapping the card. "Danae." I hadn't thought of contacting the head of the House of Swords for information on this job, but the direction seemed obvious now. Danae wasn't only a shrewd tactician, she was a witch—albeit one far more beautiful than the grim-faced queen in *Snow White* or the hideous hag she turned into. And witches and demons went way back. Maybe she would know what I was walking into in Dubai... and maybe she could help. Besides that, if we were talking about the House of Swords...then the Ace took on new meaning as well.

"Find Nikki," I told Mrs. French. "Tell her to meet me at Danae's tonight. I need to go see Gamon."

13

I crackled into existence at Gamon's cloud-swept lair—and was immediately knocked to the ground with a flurry of leathery wings and the familiar poke of a sharp beak.

"What in the *hell*?" I snapped, ducking my head into my arms to protect myself. Before I could drum up a good handful of fire, however, six more of the creatures plowed into me, sending me sprawling. I threw my hands up, experiencing the world's worst déjà vu. It was the stage in Pompeii all over again, the attack in Hell on instant rewind, and I yelped in real pain as one of the creatures dragged a long talon across my back. In a flash, without thinking, I set my entire body on fire, the burst of flames making the bird bats finally peel off and wheel back. I flipped over, grimacing with pain as my torn back hit the stone floor of Gamon's receiving area, and glowered at the squawking creatures.

"Dammit, Gamon," I groaned. "I thought you got rid of those."

Behind me, Gamon's chuckle was dry as dust. "I

wondered if you were going to try something different this time. You always forget your cuffs, you know. They worked the last time. You need to use them more often."

I sat up, glaring at her as she sat against the far wall of the bay. The creatures above us squawked and flapped, but they didn't try to approach again. Their heads swiveled between me and Gamon, and I narrowed my eyes at her as she tossed her long, thick braid over her shoulder. She leaned against a wall, decked out in her usual body armor. Because when you'd lived a life as long and as deadly as Gamon's, you never let down your guard.

"Did you make some of those things into your pets?" I asked. "Is that what's going on here? Are you training them?"

"If I am, you're the one to blame. You're the one who dropped six dozen of these fuckers on me without so much as a text to warn me. They're hellspawn, did Armaeus tell you? I had to break down and ask him. Which I did not appreciate."

"They were *cuffed*. You were supposed to, I don't know, get rid of them. All of them."

She nodded, but her eyes had gained a speculative gleam. "That was what I was supposed to do with them, wasn't it? Get rid of them. Because that's what I do. That's not what *you* do, or at least it's not what you used to do. That's changing, though, isn't it?"

I grunted as I pulled myself to a seated position. "Do I have to ask what you voted for?"

"You not only don't have to ask, I'll tell you what the rest of them voted for as well. I haven't been idle up here, isolated from all the bullshit that goes on in the Council. Instead, I've been watching. The vote was closer than you would think. The Magician, Devil, Fool, and myself all voted to act. The Hanged Man, Hierophant, Hermit, and Emperor voted to stay. The Lovers, useless meat sacks that they are, also voted to stay. That was a two-in-one vote right there, which seems like something the Council should address. Taken together, they're two brains but less than one coherent thought. Death's vote is the only one I didn't track, and honestly, she could have gone either way."

I sighed. I'd thought the same thing. "Well, they didn't ask me, and I would've voted to fight. Did they get ahold of Eshe, somehow, after all? Simon said they hadn't had contact with her."

Gamon's smile was brutal. "They did not. And yet there were other votes tallied, beyond even Death's. Three more, in fact. All voting against action."

I blinked. "Three? There are three Council members I don't even know exist? Who?"

"An excellent question, and one I look forward to helping you discover the answer to, assuming you don't die first."

With a wave of her hand, she sent the squalling bat birds back into the shadows. Apparently, there was some sort of access point into her inner sanctum, because their prehistoric cries eventually faded.

"I need to be able to hear myself think," she said. "Those hellspawn are chatty little bastards."

"And why are they suddenly everywhere, do you know?"

"Hellspawn, as it happens, are the ancient guardians of Hell, as it happens. Creatures of a very specific subset of mythology, hearkening from the Arabian Peninsula."

I grimaced. "Oh. Of course."

"It gets better. They are considered to be the particular favorites of the djinn, and their reemergence into society argues for that particular breed of demigods being awakened from a long and needful sleep. The djinn and their pets are not exactly morning people, it would seem."

"Where is the Hierophant in all this?" I groused. "Shouldn't he be policing any new demon varietals?"

"He's been busy, actually. The Syx have been sent out no less than a dozen times in the past few weeks, quelling incidents in the villages throughout the Middle East. Fear is rampant, but actual injuries and death are harder to come by. The Syx are all too often finding nothing when they go to investigate, which means most likely..."

"They're being deliberately distracted," I said. "Michael knows about this?"

She shrugged. "Who knows what Michael knows."

I looked at her skeptically. "Apparently, you do."

"I made my living knowing my enemies, and I see no reason to change that now. My targets are simply a little more advanced. Fortunately, there are fewer of them every time I turn around. It's an easy trade-off. But the problem isn't the Council, Sara, it's you. Even more so than the Hierophant and his enforcers, you've got the tools at your disposal, the resources you need to go after the Shadow Court. The Council isn't going to do it for you. A few individual members? Sure. I suspect even the Devil would love to act if he could do it on the sly, but if you want to take out the Shadow Court, you're going to have to do it yourself."

"I can't exactly blow up an entire organization on the sly, Gamon," I said irritably. "Everyone's going to know I did it."

She smiled. It wasn't a good look, but it was particularly appropriate for her. "Everyone *will* know. And yet no one will be able to prove anything, not if you do it right. Think about that. Your reputation will precede you in the deadliest of ways. You will be a one-woman agent of assured destruction. That wouldn't mean that your troubles will be over, but they would become much more interesting, now, wouldn't they?"

My head was starting to hurt, but I couldn't discount the twitch in my hands, the surge of fire in my blood. I also couldn't unhear Sariah's soft whimpers of pain as I'd peeled myself off her body. "I can't take on the Shadow Court and kill them all. That's not what I do."

"Correction, that's not what you did. Who knows what you're truly capable of? The short answer to that is *no one*. Not even you. And so...it opens up some interesting possibilities, doesn't it? If I could deliver to you the person who dismembered Sariah, the director behind that attack? Would you kill them?"

I stared at her. "How can you even ask me that question?"

"Because it's important. I need to know. Are you capable of killing someone in cold blood who desperately deserves it?"

I opened my mouth, then shut it again. The question was basic, and I wasn't the first person to ever consider it. It was a question that played out in suburban tree-lined streets and urban back lots, open plains and deep forest hollows all over the world. And I'd never given it much thought.

The answer had always been obvious, before now.

"But things have changed, haven't they?" Gamon asked again, watching me with keen eyes. "They struck close to home. Worse even than cutting you down, they cut down someone you love. Don't think they didn't notice you went after her. Don't think you haven't just given them the perfect lever. You've all but signed the death warrant for everyone you care about."

My heart jerked sideways, a flood of anger rushing in behind the wrenching tug. "Gamon," I said warningly.

"Don't you Gamon me. You know I'm telling the truth. Sariah wanted to peel back the onion, find out who was truly at the heart of the organization besides that buffoon Jarvis who's the money and the mouth, but not the real power. She didn't succeed, but you can bet she made a lot of people excited. There's a whole contingent of bad guys out there chuckling into their coffee right now. Don't think they're going to stop with Sariah. Don't think they won't even try to take her out again. And I'm not talking just the Shadow Court anymore, I'm talking every two-bit asshole in every arcane corner of the world who's thriving right now. You or me or anyone else associated with the Council has fucked up over the last few months—we've gotten soft. Even me. Your little librarian's snit over the House of Cups was well-founded. They've been very bad girls and boys since I've left, but they haven't felt the need to keep me apprised. That's not so much dangerous as tedious, and probably something I'm going to need to fix eventually. You went to Hell to retrieve someone you love. You almost died in the process, and you didn't kill a single soul to keep them from doing it again."

"There was nobody around to kill."

"Bullshit. You didn't think to *look* for anyone to kill. You didn't look to exact revenge, you only looked to save someone. Sweet, honorable Sara Wilde, champion of the afflicted, protector of the doomed. But the world doesn't just need protection, Sara. It needs someone willing to strike."

"I don't—"

"Well, maybe you *should*," Gamon cut me off. "Maybe it's time. Do you want the Council to be dismantled piece by piece? With as good eyes and ears as I have, I can't get close to Eshe right now. Who the fuck knows what they're doing to her when she's not out in the open. You certainly don't see her making a break for it, even though she's traded keepers. You don't think that's a problem? Because let me tell you, it is."

"Oh, so now you're the expert on the High Priestess too?"

"I've known people like the High Priestess my whole life. There's only one thing they prize."

I knew the answer without her having to say it. "Their freedom."

"Bingo. She's stayed too long without contact. She's not there of her own volition, not entirely. She would want to be stroked for her super-spy skills if nothing else. There's something wrong. You need to go there."

"Me?" I thought of Armaeus's direction, Sheikh Ahmad's invitation. The cries of the Connected who had the poor luck to be in a djinn's path. All roads, it seemed, led to Dubai. Was that a trap? Or simply the universe lighting the way?

"Yes, you," Gamon said, refocusing me. "You're the one who fascinates the Shadow Court more than any other member of the Council. You, not the Devil, not the Magician, though arguably, the Devil runs the Council now, and the Magician has arcane depths that even he hasn't fully explored. They don't care. They want you. There has to be a reason. It's probably not a good reason. Which means they're probably going to come at you with guns blazing. You're going to need to be prepared for that, and you're going to need to use deadly force."

"You don't know that," I finally snapped, if only to end her diatribe. Jarvis's mocking words echoed in my mind. *Was it you we should have caught?*

"I do know that," Gamon shot right back. "And if you

aren't willing to do what you have to, then you have to let me do it. Like this."

I jolted and stared across the open space at myself. It was like Sariah all over again, only I knew that wasn't possible. It was Gamon in some sort of Sara suit.

"That possibly is the most disturbing thing you've ever done," I said flatly.

"But can you fight me?" The open bay of Gamon's receiving area suddenly felt like a killing field. "Would you strike me?"

She took a step forward. The image didn't flicker or shudder like bad CGI. It was smooth, flawless. And that creeped me out more than anything.

"I told you I haven't been idle up here. I've been learning, searching. I'm Connected, but unlike the rest of the Council, it wasn't my *magic* that landed me with you people. It was my willingness to kill. To sacrifice—hell, not even that. Just to kill. In that way, I'm not all that much unlike Viktor. He's only a middling magician. You know that as well as I do. But he is one of the meanest, most cold-blooded motherfuckers you'll ever encounter in this generation or any other. He is a killer, and the Magician knew that from the start. Mix that level of sociopath with even modest Connected ability, and you've got a problem. Same with me. My Connected ability lies in my influence, and I helped cement that influence in blood. Pure magic, not really my thing. But the Magician has a big, wide library for the taking, and so does Justice Wilde. I've been doing a lot of reading in my spare time. Do you want to know the number one magical ability demons use both inside Hell and out?"

"No," I said honestly.

She smiled. The sight was unnerving, like seeing myself in the mirror doing things I wasn't doing.

"It's illusion magic. It's not even that hard. And I'm really, really good at it now. So I could kill you, Sara Wilde, kill you dead before you even realized your head had left your body, and then do the things you're afraid to do."

Even as she spoke, I didn't believe her. Or rather, I knew that wasn't what she was after. But I didn't miss the quick jerk of her body, so like my own that I knew exactly what was coming next. The knife slipped free of its sheath at her side, her arm going back with a sharpness that I never possessed. The limbs were mine, but the skill was all Gamon.

A second later, the knife hurtled through the air, spinning toward me, not a knife at all, but a throwing star. I *hated* those things. I ducked out of the way just in time, and the weapon flew harmlessly by me. But Gamon was already moving, pulling something else out of her endless bag of tricks. And I didn't have time for this.

The throwing star sprang to life behind me and came hurtling back the other direction, this time toward Gamon. Only I didn't waste time with one, I manifested a hundred. One hundred spinning blades flew across the space, straight for her. She shouted with pure delight and lifted her arms, the sleeves of her long hoodie apparently reinforced with some sort of body armor. As she deflected the first of the blades, a roar sounded over us, and once more, the space was filled with the flapping, squawking creatures.

"You can't fight me, Sara," Gamon said as I twisted away from the first wave of the hellspawns' attack. "I will always be better at direct combat than you are. You have to strike like a witch in the night and be gone again for you to have a chance."

I didn't have time to argue with her as the hellspawn circled back around. I didn't know what these things were precisely. I didn't know if they were real, illusions, or conjured bits of magic. But when the first one raked a claw in front of my face, clipping my temple, I struck. This time not to scare them, this time not to create a buffer and block them away. I set them on fire. There was one second, maybe two of a long, terrifying chorus of screams, and then they winked out, gone. Across the room, Gamon once more appeared as her real self. She grinned at me with fierce, feral joy.

"Congratulations," she said, up on her toes. "That was lesson one. It's only going to get harder from here."

"Great," I muttered.

She raced toward me.

14

The night was dark, and a surprisingly stiff breeze kicked up as I walked along the shadowed drive to the sprawling mansion at the edge of Las Vegas. Technically, this had been my headquarters when I had been head of the House of Swords. I'd given up that role when I became Justice of the Arcana Council, but for a few short months, I had been in charge of one of the world's largest syndicates of Connecteds, a syndicate that had, prior to my arrival, been dedicated to a questionable mishmash of arcane black market drug trafficking and money laundering. I had handed over the reins to Danae, a take-no-prisoners witch whose coven, known as the Deathwalkers, had been based in Chicago. Given the location, and never one to let a good moniker go to waste, Danae had also been known as the Witch of the Iron Sea. After my crash course in djinn magic, where I learned that iron was one of the few things that could stop a djinn in its tracks, she seemed like a good person to talk to.

I was here for another reason as well, and when Danae stepped into a shaft of moonlight, gesturing me to the side of the building, I knew she'd been expecting me. She was as stunning tonight as ever, her dark skin incandescent in the reflected solar lights that lined the walkway, her sleek dark hair swept off her face. She was dressed in a flowing white shift, simple and elegant at once, and she didn't speak. She didn't have to. I appreciated her combination of strength and serenity, and felt a surge of pride that this was whom I'd chosen to run the House of Swords. Danae was more than a capable leader. She was a highly skilled witch, a true Connected. The House of Swords deserved no less.

We strolled around the back of the mansion, where two figures sat huddled together near a large open fire. They talked quietly until a sharp crack of a laugh burst out.

"Ma-Singh, you have *got* to get out more. That is absolutely not how Snapchat works, and you should stay as far away from it as possible."

Danae's number one general, the Mongolian Ma-Singh, rumbled a heavy, accepting laugh, then both he and Nikki turned as Danae and I walked up. There were no other members of the House of Swords at the house tonight, save for a skeleton security crew. And those warriors were all inside. What I needed to talk to Danae about required no audience. I wasn't even sure of how to inform her.

She didn't give me much of a chance to struggle through it. She picked up a glass of wine and handed it to me, then secured her own. I squinted down at it.

"I'm kind of more of a scotch girl," I said.

"Tonight, you will drink wine," she replied, her tone brooking no argument.

"Okay, so tonight I'm going to drink wine."

I raised the glass to her, but she turned to Nikki and handed the glass to her, the two of them jostling a bit in the process. Nikki eyed the wine dubiously as Danae gave a third glass to Ma-Singh, then took a fourth for herself.

"Never was one to turn down an opportunity for a fine, ah, whatever this is," Nikki said gamely. Ma-Singh lifted his glass as well, widening his stance on his size-sixteen feet. The Mongolian warrior had been one of my staunchest supporters when I served as the head of this house, and he remained Danae's most stalwart general.

Danae finally turned to me and lifted her glass. "The House of Swords pledges itself and all its resources to you, Sara. We are here to serve as your sword and your shield."

By the time she finished her short speech, I was gaping at her. I shot Nikki a look, but she shook her head. Talk about beating me to the punch.

Danae lifted her glass higher, and for once, I had no quippy reply or sarcastic retort. Not with both her and Ma-Singh watching me with such unexpected earnestness. I lifted my glass in return.

"I accept your help, Danae. I hope I don't need it, but I suspect I will. I thank you for it."

Ma-Singh and Nikki lifted their glasses as well, and all four of us tipped the goblets toward each other. The move seemed almost ceremonial, not merely a collegial toast over an open firepit, and when the four glasses touched, I could feel the spark of magic erupt at the center. I glanced downward and realized we were standing in a sacred circle, then lifted my gaze again to Danae. She looked at me with more satisfaction than I'd ever seen on her face.

"I thought that was going to be more difficult. You've changed, Sara."

I grimaced, not even trying to understand the pinky-swear ceremony we'd apparently just completed. "It's been kind of a heavy week."

As Danae lifted her glass to her lips to take a sip, I followed suit. The wine was rich, heavy, and aromatic, a mixture of spices adding a distinct edge to it. I swallowed and gave her a rueful smile. "But I'm not sure if my changing is a good or bad thing."

"It's a good thing," Ma-Singh interjected. "A needful thing. We cannot stand on the edge of war forever. The Shadow Court must pay."

"Ma-Singh," Danae said quietly, but he shook his head, his grip tightening on his glass.

"They went after Sariah believing she was Sara. They have no right to disrespect us so deeply. They've been living like slugs under a rock for so long, they've forgotten proper manners. It's time that we taught them."

There was an undercurrent of rage to his words that startled me. Ma-Singh was an excellent general and not given to theatrics. He was also a true protector. He took the attack on Sariah personally, even though he was no longer in charge of my personal protection. I appreciated that. More than that, I needed him.

"Until I require you personally, Ma-Singh, if it comes to that, I have a favor to ask," I said.

Ma-Singh nodded brusquely, once again anticipating my words. "I will keep watch over Sariah. She will not rest if she thinks she can spur the Court to further action. Her blood runs too hot."

I sighed. "That's certainly true." Now more than ever. I didn't know how long it would take Sariah to recover from her trauma, but knowing that Ma-Singh would be there when she woke up, and would keep her from haring off without him, made what I had to do next more manageable. I met Danae's gaze. "I'm going to Dubai," I said bluntly. "I don't understand what's waiting for me. I was hoping you could explain it to me. In detail. Using small words."

She nodded, taking another sip of her wine. "The djinn are waiting for you. Summoned by I know not who. We've been trying to figure that out since Eshe was taken in Pompeii. We cannot. Which should not be the case."

She turned toward the open desert beyond the house and stared out into the starlit sky. "Since our earliest records, the coven of the Iron Sea has kept a detailed history of interactions within the community, both contemporaneous and those as far back as we can get our hands on. Whenever it occurred, the summoning of the djinn took on a very different experience than the typical calling of demons."

"You mean they had to use different spells?"

"No, the summoning process itself was not so dissimilar. There was inevitably a secret circle, specific glyphs or designs etched inside the circle, and a series of spells. But the nature of the creature summoned is where things varied. The old story of Aladdin and his magic lamp is not completely untrue. Djinn would typically not perform one act of service, like most demons, but three. It would be bound to its summoner until the completion of the third task. At that point, the summoner was obligated to return the djinn to its original vessel, or, if the summoner was feeling sufficiently generous, to release it altogether. Naturally, the djinn worked very hard to complete any requests to the summoner's satisfaction, with the hope that they would then be released from their bound vessel. Generally speaking, this arrangement rarely ended up favoring the djinn. If the djinn had been caught in the first place and confined to a vessel, it implied that they were dangerous or very powerful, and most summoners rightfully assumed that they would be the target of revenge for having availed themselves of the djinn's services under duress."

"Gotcha." I joined her in pondering the starry horizon. "And no djinn can be summoned unless they are already trapped inside one of these vessels? That's the game?"

Danae smiled. "A very good question and a very important answer. You're correct. You cannot summon a djinn who hasn't already been conquered in some way. This particular type of demon coexists in many situations with ordinary humans, who may have no idea of the djinn's true nature. Stories abound of people running afoul of angry djinn, people who have mistakenly harmed a member of the djinn's family or trampled over their lands, never realizing these lands had been claimed by a supernatural being. Sometimes the djinn are invisible, which makes it yet more difficult. Other times, they have families, jobs, positions in the community. There's no telling, unless you're a witch, who is who."

An errant thought occurred to me. "What about Eshe? She's a priestess, not a witch, and I know there's a difference. But would she be able to tell who is djinn and who isn't?"

Danae considered the question. "I don't know. Ordinarily, the answer would be no if she hadn't been trained as a witch, but her training predates my own by two thousand years, so I can't rightfully say. And further, she's a member of the Arcana Council. That also compounds her abilities."

"Could I identify a djinn?" I asked. I could pick up on demons, but generally only if they were kind enough to show me their little beady red eyes.

She smiled. "I suspect the answer to that would be no. You might well suspect the being in front of you was Connected, but whether you could make the jump to the next level is questionable." She nodded slightly. "So, yes. Of course, I'm going with you to Dubai."

"Whoa, whoa, whoa," I said, my hands coming up. "That's not part of the plan. I can't show up to meet Sheikh Ahmad with both you and Nikki tagging along. We're not Charlie's Angels here."

"Sweet Mary, we would be *awesome* as Charlie's Angels." Nikki cackled. "Talk about an instant global hit. Who would be Charlie? I mean, it's got to be Armadelicious, wouldn't you say?"

"Not the Magician," Ma-Singh grunted, his heavy voice oddly serious. "It would need to be the Devil. The Magician would act himself, not send in proxies. The Devil is subtler."

"Why are we having this conversation?" I protested, then pointed my glass at Danae. "You shouldn't come with us. It's too dangerous. I need to go in, get Eshe, then figure out what it is the Shadow Court is trying to pull and stop them. But if Ahmad is truly hooked up with the Court, things could go bad in a hurry."

Danae lifted her brows, the height of haughty cool. "All the more reason I should be by your side. We have not been idle these past months that you've given me the leadership of the House of Swords. We knew a conflict was coming. We just didn't know when. I've been in contact with the other houses. They, much like the Council, have adopted a wait-and-see attitude."

"Uh-huh," I said, remembering Gamon's concerns—and the complaints in Justice Hall. "Anything else I should know? Unofficially, of course?"

Danae hesitated, but Ma-Singh didn't. "There's been a return to the ways of darkness," he said gruffly. "Cups. Pents. Wands too, but not in trafficking technoceuticals. The House of Wands has begun to serve as enforcers for the other houses. There's been a stockpiling of resources and an upgrade of weapons. The houses are girding for a very ugly war."

I pursed my lips, but I didn't need to ask what actions Danae had taken.

"Swords are ever and always first about action," she answered anyway. "Due to your involvement in our House, we have gained standing and resources. Now we stand with you, Justice Wilde, as your house will always stand with you, regardless of your elevated station. And not just us. There are Connecteds all over the world who have stayed in contact with us since the battle of magic. They wait, some eagerly, and some dangerously so, for the call to action."

She gestured to herself with her glass. "I represent them and serve also as their proxy. If they see me with you, which you can believe they will, it will give them hope, as well as a warning that they too should sharpen their swords."

This was Sariah all over again. The worry in my gut tightened with every new stanza of Danae's battle song, until by the end, I wanted to throw my glass at her.

"Danae, with respect, think about what you're saying here. The Shadow Court isn't screwing around. They quartered and deep-fried Sariah, and I don't know how long it's going to take her to come back from that. I need to take them out."

"*We* need to take them out." I didn't miss the excitement in Ma-Singh's voice. I wasn't the only one who wanted to fight these assholes. They had caused a great many people trouble, not just me. I needed to remember that.

"But in a highly specific way," I countered. "This isn't the time to have a cast of thousands running across the open field, screaming their fool heads off. This is an operation, not a war."

"Even better." Danae shrugged. "I will still be at your side as a witch who can identify both the djinn and the horde, and as a witch who knows what to do with both of them. Freeing you to lead our party to the fullest extent of your abilities, for which you will be well prepared."

There was something in her voice that pulled me up short, a sort of smug superiority that implied she'd just pulled a fast one on me. I wasn't sure how that was possible, but I narrowed my eyes.

"Prepared how?" I said. "We don't have a lot of time. I wouldn't be surprised if the Council didn't try to clip my wings in some way if they thought I was acting out of turn."

Nikki snorted. "They wouldn't dare," she said, but she sauntered over to the fire and sat down beside it. Ma-Singh took a seat as well, and Nikki reached for the bottle of wine. "This didn't suck to start, and sucks less the more I drink it," she observed.

I narrowed my eyes at her. "You seem like you're ready to kick up your feet and stay awhile."

"Oh yeah," she said. "I figured I'd enjoy the show."

She looked at me meaningfully, and my mind flashed to the image of her taking her glass from Danae. The two women had brushed hands briefly, and with Nikki's particular skills...

"What?" I asked, suddenly on edge. "What do you know?"

"She knows that you're long overdue for a refresher course."

I barely avoided yelping as I jerked out of the way of the newest arrival to our little party. The woman who stepped out of the shadows was small, of indeterminate age, and possessed a voice like iron. She also caused a deeply violent, visceral reaction in me. Sweat beaded down my spine, and I set my jaw. Carefully. "Sensei Chichiro," I allowed.

"Justice Wilde." She nodded back, the soul of deference.

My one-time Connected martial arts instructor wore traditional Japanese robes tied with an obi, and her hands were folded demurely in front of her, her dark eyes fixed on me in the flickering light. I hadn't seen her since before the great war of magic, where she'd attempted to inspire me to up my abilities. She'd been successful, too. Because of her, I was able not only to transfer an image from my mind to reality, but also to multiply that same image a hundred times over. The magical cuffs of Justice or the throwing stars with Gamon had been the most recent examples of that skill, but it had come in handy many times.

Sensei Chichiro stood looking at me imperiously, and I bowed slightly in genuine respect.

"I didn't expect to see you again," I said honestly.

"Whereas I always knew our paths would cross once more. You cannot stop learning simply because it has become inconvenient, Justice Wilde. You do a disservice not only to your station, but to the people who believe in you. And to yourself. I could not allow that in any student, and I certainly cannot allow that in the student with the heavy charge that you carry."

I grimaced. "Yeah, well. I don't recall the actual instruction going all that well last time. I don't suppose there's just a YouTube video I could watch?"

Sensei Chichiro sighed, her lips tightening with what looked like real dismay. "It was my intention to teach you humility. Instead, I taught you fear. It was my intention to teach you self-sacrifice. Instead, I taught you stubborn isolationism. I cannot teach you in the training ground. You do not listen. You do not learn. I can only give you the crack of the rod in real life. And so, this is what I will do when the time comes. It is my promise to you, Justice Wilde."

I made a face. *The crack of a rod?* I immediately called up a vision of Yoda riding on Luke Skywalker's back as he raced through the swamp. "Please tell me you're joking."

In response, Chichiro lifted her hand and murmured something. A stiff wind sprang up between us, nearly knocking me over.

"What was that?"

"A spell of connection," Chichiro said demurely. "When you most need it."

"Oh yeah?" I fought the urge to scrub the offending magic off my face, my arms, or wherever she applied it. "And who decides that?"

"Unfortunately, it is all we have time for. Fight with your head, not your heart, Justice Wilde. I'll be watching." And then she took a step back into the shadows and vanished from sight.

For a long moment, nobody spoke, then Nikki raised her glass again. "This is gonna be *awesome*."

15

We took the House of Swords' plane to Dubai. After finding Kreios's Flamingo-flavored Tarot deck in Justice Hall, I had no interest in using any of the Council's resources, and if they were left wondering what I was up to, so much the better. The House of Swords had kept its actions quiet from the Council for millennia. They were good at it. In addition, the long plane ride gave us more time to work out a plan of action, and to run through a dozen different potential scenarios.

Finally, it allowed me the chance to sleep. I didn't want to make a big deal out of it, but my recent experience with Sariah had exhausted me more than I cared to admit. I suspected only the Magician guessed how much, and I hoped even he wasn't fully aware. I didn't want him to feel like he needed to play nursemaid, and perhaps more importantly, I didn't want anyone else on the Council to guess that I was compromised in any way.

Now, as we coasted toward the airport, banking down out of the clouds, I felt the tension building again behind my ribs. There was no reason for it to be intensifying this quickly. I glanced over to Danae, who looked equally pensive as she stared out the window.

"So let's go over it again," I said. "We were asked to meet with Sheikh Alsain Ahmad, who is currently harboring Eshe. He is sending a private entourage of security to greet us at Ahmal Lounge in the airport once we get through customs."

"Yes," Danae said. "We could've done it more elaborately, but the Ahmal Lounge is accessible to the public and gives all sides a chance to size each other up before anyone ducks into any private limos. In addition, the sheikh's security team can have their eyes on anyone watching us. There are layers upon layers of security at the Dubai airport, some obvious, some not. They're not taking any chances. We shouldn't either."

"Doesn't feel right, though," Nikki said from a seat facing us. She had her laptop open, her fingers moving rapidly over the keys. "Simon has his eyes in that airport as well. There hasn't been a lot of movement, but he's picked up members of the sheikh's public security detail. Everything looks on the up-and-up, but there's a tension in the place, he says. Something's hinky."

"And we're going to walk right into it," I said.

Danae smiled, then gestured to the ashes burning in the small salver she'd just used as a portable scrying tool. Make no mistake: witches were cool. "You were summoned to Sheikh Ahmad for the express purpose of him proposing an alliance with the Arcana Council. That feels right, particularly with his intercession with Eshe. That sets him up as a target, and, of course, you as well. In other words, there may be trouble in the airport. But what's interesting about that is that the sheikh may seek to test your abilities before he even lets you darken his door. So we could be looking at an attack from pretty tight quarters."

I made a face. "This is giving me a headache."

We argued back and forth for another few minutes as the jet landed and taxied to a stop. Given the people we knew and our friends in high places, getting through security and customs was a remarkably expedited proposition, and we were soon met by a quintet of dark-garbed businessmen, all of them sporting earpieces and serious faces.

For ourselves, we were dressed conservatively, but stylishly. Especially Nikki, who strode ahead, her impressive curves draped in a silky black half shawl that flowed easily over a knee-length dress. Matte nude hose covered her legs, and her black platform heels were positively circumspect. She also had on black gloves that extended up to her elbows, and she was clutching a baby doll pink silk purse. Her hair was swept up in a neat chignon, clasped with a thick black barrette. I'd seen the glint of steel in that barrette and wondered what material it was made of, given that it easily passed through security.

To my left, Danae looked like a Wall Street lawyer, her slender body wrapped in an ice-blue business suit with a white shell beneath, a slender blue-stone necklace around her neck, more blue stones I couldn't identify circling her wrist. She strode along easily in matte linen pumps. I moved just as easily, with a jet-black, calf-length, expensive-feeling duster over a black silk tank and trousers, my black boots polished to a high sheen. I even had a deck of cards tucked into my jacket—standard Rider Waite this time, no Disney knowledge required. The ensemble had appeared in my bedroom thirty minutes before flight, a gift from Armaeus and one I was happy to take. I generally didn't place too much emphasis on my attire, but I was walking into the unknown. At least I would look the part.

We proceeded without incident to the Ahmal Lounge, but the moment we entered, my anxiety ratcheted up a notch. Nikki had been right—something was simply off here. I could feel the tingling of fire sparking at my fingertips, so at least we weren't in a magical dead zone. That had been my first concern. But when I looked at Danae, the hard set of her jaw tipped me off that she had felt the tension as well. When we entered, a man stood at the far end of the lounge, near the bar, where a slender, dark-faced man busied himself drying glassware. The place was about half full, a mixture of obvious tourists and other smaller knots of what I presumed to be locals, all of them well-dressed. This was not a group of people who were going to suddenly start diving for their machine guns, I consoled myself. If there was an attack, it would start out polite.

The attractive older man at the bar slid his phone into his pocket and offered us a broad smile. "Hello. I am Alsain Ahmad—"

The loud crack of a gun sounded from several feet beyond us, and Ahmad's head exploded.

Shit! I spun around, my third eye peeled wide to assess the lines of energy bouncing through the room. There were dozens of them, which made sense. Even Connecteds of limited power give off some level of electrical impulse, and highly agitated non-Connected did as well. And there was no question that everyone in the room was agitated. In less than a breath, another round of bullets lit across the space, puncturing the kegs of wine that stood in artful display along one side of the bar. People started screaming, and I spun back toward the shooter, my hands out. I wasn't Armaeus, I couldn't stop time, but I could seal this problem off right now. Ahmad had been Connected. He had been shot. All these people were victims and aggressors. It was justified.

Fire shot from my fingertips in a crackle of blue flame and raced along the energy circuits bouncing around the room. The doors slammed shut, the walls became electrified, and a moment later, everyone in the lounge was shackled in the cuffs of Justice except for myself, Nikki, and Danae—and the bartender. Because: bartender.

"Well, that's a new trick," Nikki drawled.

"I've been working on it."

The bartender, who still stood frozen behind the long counter, dropped his cloth, then placed both hands on the smooth surface before raising his eyes to us. He had a serious face, I saw now, a hard face, with a long thin scar down one side. He was also quite a bit older than I'd thought he was at first glance.

He looked around the room with its two dozen patrons, wrists shackled. Easily two-thirds of the captives had started shaking uncontrollably, and Danae hissed a low warning, but I'd figured it out already. Not all the patrons in the bar were entirely human. The bartender narrowed his eyes at them before flicking his glance back to me.

"Justice Wilde, you came highly recommended to me," he said in a cultured, affluent tone. "I'm glad to see the reports were warranted."

I didn't need him to spell it out. "If you're Ahmad, who's that?" I asked, pointing to the downed victim.

"And where's security?" Nikki asked from the doorway. "Coast is completely clear, but hello, gunshots."

"Handled in advance. No one will bother us." Ahmad's face softened only slightly as he looked at the slaughtered man. "And he was a trusted soldier who knew the sacrifice he might be asked to make. A sacrifice that shall be avenged once we dispose of this problem. Unfortunately, not even you can adequately dispose of a possessor demon on your own, despite your many skills."

"Heads up," Nikki said as the men nearest to me started convulsing more violently. Their eyes flew wide, their shackled hands lifting toward their throats.

Meanwhile, Danae had dropped into a crouch, peering into the corner of the room. "Salt," she snapped, "but the line is broken."

"By necessity," Ahmad said, already in motion. He jerked up a box from behind the counter. Four large tubs sat in it, uncovered, filled with the white crystals. Nikki and I surged forward, and he tossed two of them to us, their contents spilling. We wasted no time drawing a perimeter around the edges of the room, restoring its solidity, while Danae dropped to her knees and traced letters on the floor in another spill of salt. By the time she rose again, the convulsions of the demons inside the Possessed were growing manic. I held out my hands, feeling the tension tighten.

"I can't hold them any longer. I didn't think I could hold it this long," I gritted out.

From behind the bar, Ahmad grinned. "I didn't think you could hold them at all, so that's good to know."

"Here they come," Nikki shouted.

The demons burst from the Possessed, and the moment they hit the ground, they went up in a roar of smoke and flame, black goop flying everywhere. The few tourists in the room, already traumatized, were now treated to sheets of goop. One of them fainted, and others stood rooted in shock, as layer upon layer of goop coated the room.

It took Danae another three rounds of shouted spells to

fully clear the room. By the time she was done, there was a tight knot of huddled tourists, nearly a score of dazed gunmen still in their shiny bright cuffs, and a very smug-looking Ahmad with a half dozen security guards who popped up from behind the bar and filed into the room, not paying any attention to the streaks of goop on the floor or dripping from the tables.

"You can set them free, Justice Wilde, if you would," Ahmad said, gesturing to the bound and formerly Possessed. "Most of them are my own security detail, men we suspected of turning traitor, but who had been with us for so long, their defection made no sense. It took one of the local sahiras to give us a clue as to the reason behind their sudden unexplained behavior. She was quite disturbed by the idea of an orderly, rules-following demon, but there seemed to be no other explanation for it. And then, I put the question to the High Priestess, beseeching her for oracular assistance. She was kind enough to confirm my suspicions and explain how you might assist. She said she, herself, was not as suited to the job."

"Of course she wasn't. So you brought us here to clean up your mess," I said, more irritated than I should have been. With a flick of my hand, the bracelets slid off the hapless post-possessed minions. Just as well. Gamon probably wouldn't have looked too kindly on another unexpected delivery on her doorstep, this one far less interesting.

"I did," Ahmad said. "Unfortunately, it was a very tragic gunfight. Too many good men lost their lives."

What came next happened so fast, I couldn't stop it—or I didn't stop it, anyway. Ahmad's men lifted their pistols and assassinated the soldiers who had been possessed. They fell to the floor, and the remaining tourists who still remained alert and aware finally succumbed to unconsciousness.

"Lest you mourn the fallen, we are an ancient family with ancient rituals and knowledge," Ahmad said coldly. "None of these men could have been possessed without their knowledge. They are not the victims here."

I considered that. I wasn't sure I believed him, but I had my own mad to manage. "Ahmad," I said warningly, and Nikki moved up beside me, laying a hand on my arm.

"Not now, dollface," she muttered, as Danae watched us both with narrowed eyes. "He doesn't need to know everything you can do. Just that you helped him out, yeah?"

I blew out a long breath. "Yeah," I muttered.

Ahmad turned to his men, pulling his phone out of his jacket pocket as he directed them with quick gestures. "They'll take care of the situation here, the injured," he said.

I watched with a curious detachment as the men moved around the collapsed tourists, syringes in hand. Those wouldn't be your average narcotics, I decided. Those would be technoceuticals, and probably pretty strong ones. I didn't know what these people would remember, but it probably wasn't going to be a demon exorcism, yards of goop, and a gunfight.

Ahmad directed us toward a back door to the lounge, and we followed, Nikki leading the way. He moved with utter confidence, and for a moment, I wondered if I should be more careful in following him out the door. I'd expected to be attacked by the Shadow Court, not by my own allies. And yet, maybe the two weren't as separate as I thought.

"Who possessed your men?" I asked. "Who commanded the demons to take them over?"

"A question that has haunted us now for weeks," Ahmad admitted. "You have to understand, I meant what I said when I advised that we have very old rituals and protections against such an attack. We have not lived as long as we have on the Arabian Peninsula without safeguarding ourselves from demons, particularly the djinn, which these possessors were not. For someone to have broken past our defenses, even preying upon weak-willed men, took some doing. An organization of sophistication and expertise."

I rolled my eyes. "The Shadow Court."

Ahmad shrugged. "So it would seem. I do not count that organization among my enemies, however, and we, in fact, received the High Priestess from them without issue as a show of faith. We have other discussions in progress with them, you see."

"What kind of discussions?" I asked sharply.

Ahmad continued without acknowledging the question. "We are colleagues on the same playing field, even if we rarely play the same game. So if this is the work of the Shadow Court, it would be a foolish move on their part. Men often prove themselves as fools, but because the negotiations are ongoing, we can't be hasty. If it is a third party outside the Shadow Court, it remains to be seen whether they are allies of the Court or their enemies in hiding, looking to weaken their negotiating position."

"The enemy of my enemy is my friend," Nikki muttered, and Ahmad nodded.

"Exactly so."

"So what do you want with me?" I asked. I didn't bother keeping the edge out of my voice. I was being used here. I'd been being used for a while now, but it was really starting to get on my nerves. I was in Dubai to rout out the Shadow Court and send them to oblivion, not play resident assassin for the local thug lord. A local thug lord who had indicated that *he* could help *me*, not the other way around.

Ahmad chuckled. "I am a proud man, the head of a line of proud people. I want to be heard by the strongest person in the Arcana Council in centuries. A person not so calcified in her thinking that she follows the old ways without thinking for herself. In return, I can share with you all my knowledge of the demons who are plaguing you—and the djinn who are controlling them."

I slanted a glance at him. "You know about them?"

"I know about many things, Justice Wilde."

He turned to me and, with a crook of his finger, pulled a heavy gold medallion on a thick gold chain from beneath his shirt. With a flourish, he let it rest against his sternum and lifted his gaze to meet mine. A gaze that now burned with age, knowledge, and arcane power.

"I am the Sun, a member of the Arcana Council since the time before Christ," he said quietly. "I also voted that the Council should not act. I say we take these bastards out ourselves."

16

W e moved swiftly out of the airport to where Ahmad's car was waiting for us, a long, sleek SUV that allowed all four of us plus two of his guards to enter easily, then take up positions all facing each other. The glass windows were only slightly tinted, so I braced myself for the inevitable nausea-inducing glance out the window, watching everything move sideways.

The moment we were all settled, I turned to Ahmad and scowled. "You need to start talking, right now."

He spread his hands with an affable smile. "But of course. I understand your surprise and concern. The Arcana Council has not reached out for a quorum vote in—well, it's been generations. Even their attack on the gods of magic was not something for which they sought permission. In all truth, after the war on the gods, I'd thought myself well and truly free of the Council's machinations. I suspect all three of us did."

Nikki put it together first. "The Magician didn't know about you guys until recently," she said. "The three at-large Council members. He should've, but he didn't."

Ahmad nodded. "He did not. Or perhaps more truly stated, he no longer knew what he didn't know. It would appear those memories were returned to him quite recently, and, acting on the potential of more Council members existing, he put the vote out for general response—and turned up three unexpected participants. The Sun, the Moon, and the Star, all of us—"

"The Moon and Star?" I interrupted him, seizing on the titles. At last, some real information. "You know them? Who they are?"

Ahmad grimaced. "I regret I do not. They ascended before my time, and I abandoned my formal Council position almost immediately. I'd never met any of the existing Council before Eshe...and now, you. But fear not. Once your Magician learns of their existence, I am sure he will be requiring your services again to track them down. I merely thought I would do you the courtesy of moving up the timeline. And of course, I need you as well."

There was so much to unpack in Ahmad's response, but I could only stare at him for a long, disbelieving second. Then I shook myself. First things first.

"You voted against the Council acting as a solid unit against the Shadow Court," I accused. "Your suggestion about us taking them out individually is bullshit. The Council will always be stronger together."

"Do you think so?" Ahmad asked, and settled back against the leather cushions. Across the limo, Danae studied him with an icy glare. She had also been used, I understood. Neither of us cared for it.

"The Council is bound to follow policies set in place long before our time," Ahmad continued. "Policies that may have made sense at the dawn of humanity, but not now. Not when the networks of Connected are as robust as they currently are, and the world is on the cusp of knowing who really walks among them. We have been watching the effect you have had on those communities, Justice Wilde. We are aware of the popular support you have generated."

"That support isn't..." I trailed off, glancing away. It was such an automatic response for me to discount any support by the Connected community, psychics who were not operating at the level of the Council. Those people didn't know, didn't understand what their support truly meant or what it could and could not do. I was not about to put them at risk. That had always been my thinking.

But was that the right course? Was this the time, as Sariah believed—and apparently Danae along with her—to rise up with the Connected communities, or, at the very least, help them rise up on their own? Was this the time to allow them to step into the light? It had always been safer in the shadows, but did that mean these people had to remain in the shadows forever? And was it my place to make those decisions on their behalf anymore?

All these thoughts rushed through me in the space of three seconds, and I pushed them to the back of my mind just as quickly. This was not the time to consider all that.

"So what is it exactly that you intend to do?" I asked Ahmad. My eyes tracked the movement of cars and pedestrians on the wide streets outside our vehicle. We were driving through downtown Dubai, arguably one of the most exotic cities in the world. Yet other than the luxury brand names shouted from business marquees and storefronts, and the glitzy vehicles choking the street, it could have been Scottsdale, Arizona. English signage was everywhere, and the wide sidewalks were thronged with conservatively, but expensively, dressed shoppers. Palm trees waved in the gentle breeze as we turned down another street, apparently heading for the city center. "Where are we going, anyway?"

Ahmad smiled. "I expected to pick up a tail outside the airport, but so far, we haven't. We'll circle the downtown area and head out to my residence shortly." He gestured dismissively to the opulent storefronts. "There is nothing much to see here. One day, I will entertain you at my home in Bahrain. There, you will see the soul of this part of the world. The beauty and the mystery. Here..." he flicked his fingers. "There is no soul."

He kept going before I could react to that. "Meanwhile, I intend to do exactly what the Council expected of me, of you as well, when they made their decision not to act. I expect to use you as bait. Without question, very powerful bait—but bait nevertheless. Regardless of their flirtation with the High Priestess, the Shadow Court has fixed on you in a way that is unquestionably dangerous for their future livelihood. They are poking the bear, to put it more colloquially, with seemingly no concern about getting mauled to death. There has to be a reason for this. They would not put themselves at such dramatic risk unless there was a potentially powerful reward."

I nodded. He wasn't wrong, I'd been asking myself the same questions. The first real assault the Shadow Court made on me could end only one of two ways. Either I would shut them down, or they would bring me to harm, and that would be the act that would draw the Council into full-out war. Even those members of the Council who didn't agree with me couldn't allow the possibility of an upstart organization picking us off one by one. A certain measure of respect had to be maintained, or everything was lost.

"The Shadow Court has been on the move for several months now," I said. "Why are you acting now?"

Ahmad shrugged. "Because the nature of their movement has changed. Yes, they have been acting out for several months and causing no end of difficulty. But they weren't in my own backyard. Now they are, and there's only so much I'm willing to put up with. They have extended themselves too far. So I will allow the Arcana Council to risk its most valued asset to attempt to draw the Shadow Court into the sunlight. I will soon have a great deal of resources at my disposal to strike out against them, and I am pleased to see the level of resources you have brought to bear as well."

He looked over at Danae. "Your reputation precedes you, Mistress of the Iron Sea. In a land once overrun with djinn, your skills will be put to the test. And you, Miss Dawes, are not without your abilities as well. Subtler to be sure, but we have been watching you."

"If I had a dollar for every time I've heard that line," Nikki said drily, crossing one well-muscled leg over the other. Ahmad didn't miss the movement, and his eyelids flickered momentarily before his jaw firmed.

"Exactly. And now comes the true test. Now that you have emerged into the light, how far will the Shadow Court go to engage you in battle, and how quickly will they—"

Wham!

The explosion rocked the side of the SUV like we'd been T-boned by a freight train. The vehicle jerked violently to the side and tilted, as the passengers sprawled against each other.

A speaker crackled over our group as the driver reported in.

"We've got temporary roadblocks up ahead, Sheikh Ahmad. Roadblocks. No egress. Repeat, no egress."

"Roll through it," Ahmad ordered. "Go to the Gardens building."

"Yes, sir," the man's voice came back, the words clipped. The SUV picked up speed—

Wham! This new impact was from the front of the SUV, the equivalent of us running into a concrete wall. The vehicle bounced back, then took a hard right onto a side street.

"What the *hell*?" Nikki demanded. "I finally get to play bumper cars and there's no cotton candy?"

Ahmad's security guards braced him with their bodies as a volley of bullets strafed the side of the vehicle, but the sheikh's hooded eyes were on me. The SUV careened around a corner, then jolted forward again.

"You knew this was coming?" I demanded. Fury lit along my nerves. If this bastard had led us into a trap for the second time...

"No," he protested as we lurched against each other, another slam to the side of the SUV sending everyone into motion. He crumpled against Nikki, and she grabbed his hand and set him back to rights. She looked at me and shrugged, confirming at least that much. Ahmad hadn't planned this attack. Not directly anyway. He looked up and narrowed his eyes at the view through the windshield, then jerked forward in his seat toward the front of the vehicle.

"Down, down," he shouted, pointing not to us but ahead, out on the street. A second later, I understood what he meant. He directed the driver to take us into a half-built structure, what looked like a parking garage. It wasn't a bad idea. If we were going to be attacked, this would at least keep the damage away from the public—and hide the worst of the fighting.

We bounced beneath the gaping maw of the steel-and-concrete building, picking up speed as we drove into the gloom.

"Don't you guys have *cops* in this city?" Nikki carped as the SUV screeched around a sharp turn.

"Only for certain situations." Ahmad fell back into his guards as the driver braked hard. "I own this building. There are other vehicles here. We can make the switch beneath."

I twisted in my seat to see that more cars were flooding into the construction site behind us, and still others coming in from additional openings if the flash of lights was any indication. We weren't going to lead this merry band back out again, no way. Did the Shadow Court really think trapping us in this parking garage was going to work?

I felt the burn of magic along my fingertips, then something else as well. A deadening weakness that overlay the flicker of power. *Oh shit.*

"Dead zone?" I demanded, turning to Ahmad. "You brought us into a *dead zone*? Are you out of your freaking mind?"

He stared at me with wide, confused eyes. "What are you talking about? There is no dead zone in Dubai. That magic was restrained to the old world, not duplicated here."

"Well, it is now," I grated out. "Nikki? Weapons."

"On it." Nikki lunged with brutal efficiency, ripping one rifle out of the left guard's arms and tossing it to Danae, then wrestling for the second weapon. The guard protested, shocked to his core, and she reached back and coldcocked him square in the jaw. He crumpled against the back of the SUV as I went for Ahmad's weapon, fire flickering just enough to make the Sun yelp and lurch back.

"Take it, take it," he shouted, clearly more interested in seeing what I would do than in protecting his dignity. What was with this guy? I didn't have time to care. I yanked his gun out of its holster, then spun fast enough that the vehicle blurred around me. My magic abilities were stunted, apparently, but they weren't completely destroyed. I still had speed and fire, just not a lot of it. How was that possible?

Weapons secured, we slammed against the doors and burst out of the still-rolling SUV. The one still-conscious guard leapt after us at Ahmad's order, pulling new weapons free, but at least he had the grace not to level them at us. Instead, he sent out a strafing fire, covering us as we burst into the parking area, lit up from all sides with temporarily strung lights.

We didn't have long to wait. Dozens of figures rushed from the shadows, some on foot, some on motorcycles. My third eye flipped open, and I could see the deadening impact on the energy currents that jumped and jittered around the space, yet the electricity clearly wasn't affected, either in the lights or on the bikes. If *those* worked, and if all life-forms were joined together as one, which was the true nature of what being Connected meant, then shouldn't that simply be—

"*Dollface,*" Nikki snapped as the assault group nearly reached us. "We shoot?"

"No." My hands went out toward the nearest string of lights, and I felt the current of electricity flow through me, lifting me straight up off the ground. Only it wasn't simply the current of electricity lifting me, but my own fiery wings, magic-wrought holdovers from a previous battle I'd fought between the earthly planes of this world. I generally forgot about this particular manifestation buried inside me until they decided to show up all on their own. Like now. Forcefully.

Apparently, the dead zone didn't apply to wings of fire.

I grunted in real pain as the wings shot straight out from my back, stretching wide in crackling, hissing arcs. They parted in full and lifted me off the floor a good two feet. Every single one of our attackers stopped and stared in absolute horror at me for one second...then two.

"What in the..." Danae began, but Nikki only cackled.

"*Now,*" I said. "Shoot the lights."

I didn't have to tell them twice. I flinched as Danae, Nikki, and even Ahmad, newly outfitted with his own gun, his eyes gleaming with excitement, turned their automatic rifles skyward and systematically blew out one line of lights after the other. With every new section dropping into darkness, the minions of the Shadow Court screamed and balked, running into each other in utter confusion. *Demons?* If not, they were doing a damn good impression. They were being directed through the same electrical impulses that had deadened my power, but now the balance shifted as my wings connected to the currents of energy racing through this space, and chaos reigned. As quickly as they'd attacked, they turned on their heels and started running.

"Get to as many as you can," I yelled at Nikki, and she plunged into the throng, passing her hands along arms, cheeks, necks, and shoulders as the crowd raced for the exits. Their work apparently done, my wings shoved themselves back inside my body, and I dropped to the concrete floor, staggering a bit as I sucked in a tight breath. *Damn,* that'd hurt.

"This way," Ahmad shouted, and jerked his gun toward another ramp toward the back of the structure. We raced up it to where new vehicles sat, pristine and unharmed, all of them ordinary SUVs, though oversized ones, not limousines. We piled into the closest one and were off again.

"Will there be more?" Ahmad asked, his eyes wide as he turned toward us. His skin was flushed and his teeth chattered. "I'll need to call the authorities if so. Even in Dubai, there are limits." He didn't seem too upset about it, and I glanced at Nikki.

"There won't be more from this crowd," she said. "Not demons, but low-level Connecteds, and amped to the nines. They had one assignment, and they all had it down with the same level of fervor. Like they've been hypnotized or drugged with a combination prime directive and flash-mob technoceutical. Their job was to attack Sara Wilde, overcome her and anyone she was with. They literally were supposed to overtake you with boots and stones, though. No magic. No power. Nothing but the might of the people. They were told you wouldn't fight back." She grimaced. "That's some seriously creepy shit."

"You got that right," I muttered.

"No—no, it isn't," Ahmad said, flapping his hands at us. "It makes perfect sense. If they came after you without magic, you should only have been able to counter them with guns and violent force. You would have become the thug that you rail against, Justice Wilde. The Shadow Court knew you would not do that. They didn't know you would beat them at their own game, though." He looked at me. "How did you negate the power of the technoceuticals they were under, though? How did you have that ability?"

I shook my head. "I have no idea." That wasn't exactly true, but I wasn't in any mood to split hairs with Ahmad.

He slapped his hand to his ear and nodded. "We are clear," he said. "There are no more roadblocks, and in this vehicle, we should not gain so much notice."

"And no cops either?" Nikki asked, still clearly put out about that.

Ahmad flashed a triumphant grin. "No. And most importantly, we beat the Shadow Court at their own game. That's what's important."

"No," I countered, not bothering to hide the bitterness in my tone. "We didn't stop them. We *taught* them. Now they know one more way I can react when they attack. Eventually, they'll figure out all my tricks. This isn't a game that I want to keep playing. Not with them."

Not with you either, I said in my own mind. Ahmad was the Sun, the bright ray of hope on the horizon, a god to the ancient world, even. But right now, he was nothing but a mystery to me. And he was the one who held all the power. That wasn't going to last long.

"Easy, dollface," Nikki murmured, her manner shifting as she picked up on my darkening mood. I glanced her way, and she met my gaze, Danae equally still and certain beside her. We needed to understand what was going on here.

Beside me, Ahmad relayed another volley of orders to his men, practically chortling with delight. I grimaced. None of this was going to be easy. And it was all going down faster than I was ready for.

17

We reached Ahmad's residence an hour later. Surprisingly, it wasn't within the city limits, but perched just beyond the far northern edge of Dubai, an elegant estate that spread over what had to be a billion-dollar seafront. Man-made hills and ridges rose on either side of us, artificial follies to obscure the palatial home beyond the walls of turf and stone. The house itself was relatively low-slung, but then it didn't need to be a skyscraper when there was nothing to obstruct it from the stunning view of the Persian Gulf. Its white walls and huge panes of glass served as a perfect counterpoint to the sandstone walkways that were threaded throughout the property, leading down to the beach and over to what look like a walled garden.

"I hadn't planned for such an exciting introduction to my home." Ahmad gave a rueful chuckle. "But I hope you find it to be restful after your long journey. We have much to discuss, but you will need time to relax and refresh yourself. My entire estate is at your disposal. I beg you to take advantage of all I have to offer, and we will talk of our plans this evening."

We glided around the corner of the main house, only to find a second structure waiting beyond fountains and a perfectly manicured lawn. Even if Ahmad was repurposing seawater to irrigate this place, it must cost him a fortune to maintain the lush exterior.

Then the SUV slowed, and I noticed a group of people gathered beyond the central fountain—a semicircle of women all arranged around another striking female, this one dressed in a gorgeous white pantsuit with wide, draping trousers and a coat-style jacket so light, it fluttered in the breeze. Her hair was long and shiny, her face radiantly beautiful even from a distance. The young women stared at her with undisguised admiration. I couldn't blame them.

"Eshe being Eshe." Nikki drawled. We'd known she would be here, but I still felt a surge of relief at seeing her safe and apparently unharmed.

Ahmad beamed, turning back to us again. "It's my first gift to you, and one I am very happy to grant. As I'm sure you are aware, we located the High Priestess yesterday, shopping in Dubai. It was a simple matter to extract her from her guardians. Too simple, if truth be known. We suspect they anticipated her rescue, and sought mostly to draw you here. But to our knowledge, she has no recording devices or magical wards of any kind placed upon her. We do not believe she is a threat, and she assures us she is unharmed."

"They let her go," I said. "They were done with whatever they needed her for."

Ahmad nodded. "I believe so as well. And again, Justice Wilde, you are here. That was the ultimate game for them, wouldn't you say? And to all indications, she is healthy, well-fed, and quite satisfied with her experience with the Shadow Court. She has been unwilling to share that experience with us, and I, of course, have not pressed."

Nikki snorted, and I managed to hide my smile. The High Priestess was not likely to spill her candy to this guy, even if he was the Sun. Which begged the question...

"Does she know who you are?" I asked. I was pretty sure she hadn't told Kreios, if so...and if not, why not?

Ahmad modestly inclined his head. "I confess I was most eager to tell her. It has been a long time since I have interacted with anyone on the Council, and though I had no interest in reestablishing that contact or submitting to anyone's will but my own, I missed the stimulation of speaking with a true peer. Being immortal is an incredible asset in building a fortune, but it can be lonely as well."

I wasn't quite ready to play the violins of sadness yet, but I kept my peace. With a murmured word to his driver, Ahmad ordered the SUV to slow and then to stop. The doors opened, and Nikki, Danae, and I stepped out as Eshe stood, dispersing her followers with an imperious wave. I studied the girls closely as they drifted away, but I couldn't recognize any of them. Where were the girls from the Pompeii gathering? Surely Eshe would know...assuming she was okay, and not merely putting on a haughty show.

She waited for us with primly folded hands, smiling as we approached. But once Ahmad gave us a final happy wave and drove on, she fixed me with a pointed glare.

"It took you long enough."

And just like that, I no longer worried about her. "I'm sorry, did you send up some sort of flare? From what we could see, you were liberated from a shopping trip, not some sort of prison camp."

"You've no idea what I've endured," Eshe said, but she

sounded mostly bored as she surveyed us with a shrewd glance. "We have a suite of rooms assigned to us. I'm glad to see that at least Nikki dressed you appropriately for once. Did you have any difficulty getting here?"

There was an amused lilt to her voice with her last question, and I narrowed my eyes at her.

"Don't even tell me you knew that was going to happen. A little heads-up would've been handy."

Eshe lifted an unconcerned shoulder. "I couldn't run the risk of either the Shadow Court or Ahmad knowing exactly how advanced my skills are. It does me no favors to show my hand completely. I'm sure this will not come as a surprise, but the rooms we have been assigned are all wired to the rafters with eyes and ears. It seems our host is willing to take no chances and wishes to shine his lovely rays of curiosity down upon us at all times. The only place that's free of surveillance I've been able to find is the spa."

Nikki turned toward her. "Back it up, Buttercup. There's a spa?"

Eshe favored her with an amused smile. "Staffed by very watchful personnel, but not bugged, that I can tell. All the members of the facility are women, of course, all very circumspect. I would not misjudge them, and I would also not underestimate them, but there is privacy to be had there. Privacy we need. There is much we should discuss before the proposition that will be made to you this night, much I need to share."

My brows lifted. "What kind of—"

"As I said, we would do better to wait," Eshe said, cutting me off with a dismissive wave. "In half an hour, then? The staff will show you the way. Don't dawdle too long in your rooms, and have a care—there *are* cameras. Trust me on that."

With that, she swept off in a swirl of silk, the long lines of her pantsuit somehow seeming even more suited to her than her typical toga. Nikki flipped her hair over her shoulder, Danae smiled inscrutably, and the three of us followed in Eshe's wake, not speaking as we entered a low guesthouse compound. It appeared that our suites were all interconnected, one after the other down a long hallway, the doors between our main sitting areas all linked.

"Wow," Nikki said, lifting her gaze to the glittering chandeliers beneath a series of open skylights, before poking her head inside the first bedroom. "Ahmad sure knows how to show a girl a good time."

I had to agree. The rooms were sumptuously outfitted with low cushioned chairs covered in pastel shades that evoked pearls and sea glass, the walls covered in fabric wallpaper, making the chambers feel like the inside of a jewelry box. A peek into the sleeping areas showed similarly outfitted spaces, with doors standing open to dressing alcoves.

"We've got spa robes, ladies. And slippers and, like, pajama pants, and I don't even know what this is, but I am all in," Nikki announced from inside her dressing chamber. I couldn't help but smile, but when I shut the door on her and Danae's chatter, it was to draw in a deep and unsteady breath. The lines of fire where my wings had burst free from my shoulder blades had never stopped throbbing. I'd accessed a different kind of energy today, one that I did not understand. I lifted my mental barriers slightly, unexpected tears sparking behind my eyes as the Magician immediately responded.

"You're hurt," he said. *"I should be there."*

Not yet, I replied mentally, startling myself with my choice of words. Not "No," full stop, but "Not yet." My heart

179

JENN STARK

gave a hard tug at the idea that the Magician was only a quiet call away. Even if I would not put him in danger, that gave me strength.

Instead, I focused on my primary concern, though I wasn't a hundred percent sure he could help me. *What magic did I tap in to today?* I asked. *Could you tell from so far away?*

As usual, I should never underestimate the Magician's ability at telehealth.

"It is an old energy, one that has not been fully utilized for centuries, possibly millennia. I mentioned that the Shadow Court was not active in the Arabian Peninsula, but their prejudice was not isolated. We haven't explored the arcane powers of those lands, or those who have learned to wield those powers, nearly enough. All of us on the Council tend to stick to the magic we know best."

Yeah, speaking of the Council. Were you ever going to get around to letting me know about the Sun?

The Magician was quiet for a long moment.

"So it is Alsain Ahmad," he finally said, as if I had just given him the news. *"The Sun reveals itself, at long last."*

Apparently, I had.

You didn't know? I protested. *How could you not have known that he was a member of the Council? I mean, seriously. It's not like he's doing all that much to hide. And what about the Moon and the Star? Who are they?*

"Ahhh...the Moon. The Star...there is a symmetry there, of course. And their identities remain unknown. Some of the most effective disguises are those you wear in plain sight," Armaeus said, but his voice was distant, and I knew I was losing him. There clearly was much important thinking to be done about this discovery, and he was already fading, doubtless to

go wall himself up in his fortress of solitude until he could figure everything out.

Hey, hey, hey, don't feeb out on me yet. What do I need to know about Ahmad? How dangerous is he? What does the Sun do, anyway?

Armaeus's voice strengthened. "*Fortunately, the ancient powers of the Sun are well documented—fire magic, of course, and powerful influence. He can lull you into coercion or scorch you into it, you might say.*"

I grimaced. *Charming.*

"*There is also mention of weather magic and an interconnectedness through light rays, though that is less certain.*" Armaeus's words picked up speed, probably reflecting his growing intrigue over Ahmad being the Sun. "*I have much research left to do. The Sun, the Moon, and the Star were once a trinity of power on the Council, but that was millennia ago. They fell away from the Council almost as soon as the battle with Atlantis ended. The Moon and Star were lost to history well before Ahmad's ascension.*"

Yeah, he said he didn't know the other two.

"*He speaks the truth in that. I realized only recently, after reclaiming my memories, that all three members had been part of Council lore up until the mid-1800s, but I had no idea how to find them, or even if they remained alive. When the call went out for the full vote, not even the Devil expected them to respond.*"

But they all did, I said.

"*They all did. Unfortunately, they elected to use a mail-in ballot, you might say. We had no way of knowing where those votes came from or who generated them.*"

I grimaced. *You people seriously have to get a better system.*

Armaeus chuckled. "*I will take it up at the next bylaws meeting.*" Then his words grew more serious. "*You need to rest,*

Miss Wilde. You are very drained from your efforts today. More drained than you should be."

I shrugged, though he wasn't here to see me. *Well, I didn't have much of a choice. How's Sariah doing?*

"Resting and healing. As you should be. In fact..." Armaeus's voice faded again, and I shook my head.

Fine, I'll rest. We're about to take a spa day, actually. With Eshe. It'll be great.

The Magician's voice filled my mind with a new urgency, as well as a definite sense of satisfaction. *"I'm sure it will be. But not as refreshing as a moment spent elsewhere in this world..."*

I felt an unexpected tug then, and, more surprised than alarmed, I gave in to it. A moment later, I found myself in Armaeus's arms, smack in the middle of his office in Prime Luxe. It was full-on night outside, the Strip lit up like Christmas, which only added to my disorientation.

"Whoa!" I managed, my mind spinning as all my cells reconstituted. "How did you do that?"

"I never stop learning, Miss Wilde. But shhhh..." With a long, soft sigh, he sent rivers of healing energy through me, flooding over and under and through injuries I hadn't realized I still carried, and I sagged against him, spent.

"Oh...oh wow," I managed.

"Somewhat better than a spa day, I hope you'll agree," Armaeus said. After a few blessed moments more, he held me away from him, his gaze soft as he studied me.

"You must return," he said, as if trying to convince himself. "A battle awaits that must be fought."

"But not yet?" I asked too quickly. Then I bit my lip. Armaeus's eyes widened, and he gathered me close again, pressing his lips to my temple.

"Not yet, Miss Wilde, no," he murmured into my ear.

"Not yet. If I could create a world away that you and I could share for an eternity, I would do it. My magic only goes so far, unfortunately. But for a space of minutes, perhaps the half hour Eshe has allotted you before you meet again? Yes. That I most assuredly can do."

He lifted his hands to my face and cupped my chin with his fingertips, leaning down as if to brush the softest kiss against my lips.

I didn't give him the chance. I threw my arms around him and shoved him backward against a pile of pillows that appeared a half second before we landed on top of them, sending him sprawling as I came down on top of him. My mouth found his, and I pressed against him hard, hungering, dying of a thirst that overwhelmed me to reconnect with this man who barely knew who I was anymore, and yet who was as bound to me as my soul to my body. Armaeus, never one to hesitate once a decision had been made, especially one he supported, murmured something else, and a moment later, we both sank not into enormous pillows on the floor of his office, but into his luxurious bed, our bodies naked and entwined.

"I really need to learn how to do that," I muttered, lunging for him.

He laughed, the sound rich and full, and took my momentum as his own, catching me and turning me over on the bed until he pinned me with his body, his hands shackling my wrists and stretching my arms high, his breath a sweet mix of cinnamon and citrus.

"I think I should be careful of exactly how much you have learned to do already, Miss Wilde," he said, staring down at me. He looked like he should be the one trekking across the Arabian desert, spiriting chalices free from ancient ruins, and for just a moment, I let myself long for that possibility, the two of us setting out side by side, partners not of a great and mighty Council, but on some clandestine midnight raid for a shadowy client whose intentions we couldn't fully trust. "I have long known you are more capable than even you suspect."

"Maybe I know exactly how capable I am," I challenged, and I sent a pulse of magic through my hands, directed at him, lifting his body more fully and shifting it a few crucial inches until it was better positioned above me. Just as quickly, I swept the magic away, and the Magician settled down heavily over me, our bodies fit perfectly together. He reacted with gratifying speed, his shaft hardening against me and his eyes heating, glittery with purpose.

"Then I definitely should be more careful," he mused. "But not yet, I think. Not yet."

He tilted forward and slipped inside me, and it was my turn to arch back on the bed, my mouth dropping open on a groan, my eyes drifting shut. I moved against him in a swift, rolling rhythm, wanting—needing more. I knew I should meet his gaze, knew I would regret not watching the rush of emotions chase across his face as we joined together, but I couldn't share my focus right away. I couldn't do anything but revel in the explosion of sensations that his body was evoking in mine. His body and his magic.

Armaeus murmured something low and arcane, and I increased the rhythm of my movement, the speed, my breath coming more fitfully now. This, *this* was what I'd been missing, almost without realizing it. The sharpness of our connection, the immediacy of it. Armaeus had been my introduction to the fullness of my magic and also its strongest prod, and I craved that insistent drive now, craved it like I craved his body.

I pushed against him, and he rolled easily until he was

beneath me. I braced my hands on his beautiful bronzed shoulders, my fingers pressing into the taut muscles. I stared down, feeling myself fall into the endless mystery of his gaze, his eyes widening as something opened deep within me, filled with joy and power.

I clenched my eyes tight and breathed that power in, let it fill me, let *him* fill me, the movement right and true. We slid out of time and place and back again, my skin growing frigid, then fiery hot, then drenched in rain and whipped by wind. And all the while, the open space within me reached hungrily for more, more, more—

"Sara," Armaeus gasped, and his use of my name made my eyes shoot open, my own sudden need for oxygen overwhelming as I sucked in a startled breath. His eyes had gone completely golden, the darkness of his magic that had haunted his expression for months now, a darkness that had always been there, but had grown so much more intense as we'd fought the war against magic and dealt with the subsequent fallout—suddenly, crazily gone.

"Sara," he gasped again, his voice more urgent. He looked at me with wonder and surprise, and his own pulsing rhythm increased until he was driving into me. "You can't take all my darkness, no matter what you think. I need it—and you need me to have it. You have to know that—"

At least, that was what I thought he said. I couldn't fully process his words as I exhaled not only breath but power, and the world tilted back on its axis again, time suddenly resuming its rush and tumble around us. Then Armaeus was filling me once more, spiraling me to a climax I felt myself clawing toward, desperate to have and desperate to stave off at once, but one I couldn't delay any longer. I jerked hard, and he shouted with an exultation that seemed to stretch far beyond sexual into something dark and unfathomable.

I fluttered my eyes open again, not realizing I'd clenched them shut, and I saw not only the Magician, but an entire night sky around him, filled with shimmering stars. *This, this,* the magic within me seemed to whisper. *This.*

And then—we were flying.

18

By the time I returned to Ahmad's pleasure palace in Dubai, I had absolutely no need of a massage. But I also wasn't in the mood to explain why I now felt... uniquely relaxed, so I dutifully reported to the spa a half hour later.

The personal care facilities at Ahmad's residence were every bit in keeping with the rest of the accommodations. Eshe, Nikki, Danae, and I met up in the lobby of the facility, which looked like it had been designed to hold fifty such guests, not four. There were half a dozen staff lined up to greet us, all young women of startling beauty, in flowing outfits of shell pink and sea-foam green. I was beginning to seriously miss my grungy hoodie.

"This way, this way," the lead woman instructed us, and from hearing her voice, I realized she wasn't the teenager I had suspected, but a full-grown adult. I amended my reaction to the place. If this was the effect the spa had on its patrons, I might need to stay here longer.

She ushered us all into a large room, where showers were set deep into the wall, each with its own curving alcove. Her instructions transcended the need for language, but we waved her off, pointing to our already damp hair. Even Eshe had elected to shower in her room, clearly eager for us to be left to our own devices as quickly as possible.

Our guide brightened, nodding quickly, then took us to the next room, where four tables had been set up in close proximity to each other. Another quartet of women stood at the ready, and the space smelled of jasmine and sunflowers.

I stared at the table, confused, and Nikki nudged me forward. "Girl, I haven't had a massage since God was a child. Go with it."

All I really wanted to do was get information from Eshe, but this was clearly the path of least resistance. I stretched out on the table, facedown, and winced only slightly as my masseuse laid her hands on my shoulders. Not surprisingly, she flinched back. Armaeus had taken away the pain of my impromptu Winged Victory impression, but not the heat.

"Sorry about that," I managed as she dipped her head down to look at me with wide eyes.

Her smile was reassuring, if a little tremulous. "No, no, it is no trouble. No trouble," she said breathlessly. "I will start elsewhere." She did, and my overheated shoulder blades cooled off enough for her to brave my back a few minutes later. Small wins. Against all expectations...I relaxed. Deeply.

It was another hour before we were set free from the careful ministrations of Ahmad's staff. We were rolled off the table, our conversation barely intelligible with our level of stupor, and led into yet another spa room. Here there was a pool of crystal clear water, shimmering beneath a pergola of wood and more fluttering fabric. Nikki and Danae wasted no time submersing themselves in the water, their groans of pleasure audible, but Eshe and I moved to the far corner of the pool.

"Do they have ears here?" I asked.

"Not that I can tell," Eshe said. "And I think I would be able to notice. My ability to sense the magic of a place is amplified away from the Council. I never knew that, since I rarely leave the Council's base. It simply seemed better for me to stay hidden away."

I glanced at her, surprised. "All these centuries later? Why's that?"

The question was rude, but Eshe didn't seem to mind. "I think there are those who are meant to fly, and those who are meant to hide," she said, not without a hint of sadness. "Something I shall have to consider more deeply when there is time. Which is not now."

She refocused on me. "Ahmad puts on a good act, but he is flat broke. He made one too many poor decisions in his dealings with the newer families, and they have made him pay for it. Accordingly, he needs money, and a lot of it. He is hoping that you will help him get it."

I blinked. I never thought about a Council member not being loaded, but Ahmad had been cut off from the mother ship for thousands of years, and this arguably was some pretty pricey real estate. Still, those must have been some epically poor decisions. And more to the point... "Me? How does he think I can help him out with that?"

"That, I don't know," Eshe allowed. "Suffice to say that you are his number one plan, though. It would not surprise me if he is using the distraction of the Shadow Court as a cover to get this help from you. He is not to be trusted. I don't care if he is the Sun."

"And he is, right? That's not bullshit?"

Eshe made a face. "Sadly, it is not. When I was in

Pompeii, I was visited with many visions. They came all at once, a jumbled mess. It has taken me some time to unravel the first few, but what does seem to happen is that when I'm faced with a person or place who figured prominently in the vision, it becomes clear. When Ahmad's staff approached me at the Dubai bazaar, I knew immediately who and what he was, even though I also understood that no one else did. Not his own people, and, importantly, not the Shadow Court. At least, not my low-level keepers. To them, he appeared to be a person of some importance, a Connected player whose use they have not fully determined, but not the Sun. Certainly not a member of the Arcana Council."

I considered that, but it wasn't my only question. "Yeah, about that. What the hell happened back there in Pompeii, anyway? You were supposed to go under and report back. Instead, you ghosted. Did they hurt you?"

"They didn't hurt me," she said. Then her lip curled. "Though they kept my acolytes, which infuriates me. Those girls should be returned to their guardians."

"They will be. You're still in contact with them?" I remembered the plea from the wizard, begging for his daughter's safety. It had only been a few days since the Pompeii festival, but for a parent, it must feel like a lifetime.

"I am, though distantly. They are not in distress but they are in—confusion. I suspect they're drugs."

"Of course they are," I muttered. Jarvis would pay for that. "Were you?"

Eshe sighed. "I...I don't believe so, but I'm not certain," she said, though the admission clearly cost her. "I know only that I was treated well, made comfortable—and then the visions came. I awoke in Dubai two days later."

I stared at her. "Two *days*?"

"It's completely normal," she said, though her voice

wasn't as firm as I would have preferred. "When I am in the exalted state, I do not eat, I do not sleep. I do not age or suffer in any way. It is like...a stasis."

"Yeah, but what if someone was dialing into Radio Eshe? Ahmad said you ran some visions for him earlier today."

She shook her head. "That was different. We spoke early this morning, when he put to me questions as a worthy querent. But the other..." She glanced away. "There was no one there. And even if there was, they could not have interpreted my fugue pronouncements. I am sure of it."

I was equally *not* sure of that, but I didn't want to completely harsh Eshe's mellow. She'd been through more than I realized in the past few days. Her eyes were shadowed, almost bruised, and her manner curiously fragile. Even as I watched, her eyes shifted, strands of milky white slipping across her irises, sending a chill through me.

As gently as I could, I pushed on. "Ahmad says there are two other Council members in the wind—the Moon and Star. Did you have any visions about them?"

"I saw only chaos and betrayal," she said, the words curiously flat and hushed, like a muttered prayer. "An ocean of death in the wake of the night witch."

I stiffened. "Whoa, whoa, whoa. Hold up there."

Eshe jerked back a little at my harsh tone, then shook her head, glancing around quickly. "What?"

"You've mentioned that term before. The night witch. Who the hell is that?"

She blinked at me, tilting her head. "Well—it's you. Or the shadow side of you. How do you not know that? Did you not look at all into the history of your own position?"

"I didn't make it that far back," I said drily. "And Mrs. French has found impressively little on the subject, no matter how hard she looks. So enlighten me."

She sighed. "I forget sometimes how old I am and how long I've been a member of the Council. But the basic truth is this: Justice, the original Justice, could not always serve in her given role. From the start, she was overwhelmed by the needs of those who called for her aid. But not everyone who is harmed needs Justice. Some require only revenge. And revenge is swiftly done."

"So Justice had a sidekick," I said. "This night witch. And she would...what, just go kill people Justice couldn't get around to? Take them out?"

I asked the question almost flippantly, but Eshe nodded. "The night witch walked where Justice could not and struck where Justice would not. The Council evolved, and the role vanished. But if whispers of her are returning, there are clearly those who remember...perhaps those who see the value in a willing sword in a hopeless battle."

"That's beautiful." I shook my head. "You guys really need to do a better job of onboarding with this whole Council thing."

Eshe waved me off. "You've little likelihood of being drawn into vigilantism," she said, and the disdain in her voice brought to mind Gamon's sneering accusations. But Eshe pushed on.

"Truly, you have to focus. Jarvis and the way he's positioning the Shadow Court—it's not the end game. I know that much in my bones."

"Yeah? You remember it from your visions?" I asked. Now we were getting somewhere.

Eshe nodded. "There was so much chaos. So much anger. And a power far beyond any ordinary mortal scope."

I made a face. "Do *not* tell me the Court is tied up with the gods in some way. Not after everything we did to get rid of those guys."

"I don't believe so. I think it is an earthly force. A government, a corporation, a family, I don't know. But they are powerful, rich, and very old. And they want you out of the way—your strength, and the Council's strength as well. They seek to rule, and they sense their chance is coming, finally. That's all I've been able to interpret so far from my visions. I sense there's more, but it remains just outside my grasp."

She bit her lip, looking frail again, and I forced myself not to push her. It wasn't nearly enough information to act on, but it was more than I had coming into this conversation, and for that, I was grateful. It would have to do until Ahmad showed his cards.

Fortunately, we didn't have to wait long for that.

19

My first dinner with a sheikh was a weirdly casual affair, with Eshe, Nikki, Danae, and myself joining Ahmad in his private dining room. *Private* was a little bit of a misnomer, as the room could've easily seated seventy-five people, but it was intimately staged, with Ahmad at one end of a heavy olive-wood table, Nikki, Danae, and Eshe arranged around him, and another man to Ahmad's left. I hadn't seen this man before, but he looked both nervous and uptight. I figured he was probably Ahmad's accountant, based on what Eshe said.

I sat opposite Ahmad at the end of the table, which was all right with me. I didn't exactly trust my mood. Despite my epic massage and Eshe's continued assurance that the young women still being held in Pompeii were whole and healthy, I found my nerves were wound tight, anger simmering right beneath my veneer of helpful Council representative. If Ahmad did anything to piss me off, I didn't know how well I would handle it. My irritation was actually a little concerning. It wasn't like me. After the Magician's report on Sariah, I should've felt better. Instead, I found myself getting more and more unsettled the longer I thought about it.

There was no reason for Sariah to have been attacked. I couldn't get past that. Anybody with half a brain would've been able to figure out that she wasn't me, the fact that she thought her plan would work notwithstanding. So why? Why do it? Why piss me off? Was it truly that the Shadow Court hadn't been able to get enough of a rise out of me up to this point? Was this all some sort of meaningless game to them?

Even as I thought that, I rejected the idea. Whoever they were—and there was simply no way Jarvis was behind all this, I was...almost certain—they were not dumb people. They wouldn't simply irritate me because it made them giggle. There had to be a reason. Every single attack they'd leveled against me had been set up with a specific goal—and I'd responded each time, advancing my abilities without intending to. And each attack had brought—nothing. No retribution, no countermeasure. We just took it, and took it, and took it.

I thought about Death's warning, that no action was without consequence. Yet the Shadow Court hadn't paid for any of its crimes. Was it time for me to change that?

"I could not be more pleased to welcome you all here," Ahmad said, recalling my attention with a jolt. He'd waited until the meal had been served, savory-looking dishes nestled in elegant bowls. Not too ostentatious, but I suspected that the china alone would cost a king's ransom. Everything about Ahmad's palace was over-the-top luxurious to a fault, giving the impression of minimalism on the outside, but grandiosity at a closer glance. No wonder the guy was broke.

"I trust that you've found everything to your satisfaction?" he asked.

He might have intended the question for all of us, but it was Eshe he looked at first, and then Nikki, surprisingly enough. Both of them smiled in return, murmuring soft, approving platitudes. Eshe because she was cool enough to know what was going on here, Nikki because I was making her nervous, I suspected. Her normally bright, flamboyant style was restrained, and the way she kept glancing at me was a dead giveaway as to why. I felt bad about that, but I couldn't shake my growing tension. I suspected I wasn't going to like what was about to happen.

"I hope you forgive the intrusion on our private dinner, but I have asked Hassan, my closest advisor, to be with me. He will serve both as a witness to our arrangement today and also provide any necessary history, in case I misspeak."

"It is my pleasure to serve," Hassan said, his voice shivery and cool. Beside me, Danae stiffened, but she kept her gaze across the table on Nikki another moment before glancing casually to the right. My third eye flew open. Hassan's energy crackled, but my first guess, that he was possessed or maybe even a full-on demon, didn't seem to be borne out. He was definitely Connected, which made sense as the right-hand man of the Sun, and his energy was decidedly dark, but not demon dark. Still, there was no denying the tension in Danae's body. Maybe he was a witch as well—but a sketchy one? Some kind of Arabian warlock?

I regarded Hassan coolly. "How long have you served Ahmad?"

"I have had the privilege of serving him my entire life," Hassan said, and I had to give the guy props. It was a great answer. That could've ranged from the approximately forty-five years that I judged the man's age, up to a millennium. I was willing to let it go for now, either way. I'd follow up with Danae later.

Ahmad beamed approvingly at his lackey, then refocused on me. "As is appropriate in the land of a thousand and one tales of Arabian Nights, I have a story to share with you. A tale of a great kingdom that never was. I was not born the Sun, as you may imagine. My kingdom came into power at the time of the great Queen of Sheba, around 900 BCE. My father was the queen's greatest fan. They were to be wed and rule over the entire Arabian Peninsula, or so he dreamed. My father, however, was a careful man as well. Some would call him cunning. He knew he was not the only sheikh vying for the queen's hand. And so he decided to get a little help."

At this, Hassan leaned closer to his master, murmuring in his ear.

"Of course, of course," Ahmad said before turning back to us a little apologetically. "My advisor reminds me that as with many great households, there are some rules of hospitality I must ask you to follow before I speak further."

Another spark of irritation flared up, but I merely nodded.

"Such as?"

"I would ask that none of the stories I am about to share with you leave your own hearts. I have survived many lifetimes as a result of my discretion. I would hate to have that discretion compromised now."

It seemed like a reasonable enough request. "Whatever's spoken here, we will hold in our hearts," I agreed. I thought about giving caveats, but there was no real need. Should the Magician wish to review the highlights from today, he could do so without... I paused, regarding Ahmad more steadily. "Provided that we all remain healthy and unharmed."

I didn't miss the tremor of annoyance that passed over Ahmad's face, though his advisor merely regarded me with cool amusement. *This had better not be a trap.* I seriously wasn't in the mood for traps.

"Very well," Ahmad finally said. "It was never our intention to bring you or any you care for harm, Justice Wilde. We merely need to ensure the safety of our holdings."

"Of course," I said, matching him with a smooth smile of my own. "Set within those parameters, your stories are safe with us."

"Excellent, then. As I was saying, my father had set his sights on marrying the Queen of Sheba. While many today say the fabled Queen Makeda did not exist, she was one of the grandest and most knowledgeable rulers of her time. My father knew he had to act quickly and decisively if he meant to gain her hand in marriage. He enlisted the aid of a djinn."

"A djinn?" I echoed. Not what I was expecting. "He was able to do that?"

Ahmad nodded. "Unlike the demon summoners elsewhere in the world, one does not require witchcraft to summon a djinn, merely profound intent and the correct words. Likewise, the djinn is not bound by chalk circles or spell craft, but by the simple construct of the summoner's three wishes. Once those wishes are met, the djinn returns whence it came. Until those wishes are completed, however, it remains restricted in a vessel of the summoner's choosing. My father needed the most powerful djinn he could conjure, and he aimed high. He called—"

Here Ahmad broke off, smiling like a showman. "I won't share his name aloud. Names have power, especially here. But rest assured, it was one of the mightiest of the djinn realm. He came with all haste and gave my father the two things he most needed to entice the queen: money and influence. My father's third wish, I am told, was Connected ability beyond any of his rivals. But what we did not know was that the djinn had been constrained against completing such a wish. He could not do it. And my father, having made his wish, could not change it. As he was thrashing about, trying to reconcile the problem, or at a minimum determine who had crossed him so neatly, he was attacked and killed."

"Ouch," Nikki blurted—and I couldn't have agreed more. Ahmad smiled a little sadly.

"Indeed. The queen, of course, vanished into the sands, to make other marriages and start other kingdoms. But at the moment of his death, all the power my father had accumulated through his work with the djinn was released to me, and I, by a twist of fate, had been born Connected—powerfully so. I was merely a babe at the time and did not understand, but when I was still a child, I was approached to join the ranks of the Arcana Council. I accepted, and retreated to security ever since. It took generations for me to reach my majority, and then I seemed to stop aging entirely, at least to those with a less discerning eye. I cannot argue that point. I am happy enough to stay young, but that is a tale for another day. What is important is that the djinn bound to my father was never heard of again. I believe, as does my counselor Hassan, that it remains hidden in one of Sheba's palaces, awaiting the granting of its final wish, and its release."

I narrowed my eyes. "Please don't tell me you want me to find your genie."

Ahmad spread his hands. "For many hundreds of years, I was afraid to look myself. I did not want to call attention to such a prize. I watched as kingdoms rose and fell, barbarians rolling across the land like a bloody tide. I watched once-proud fortresses descend into ruins and mighty empires rise up on their ashes. But no one came. No one looked. My father's djinn remains trapped in Sheba's palace. I am sure of it."

Despite myself, I couldn't deny a growing interest in this story. "But you're already Connected. What would be the benefit of more magic?" It was a somewhat facile question. No magician on earth was ever satisfied with his current magic if he could somehow gain more. But I wanted to hear Ahmad's specific answer.

He lifted his glass and took a long, considering sip before he answered. "The kind of magic that the djinn was to gather for my father was regenerative. Its purpose was to grow within whatever vessel held it—ideally, that would have been within my father's body and soul, but that was not meant to be. Instead, it grew within the djinn's vessel, doubtless infusing him with terrifying strength. All these thousands of years later, it would be a rare and mighty power indeed, an unknown magic entirely, and one that only a few bearers on this earth could control. You are one of them. The Magician of your Council is another. I, sadly, am not."

I narrowed my eyes. "You want me to find this djinn— and take its magic *from* you?"

And then, of course, I got it. "You want to sell it. To the Arcana Council."

"I do," Ahmad said without embarrassment. "My decisions do not always keep pace with my dreams of late, and I would not come into active involvement with the Council as a poor relation. I am as proud as my father once was."

I blew out a long breath considering that, and Ahmad kept going. "Of course, there is another concern."

I grimaced. "Which is?"

"As long as this reservoir of magic remains in the world,

we are at risk. I cannot overstate how powerful it is. If it were to fall into the Shadow Court's hands..."

"It cannot."

I was already lifting a hand to wave off Ahmad's concern when Eshe spoke, her voice thick with an odd, otherworldly intonation. I jerked my attention toward her to see her eyes wide, unfocused, and milky white. Her hand was loose around her chalice, her lips stained with wine. A lick of fury ripped through me, but Ahmad lifted both hands, warding me off.

"There's no poison," he declared, accurately guessing my concern. "I do not..."

Both he and Hassan looked at Eshe with worship in their eyes. It took me aback for a second, but it wasn't the first time I'd seen her generate that reaction, even among the Arcana Council. The Emperor could be a fangirl as well.

"They are close. Too close, Sara Wilde," the High Priestess continued. "They seek to distract and destroy, and on your bones make new magic."

I curled my lip, but it was Nikki who gave voice to my thought.

"Well, that took a dark turn."

"They are close," Eshe said again. Then she slumped a little in her seat, blinking. Reaching for her glass, she took another long draft of her wine, and Danae leaned toward her to put a cool hand on her arm.

Ahmad turned to me excitedly.

"You see? You see. You must find the djinn before the minions of the Shadow Court do. There can be no other reason for them to have come so close to where I believe my father's djinn to have been buried. I never would have broken my own silence unless I was truly worried."

He seemed earnest enough, but I couldn't stop my

unease. "Then why are they poking me at all?" I asked. "If they'd left me alone, I may or may not have come at all, and certainly not this fast."

"You misunderstand the true desire of the Shadow Court," Hassan spoke up. "The magic of the djinn is great, countered only by a few who walk this earth. But your magic is great as well. If both could be constrained in one stroke, if the Shadow Court could amass not only the magic of this ancient carrier but conquer yours as well, there is *no one* in the Arcana Council, either singly or together, who could withstand them. In one swift act, they would have the power of a god. Perhaps, the power of the one true God. And unlike the Council for all these long millennia, they would not hesitate to use it within the world of man."

"Sweet mother Mary on a tricycle," Nikki muttered, while Danae had gone still again. I stared at Hassan, struck by how forcefully his words rang in my ears. He was telling us a fact, not merely a truth. He definitely had some witch magic in him.

"Where are they now?" I asked.

"The Shadow Court?" Ahmad grimaced. "They are being feted by three royal families of the Emirates at once. You should consider that. It is very likely that the promises they have made are extreme and the action they will take immediate, the moment they have the magic of the ancient djinn in their hands."

That...didn't sound good.

"It gets worse," Ahmad said, reading my reaction exactly. "Where I'm sending you, it is not merely an abandoned tomb. It is occupied by an army of djinn...and possibly other creatures too. The queen's burial chambers have become a stronghold for the defiled, probably drawn by the deep magic the place possesses. I didn't mind so much for a long time, because it kept out any enterprising artifact hunters. But it is a den of cobras, make no mistake.

"All right," I said. "Then I'll need a full team."

Ahmad brightened. "Of course, of course. I can offer any of my men."

"No," I said. "I'll get my own men. But Eshe, here, I will need returned to the Arcana Council. Immediately."

The High Priestess blinked at me, clearly startled by my order.

"I need you with the Magician," I said, and to my surprise, she merely nodded. In fact, I saw something approaching relief in her expression and once again, I wondered how drained she truly was. I slid my gaze to Ahmad, and was equally surprised to see anger ripple across his face.

"You don't trust us to take care of a member of the Council?" he asked stonily.

"I don't trust myself not to be distracted," I said. "She'll go back. What she does after that is on her."

Ahmad blew out a long breath. "Agreed. But I implore you, summoning outsiders to assist you is not only unnecessary, it is very dangerous. Djinn magic is very subtle. My men have been trained against this very task for generations, their skills transferred from father to child. They're ready for this challenge."

"I'll take my chances."

A tiny flare of panic sparked in Ahmad's eyes. "I'm telling you, these are not demons you're dealing with here. In many ways they're human in their temperaments, their needs, and their emotions. But when they act, they are fully magic in their manifestation and might. There are no ordinary humans who can face the kind of danger they present."

"Well, lucky for me, I'm not going to rely on any ordinary humans. I'm calling my own people. That's final."

Ahmad exhaled heavily. "Very well," he said. "But you leave me without any reassurance that you will return with my djinn. After all these millennia, I must have that reassurance. My father lost his life for that djinn, and I've never known who betrayed him. Along with the magic that is rightfully mine, I demand the right to learn the truth about my family's betrayer."

I made a face. "That's ancient history, Ahmad. That villain's family is doubtless long dead and buried."

"Nevertheless, it is my *right* to know," he said again, sounding ever so slightly unhinged.

"And I will bring the djinn to you. I have no problem with that," I countered.

"I would like to believe you, but I still need my reassurance that you will return," Ahmad said. His eyes shifted to the left, and I felt more than saw the caress of them against Nikki's jet-black hair. Fury licked up within me, quick and hot.

"*Don't,*" I said.

Ahmad's gaze returned to mine, startled. "It is customary—"

"*Fuck* your customs," I snapped, and everyone in the room froze. "I will find your djinn, Ahmad. I will keep it from the Shadow Court. I'll even give you your moment of absolution. But do not threaten my people, and do *not* piss me off. I'm only warning you once."

Nobody said a word.

20

"You have to understand what I'm dealing with here," Ahmad whined for about the fifteenth time nearly an hour later as we walked down the back corridor of his home and out to the veranda. Night had fallen, and the entire expanse of his palatial residence looked serene, leading out to the silent sea. The skies above sparkled with stars. "It's important for us to go about this as carefully as possible. I've been planning against this potential opportunity for quite some time."

"I told you, I'm good with—Oman? Was that his name?" I hadn't expected to be able to go into the ruins without a local guide, I could even accept it would be one of Ahmad's choosing. But I was itching to move. "We start tonight?"

"Yes, yes. Oman," Ahmad said. "But timing is important. It is not a site that draws a great deal of attention, mainly because it is so plain. It's not an active dig site either. Far from it. A search party going out at night might be noticed. A crew going out during the day, however, has a greater likelihood of success, particularly if it can be assumed to be something else."

"Are the ruins open to visitors?" Nikki asked.

He turned and favored her with an approving smile. I fought the urge to roll my eyes. "It is, and only a short drive north of here. I took it upon myself to win the contract for maintaining the grounds and have managed to make an important find, which I've kept hidden from the authorities. A gallery room that, when it is eventually discovered, will bring a host of activity to the ruins. It's only a matter of time before I'll have to stage an unfortunate accident at the site, a cave-in, to reveal the room to the authorities. But I have held off. I simply...could not share it yet."

"Well, you'll definitely be sharing it if you send a crew in during the daytime," I said, shaking my head. "As it is, the Shadow Court knows I showed up this afternoon. An even slightly strange-looking crowd of workers going into the ruins tomorrow morning is going to attract attention. We should go now, if your guide is ready."

"If...I don't know." Ahmad sighed. "I simply cannot be certain that you'll get into the ruins unseen."

"Why don't you let me worry about that. You think your guide is ready?"

"Yes. Oman is one of the best guides in the Arabian Peninsula. He knows each of the castles attributed to Queen Makeda, most notably this one. And he knows its secret ways."

"Excellent." I considered Ahmad again, my mind working through the angles. "You've been cleaning these ruins for over two years, you said. Why haven't you searched it yourself? Beyond this gallery room that you've found?"

A smile flickered across Ahmad's face. "We have, to the extent that we can. We know there is one subterranean chamber, likely part of a larger level that does not show up on any architectural renderings of the queen's castle. The archaeologists did not find it or the welcome gallery, and we have taken great pains to ensure they still don't know these rooms exist."

"And how did you pull that off, again?" Danae asked.

"One of my skills as Sun—I can manipulate light and energy as a distraction," Ahmad said modestly. "Interfere with readings, deflect attention away. The illusion has been draining to maintain over time, but I would have gone much further in the ruins if I could have. There are guardians beyond that first chamber, however, that have proven sufficiently difficult to overcome without drawing undue attention to the effort."

I lifted my brows. "Demons?"

"Not in the traditional sense," Ahmad said. "Very old, and very dangerous. Oman can tell you more when you see him. I suspect you will find him very helpful."

He turned and gestured to one of his staffers, who nodded and hurried away.

"Suffice to say the danger proved too great on multiple fronts to carry on the search," Ahmad continued. "We instead turned to researching spells that might deter the guardians. We suspect they are only the first layer of protection, but they are a formidable one."

"That usually seems to be the case," I said.

He nodded. "I believe you will find that the public access point holds no information you will need, and the subterranean chamber itself is quite barren, though the gallery in between remains an interesting study. I remain convinced there is more beneath the chambers we've found, however, an entire network of tunnels and ancient rooms said to hold great secrets. We've attempted ground penetrating radar from the air to determine if we can see anything beneath the earth's surface. The results are indistinct, but to me, significant. There is something down there. Whether natural or man-made, I can't say, but definitely something there. Regrettably, we'll only have one opportunity to find it. And you'll need to be quite careful. If you're discovered, the local governmental response will be...unfortunate."

"Understood." I moved to turn away, eager to start preparing for the trip, but Ahmad raised a hand.

"I know it goes without saying, but there is one more thing I need to remind you of. It is through the generosity of the house of Ahmad that I'm releasing the High Priestess back to her home. We will arrange for transportation, of course."

I shrugged. "I think the Council probably can handle that."

"It is a grace I'm extending to you in good faith," Ahmad pressed. "When you find the vessel of the djinn, I must insist that it be returned immediately to me. You dare not betray me in this."

Irritation didn't just spurt, it *rocketed* through me. There were a great many things that I dared, and this really wasn't all that high up on the list. But I was a game girl. "Fair enough." I shrugged. "I will return the vessel to you and no one else. Anything else we need to clear up?"

Ahmad smiled broadly. "I think we understand each other perfectly. I appreciate it very much."

With that, he released us, but, wary of the surveillance equipment, we did not discuss much on the way back to our rooms together to gather what belongings we needed. By the time we met again behind Ahmad's palace, only a scant hour had passed. Ahmad stood there with his usual entourage of security guards, but with him now was a small man dressed in overalls and a cap with long tails intended to keep off the sun. We'd been given similar outfits to wear, in case we were detained on the way to the dig site, but the caps were particularly foolish given the fact that night had long since fallen. Still, we had all donned the heavy uniforms. Nikki walked as if she might catch a rash from the material.

"This is Oman," Ahmad said. "You'll be in good hands."

Oman, for his part, surveyed our small group distrustfully, which made me like him instantly. "None of these are warriors," he said, his voice as dry as sandstone. "Sorcerers, yes. Fighters..." He gestured to Nikki. "Yes. But not warriors of the caliber I told you we would need."

Ahmad drew in a breath, but I cut him off. "We'll talk about that later," I said gruffly. "If we're gonna do this, we need to go."

Ahmad lifted both hands in a conciliatory gesture, and there was no denying his excitement. "Of course, of course. You are eager to get underway, and after so much time, I should be eager to let you. But I cannot deny wanting to savor this moment. I've waited so long to have hope again. And knowing the end result of your efforts, I believe this quest will succeed. It is an auspicious moment."

It was everything I could do to resist a snide comeback, so I contented myself with nodding.

"We'll be back probably before daybreak," I said. "Sooner if there's nothing there."

Oman turned to me, a fire in his eyes now that matched Ahmad's. "Oh, there's something there, I promise you. Finding it will not be the challenge. Spiriting it out from beneath the guardians of the ancient queen, that is another question altogether."

"Roger that," Nikki said, saving me the trouble.

A bulky cleaning van was waiting for us beside Ahmad's mansion when we exited several minutes later from the service doorway. We entered the vehicle without speaking, leaving the High Priestess and Ahmad standing side by side, surrounded by his minions. I couldn't help myself. I turned and watched as we sped away, wondering exactly how...

Eshe disappeared in a sudden whirlwind, smoke bursting up around her like a dust devil, disappearing just as quickly into a scatter of birds. One second she was there with Ahmad, the next, she was gone with Ahmad jerking around, his robes flying and his hands raised, his head tilted back in alarm.

I chuckled as I settled into my seat. Whether Ahmad was a long-lost Council member bristling with mystical powers or not, the Magician would not have been able to resist a show of strength. Ahmad would have to figure out how to play better with the Council after all this was said and done.

I glanced up to see that Oman was watching me carefully, his mouth set in a grim line. "I know Sheikh Ahmad has filled your ears with magic and hope, and he is right to be awed by the mystery that lies beneath Sheba's palace," he said. "But there is great danger, too. We are not the only ones interested in the vessel you are seeking. There will be watchers."

"Yeah, I figured that. So, how well do you know the ruins? The subterranean chamber and, more specifically, the room that leads directly to it, the access point?"

Oman tilted his head. "The subterranean chamber, not as well as I would like. I've been there several times over the past few years, of course, the most recent visit perhaps two or three months ago. It never changes. It is a room about fifteen feet square and just over six feet in height. The people of that time were small in stature, and there would be no reason for a room of such height that deep underground, unless..."

"Unless they built it as a demon lounge," Nikki said. She'd already removed her coveralls, leaving her in skintight black fabric from head to toe, with a slender draping tunic that managed to add another layer of discretion while still looking badass.

Oman glanced at her and blinked, startled. "We need to remain in uniform."

"Maybe, maybe not," I said. "Back to the access point and this gallery room. How well do you know that?"

He refocused on me. "Much better. I am there every day. I am convinced there are secrets in that room that will guide us down below. Secrets I have yet to find. Ahmad would not let me assign any ancient scholars to this task, for fear of the secret getting out. I respect that, but I am a historian and a guide, not a sorcerer. This room was not meant for me."

"When was the last time you were there?"

He didn't hesitate. "Yesterday morning."

"Excellent. Could you give me your hand, please? I promise this won't hurt."

Oman stiffened, but he held out his hand to me. I took it, then turned to Nikki. Wordlessly, she reached for it as well and grasped it hard.

Oman jolted, doubtless taken aback not only by the intimacy of the gesture, but by Nikki's strong grip, and his eyes shot wide. She grinned and nodded at me, and I reached for Danae, pulling her in close.

"So, I lied," I said. "This part is probably going to hurt a little."

And we crackled into nothing.

We rematerialized a second later in a dimly lit chamber of rock that ran about twenty feet long and ten feet wide, a gallery of sorts. The walls had been carved with interconnected pictures, roped off and marked by small makeshift placards at each new carving. A single tiny candle guttered in a lantern by the doorway.

"The welcome chamber," Oman breathed. It was a testament to his excitement that he made no mention of how we arrived in what was clearly his favorite room in the world. "I should not have the candle or placards here, in case the room is discovered, but Sheikh Ahmad instructed me to set them up for you."

Oman turned to us and noted that we were divesting ourselves of our heavy coveralls. Nikki was way ahead of us there, of course. Nikki usually was. Now she flipped her long black braid over her shoulder.

"We can use lights in here?" she asked.

"We can," Oman said. "The guards do not venture this deep into the ruins at night. It is considered..."

"Haunted, sure, that makes sense," Nikki said. She flipped on a second Maglite and handed a third to Danae, who headed for the wall.

I looked around. "Where is the trapdoor into the next chamber?"

"Hold up a second," Danae said. She was moving from image to image, taking in the faint remnants of what had once undoubtedly been brilliantly colored art and scanning the placards. "Why are these so degraded?" she asked. "These images have been underground all this time, and you said they'd never been discovered."

Oman brightened with approval, a delighted teacher encountering a particularly astute student.

"This room *has* been underground all this time, and I do not believe it has been discovered. The outer edges of these carvings have been purposely dulled. It is my best guess that it was at the request of Queen Makeda herself. She wanted to give the impression that the grave had been robbed and desecrated, everything of value taken away. It was not a bad idea. The problem of grave robbers was becoming more and more prevalent even in her age. And this was but one of her many palaces."

"So why create a grand funerary welcome chamber, or whatever this thing is, at all?" Nikki asked. "Seems like kind of a lot of work for nothing."

"There are many possibilities. One is simply that the queen enjoyed a game of misdirection. Another is that her pride would not allow her to bury anything of significance without proper rituals and respect. And then there is also the possibility that we're wrong, and this site was, in fact, desecrated by real grave robbers who simply never got past these walls to see where the true treasure lay."

He looked at Danae, ever the encouraging instructor. "Is there anything you are seeing that can lend us aid?"

"No, other than her entourage here are all members of the same coven. Which means she was a witch."

"Probably explains why she was able to summon so many demons." Nikki chortled, but Oman's eyes widened as he stared at the images on the wall.

"What? No. There has never been any whisper of the Queen of Sheba being a sahira," he insisted. "There's nothing at all like that in any of the accounts of the time either. There would be."

"Would there?" Danae asked. "It's not exactly something I would advertise, I'll tell you that right now. And if your assertions about the queen's level of ability are correct, it only makes sense that she would have a few tricks up her sleeve. In this case, literal tricks."

"The idea that she would employ witches—of course. But be a witch herself? No. No, I cannot believe it."

"Oh, but you're cool with her taking control of a djinn?

Like, that doesn't faze you?" Nikki observed drily. "Makeda wearing a pointy hat doesn't seem all that far-fetched to me."

I smiled, letting them banter, but I'd flipped open my third eye and was scanning the room with far more interest than I was following their chatter. There was something wrong here. Oman was correct—this was a dark place. The room had been covered in elegantly worded curses. And the general gist of those complaints? Over and over again?

Let no witch pass this threshold.

"Ah...guys?" I murmured, squinting to peer more closely. Was I reading this right? I didn't even know what language it was, but it seemed like—

"Did you never notice this?" Danae asked, her voice rising with excitement. "It's right here as plain as day. You have to look at the two images together, not apart. But this is definitely a queen, and she is definitely—"

"*Guys,*" I said more fervently this time. But Oman was already moving.

"That cannot be," he said, nudging her to the side, trying to move past her to get to the wall. "You must be reading it wrong."

Danae stepped out of his way, then seemed to stumble, the section of floor she was standing on dropping with an audible thunk.

"Uh-oh," Nikki muttered.

With a loud, sickening scrape, the floor slid out from beneath us.

21

Our shouts of alarm were cut short almost immediately as we connected with a second stone floor a few seconds later, surrounded by smoke and darkness. Above us, the floor ground back into place, the sound deafening.

"You mean to tell me that nobody's going to *notice* that?" I demanded, but Oman merely looked panicked in the light of Nikki's Maglite. "This is not the correct way into the chamber," he whispered. "Not the safe way, the way I know. This way is cursed."

"Well, that's reassuring," Nikki said. She stood and dusted herself off, though with the rock dust still flying, it was a losing battle. I looked around, scowling at the room. It was roughly fifteen by fifteen feet wide, as Oman had explained. Even more interesting, the ceiling was easily seven feet tall, not six. Probably still kind of cramped for your average demon, but definitely something they could manage.

Oman was right on the third count as well. "Not much going on in here, is there, magicwise?" I asked. Even with my third eye firmly open, there was very little electrical signature happening at this depth. All the gyrating energy from the room above had been cut off. The place was...

"Oh *crap*," I muttered. I reached out my fingers experimentally, waiting for the familiar crackle of heat, but there was nothing.

Nikki turned to scowl at me. "A dead zone?" she asked, entirely too chipper. "You know, that's happening *way* too often in this neck of the woods. I wonder if there's some sort of kryptonite they've got buried in the bedrock here." She kicked at the stone floor with the toe of her boot.

But Oman was shaking his head. "I have never experienced the touch of magic in this place, so I cannot tell you whether it is this dead zone you speak of, but I do know this: here, we are safe. Ordinarily, I enter through a trapdoor in the floor, and therefore, I can get out fairly easily. From all my research, it seems that unwitting explorers only come to harm in similar tombs if they attempt to leave the chamber through the wrong corridor." He gestured to four archways, barely discernible in the gloom. "Of course, we didn't use a trapdoor, so..." He frowned, looking upward, but had the grace not to finish the sentence.

"If you're right, then we'll be okay—until we leave this room," I said. "Our theory still holds. The guardians of the Queen of Sheba can't enter this particular chamber because they're constrained as much as we are. They come in, they've got no mojo. We go out of the chamber, we're fair game."

I looked at Danae, who was peering at an inscription above one of the archways. "You got something there?"

"Something, yes. But nothing I like." She pointed to the marking, then gestured to the archway on the opposite wall. "These openings each have a symbol etched over them.

King, Child, God, Servant. There has to be a reason for that."

I frowned. "None of them are female?"

"The servant is, and Makeda was a witch. The servant's path would come naturally to her."

"She was also a queen," Oman said. "And to some, doubtless, a god."

Nikki snorted. "I begin to see the problem. Sheba was no ordinary woman, and during her time, she was as revered as a king—and a god. But that sounds exactly like what a greedy gold digger would think, right? So you gotta go with servant."

"Maybe—or you could go with child," I countered. "The path of the curious leads to the ultimate reward. It's a riddle, basically."

"Not a king," Danae contended. "She would have been too proud of her feminine strength for that. Or at least, most witches I know are."

"And it wouldn't be the god," I decided, reaching into the pocket of my thick-knit black pants. They weren't anywhere near as stylish as Nikki's were, of course, but all I really needed them to do was stay up—and carry a Tarot deck. I drew my thumb across the edges of the cards as Oman spoke up.

"From the ancient texts we've been able to find in a similar riddle passage placed in another of her burial chambers, the path of god is by far the most popular route taken by grave robbers. However, there's no record of anyone succeeding down that path. The path of the king then followed, with equally poor results. I am sure that over time, the other pathways were attempted as well, but we have scant information about either the servant woman or the child pathways. And we have *no* records of this place."

"Nifty," Nikki said. "But we're gonna have to choose one of them, right? We can't stay here all night."

"We can't," I agreed. I pulled out three cards as she shifted toward me. She shone the light down.

"Huh," she said. "The Sun, Moon, and Star? That seems...kind of heavy for what we're needing."

"Very heavy." I grimaced. This wasn't the time for the cards to be cute, but I couldn't dismiss them out of turn, considering had recently shown up to the Arcana Council slumber party. So I ran through the options they suggested.

"Three Major Arcanas. Just on the face of it, you're looking at a god option, full stop. If you're taking the meaning of the cards, it could argue for the child, since the Sun is usually represented by a child on a white horse, or a young woman, given the traditional depiction of the Star. The Moon is murkier. Three creatures are represented, none of which seem to apply here, and the card itself is steeped in deception."

Danae sighed. "So it could be the god corridor, or the child, or the servant woman. That doesn't narrow it down all that much."

"It does not. Unless...unless that's maybe the point. There's no answer to our question because our question needs no answer. Nikki, help me out here." I moved toward the archway emblazoned with the child figure.

"Gotta say, I'm all for Team Answer here," Nikki said, but she followed me, gamely swinging her light toward the corridor. The beam of light shone about twenty feet down the passage, and I glimpsed the barest shadow on the right.

"What is that?" I asked. "That shadow thing?" She angled the light farther, even as Oman walked up to us quickly, hissing a warning.

"Do not breach any of the openings until you are ready,"

he urged, glancing over Nikki's light, then frowning. "The old texts are clear on that point—and I see no shadow."

"You don't see that?" Nikki squinted down at him. "For reals? Because to me, it looks like another hole in the wall, maybe an opening to another corridor."

"I'm seeing something similar," Danae said, streaming her light into the servant corridor. Mine has openings to the right and the left."

Nikki swung her light to the side. "Huh. Same here. Keep that light steady, Danae." She crossed the room and peered over Danae's head, then glanced back to me. "I'm thinking they're connected, dollface. Which means ultimately..."

"Check the others," I said, and as she did, I narrowed my eyes on Oman. "You mean to tell me you never stuck a flashlight down one of those corridors? You didn't notice the openings?"

He lifted his hands helplessly. "I have shone powerful lights, yes. But I have never seen such entryways—it has always been flat rock, going on until the shadows take hold. I still don't see what you're seeing." He bit his lip, and I belatedly noted he had begun to tremble. "I do not understand."

"Something hidden," I murmured, thinking about the Moon, even though I was pretty sure the cards were just screwing with me—or putting me on notice that the three "missing" Council members were what I should be focusing on.

I sighed. "Gotta get out of here first, guys." I stuck the cards back into the deck, and pulled another one free. Technically, that was cheating, but I wasn't about to split hairs. I flashed my penlight over the card, and sighed. "Freaking great."

"Anything useful?" Nikki asked.

"Not really," I said. "Five of Wands. We'll have a fight on our hands no matter which way we go."

"A fight would not go in our favor," Oman said, a hint of fear in his voice. "We should have warriors with us."

I wanted to roll my eyes at him, but he wasn't Connected. He couldn't see—

I frowned. *Couldn't see.* A pathway that could only truly be seen by a Connected? Would that matter to Makeda?

"Another consideration..." Danae stepped back, turning in a tight circle. "If there are four corridors, and they're all linked together with a passage that surrounds this room, that could be a sacred circle. We could be safe no matter which direction we take, so long as we stay within that circle."

"Kind of a big 'if,'" Nikki pointed out, but I liked Danae's thinking. Regardless, there remained the problem of which passageway...Sun, Moon, Star. Heavenly bodies and ancient gods—but not Death, not the Devil...

"Up," I said abruptly. "We should head up. Which of these is on the cardinal point of north?"

Oman pointed to the archway marked with the symbol of the god. "This."

"Then that's the one," I decided. "Brace yourselves. Nikki, you good?"

"Always. Danae?"

"I still wonder if servant is a better choice," Danae said, shaking her head. "If she was a witch, in the end, it's how she would have seen herself. No matter how great her personal strength or how mighty her influence."

"She would," I agreed. "But she didn't set all this up for herself, I'm thinking."

Danae shot me a quick look, understanding lighting her eyes. "Fair. Very fair. She set it up for a god to claim a god."

"But—" Oman protested weakly. We didn't give him a chance to object. We moved single file through the portal of the god. It was equally dark beneath the archway, and we stayed close enough to each other to touch the next person without resorting to holding hands. Nikki led, I followed, then Oman, and finally Danae, who had started to murmur quietly beneath her breath. I could see the opening up ahead, clearer now that we'd stepped into the corridor. It was definitely some sort of access hallway, and it definitely opened both to the right and left.

Something else resonated as well, and I perked up. "We're back online," I said. "I can call the—"

The walls exploded around us.

Nikki yelped in surprise and threw her Maglite. As it went skittering down the corridor, I realized the stone ceiling above the passageway wasn't an arch of stone at all, but made of demons stretched into impossible proportions. They were tall and emaciated, wrapped in leathery skin, their arms and legs far too long for their bodies, their hands curved into claws. They dropped behind us, blocking our exit, then chased us forward as another pile of demons crashed down onto us. They leapt on us in a flesh-eating frenzy. I flung my hands up, desperately relieved that we'd apparently moved out of the dead zone, as I managed to get off a couple of fireballs to clear us a hole.

Unfortunately, the demons didn't scatter. Oman howled with pain, and Danae started throwing spells strong enough to push back the demons nearest her, but no sooner did I catch my breath than a loud boom sounded from deeper in the ruins, followed by the unmistakable pounding of something racing up the access corridor.

"Seems like a good time for backup," Nikki shouted.

"You do it," I shouted. "He likes you better."

"Ha!" she cackled. "You know what, he does. Warrick, love chop, get your enforcer asses down here!"

The arrival of the Syx was more spectacular than I expected it to be. I honestly assumed we'd have one or two lent to us by the archangel, whose disdain for this effort was undoubtedly high. To my surprise, the entire crew showed up. In the tiny hole I'd managed to carve out amidst the screaming demons, six enforcers burst out, their faces alight with joy, their fists clutching weapons I'd never seen them use before, jagged knives that cut through the wall of demons like butter.

"Infernal beasts!" howled Warrick, and he struck out, arms flying. Behind him Finn and Stefan were full-on laughing as they cut through the creatures.

"Man, you guys got to get out more often," Stefan chortled, beating back a creature that seemed to be all mouth. "Maybe order in a little takeout."

"I said *move*," a fourth demon enforcer roared, and I turned to see the largest of their team, Gregori, bodily push back an entire wall of fire-breathing monsters. Every time he connected with one of the creatures, it disappeared into a massive splatter of goop, and within seconds, the corridor had become a slippery slide of horror.

"Run!" ordered the last of the enforcers, Raum—but I couldn't help myself. I stopped. Raum was the most enigmatic of all the enforcers, and as he and Hugh threw up a great wall of white fire, blocking off the access corridor, his voice almost brought tears to my eyes. It was low and resonant, and it rolled across the open space like a benediction, despite the murderous intent of the demon enforcers.

"Kick it, cricket," Nikki shouted, breaking through my

thrall. She shoved me from behind, and then I was running too, down the long corridor, past the access point where yet more demons had come boiling out in force, and, at length, into another chamber. The sounds of carnage continued behind us as Oman sank to his knees, Danae by his side.

"He's been cut, and pretty badly," she said. I turned, surprised and more than a little chagrined. What had I just subjected this poor man to? He was a civilian, not even remotely Connected, by his own admission. I rushed to his side, dropping to my knees beside him. His injuries were numerous but not deep, and even on a bad day shouldn't be life-threatening.

Fortunately for Oman, this wasn't a bad day. I took his hands in mine, more to reassure him than anything, and breathed out a pulse of healing magic. His eyes shot wide, the expression on his face going from terror stricken to awed.

"It is true, then, it is true," he murmured, and I glanced from him to Nikki. She shrugged.

"You're going to be just fine. Just breathe through it," I said, not really knowing how else to direct the process. Oman's eyes cleared, and he jerked his gaze down, his mouth dropping open as he saw the bite and slash marks on his arms and torso close up, the skin shifting from dark and angry welts to a light pink as it healed, before deepening to its normal color. Tears sprang briefly to his eyes, and he scowled, dashing them away with his newly healed hands.

"There you go, that's right," Nikki said, her voice gruff, almost cop-like as I sat back from Oman to consider the room around us. The corridor of demons and enforcers still rang with both shouts of joy and snarls of pain and rage, sounding like a frat house on a bender, but Nikki rose to her feet along with Danae and flipped a second penlight around the space.

"Now we're getting somewhere," she said.

I had to agree. The chamber was small, almost like a grotto, the walls inlaid with dark chunks of what looked like lapis lazuli, interspersed with shiny white points that caught the light, rendering the room into its own starlit grotto. Rock dust hung in the air, perhaps the result of the disturbance in the corridor, but the motes merely added to the surreal sense of the space. We stepped onto a thick woven rug that, interestingly enough, had been made of rushes, not fabric.

I flipped open my third eye and focused on the space around me. My lips curled slightly. Oh *yeah*. There was all sorts of magic going on here, none of it as dark and dire as the energy I felt in the welcome gallery, but still very old, and dangerous in a way I couldn't quite place. As if it had been magic sprung from the dawn of time, and therefore wild and untried. Wild, untried, and cooped up for far too long. That could prove dangerous all on its own.

Oman stood and turned slowly in a circle, his hands out slightly, his eyes wide. "Yes, please, this place..."

I looked at him sharply. "You know it? You said nobody had ever gotten past the dead zone room."

"Not here, no, but it is built to the exact specifications of a room Queen Makeda had built into the palace itself, a room of starlight where she went to pray."

Danae snorted. "You just keep telling yourself that's what she was doing if it makes you feel better," she muttered. "Praying."

Oman wasn't deterred. "She might well have created a sacred space down here, though again, it was never her intention to be buried here."

"Maybe not all of her," Danae said, but now her voice

sounded strange and sad, and I turned her way. She was standing over a small salver that stood on a narrow pedestal. And she held her hands above the dish without touching it.

"There are pieces of her hair," she murmured. "A lock of hair tied with a golden thread, jewelry, a scrap of cloth. She wanted her presence to remain in this place long after she left it."

I glanced at Oman, grimacing as a particularly loud crash rocked the corridor beyond. "Is the chalice here?"

"In truth, we have no idea what the vessel is that holds the djinn," he said, but he was overcome with new excitement, his eyes brightening as he glanced around. "Light, light, we have to have more light."

The room had several sconces built into the walls, and Nikki cracked a flare. I felt my own fire crackle in my fingertips, but until I knew more about the nature of this room, I didn't want to act out of turn.

Another crash sounded outside, and then the corridor beyond grew eerily quiet. We all turned as the Syx pushed their way into the small prayer room, the space suddenly too tight for all of us.

Warrick grunted. "Hugh, Raum, stick around. The rest, you're out."

"I've got other places to be," Hugh said tersely, but Warrick shook his head.

"Your place is here, sending more of these bastards back beyond the veil. With any luck, it'll keep the archangel from yanking your chain—for a minute, anyway."

I blinked, not missing Raum's soft, sad smile as he stood behind Hugh, and once again, I was struck by the expression. Demons had the ability to effect glamour, and none of the guys were hard on the eyes. Warrick and Nikki had even developed a bit of an attraction for each other, and even though he towered over her, he was one of the few males on this earth she didn't threaten just by being awesome. But Raum was more than simply a strapping, six-foot-six demon in the body of a superhero. With his blond, swept-back hair, his sea-green eyes, and his deeply tanned skin, packed tight with muscles beneath his dark leather gear, he should have been fierce, almost frightening. He wasn't. Instead, he possessed a sense of almost ethereal beauty, his body held in relaxed stillness, his manner reverent, and a soft, somehow desolate twist to his smile. Beside him, the dark-haired, dark-eyed, porcelain-fair Hugh—every bit as large as Raum, but possessing not even an ounce of his brother demon's tranquility—burned with an almost feral rage. We might have need of that rage, so I felt good about Warrick's selection for our honor guard, though I had respect for the entire demon enforcers team.

The others gave no arguments, and a second later, they disappeared into puffs of smoke.

Warrick folded his arms over his chest. "So what's the game here? Those demons were nasty, but easy to break. Will we have higher-grade security from here on out?"

To my surprise, Oman stepped forward, his manner uncowed. "Who summoned you, demon? The witch? You will take orders from her?"

Danae gave a short, startled laugh, and Warrick answered for her.

"If that helps you sleep better at night, go with it. All you need to know is that we're here to protect your ass."

Oman turned to Danae. "You cannot trust these creatures. I don't know if they are ready for this trial. The djinn we face is trapped in a vessel of great power, yes, but magic as strong as his will have doubtlessly drawn others to his protection as well."

"Then all the better that we have support," Danae said, reasonably enough. "What happens next, do you know?"

"I know only what has been found in other chambers this queen has built. There are two paths to defeating the djinn warriors who protect their trapped brother. One is to provide the promise of release. Then, as a gesture of good-will, the protector djinn might allow you to take his chalice from this place. That is the best possibility."

"Fair enough," I said. "The other?"

"In that scenario, you will have to fight to free the chalice, fight to return up through the corridors to your eventual escape, and fight to ever see blue sky again."

"So we're hoping for option one is what you're saying," Hugh supplied.

"Is what we're looking for here?" I pushed. "I mean, it's a pretty place, but if this isn't the end game, then we need to go."

"This is the place," Danae said quietly, and we all turned toward her, her hands still hovering above Makeda's offerings. "It is not the end, but it is the beginning. And to find what we seek, we will do what Makeda would have us do."

She smirked at Oman. "We will...pray."

22

At Danae's direction, Hugh and Raum pulled back the rush mat, revealing polished stone beneath. Warrick muttered his distaste as it became clear the stone was also inlaid with another ring of lapis lazuli, this one set into the stone as a sacred circle. A series of arcane runes ringed that circle, and both Oman and Danae murmured with excitement as they pored over them, while Warrick shifted closer to me, near silent in his movements. A pretty impressive feat given his size.

"I've got to tell you, I don't recognize this," he said. "These symbols don't resonate with me."

I lifted my brows and frowned over at Danae. "Do you know what they are?" I asked her.

She didn't respond to me directly, but her muttering started coming more quickly. I couldn't tell if she was whispering spells or translating, but as we watched, Hugh rocked back on his heels. "Arguably, the djinn are a different kind of cat. We haven't had much call to go up against them. They keep to themselves and interact with humans in a different way from your Garden of Eden-variety demon."

"Yeah?" Nikki asked. "Even locked away like they have been? I don't think there's going to be an awful lot of interaction with anyone if they've been stuck down here in the Queen of Sheba's rec room."

Across the room, Raum chuckled, the sound like the slow strum of a harp. "The djinn who elected to remain down here with their compatriot did so for a very good reason. They recognized it was a gamble, but it was a gamble they were willing to make."

Warrick scoffed a short laugh. "If they were thinking of winning their deliverance, it wasn't such a smart gamble."

"We'll find out quickly enough." Danae stood and brushed her hands against her clothes, clearing them of rock dust. "This is a summoning circle. But not for the chalice. More so for the guardians of that worthy vessel."

"Well, why do we need to talk to those guys?" Hugh asked. "Shouldn't we just be able to go to the source?"

"You don't understand," said Oman. "These are not the mindless demons you found in the corridor that led us here. The djinn at their heart are thinking, rational—"

Warrick grunted again. "Well, maybe I wouldn't go that far."

"They have feelings, desires, and wishes of their own," Oman insisted. "We should hear them out."

Danae raised her hands and lifted her chin. When she spoke, the language was ancient, but one I was able to translate easily enough. It was also brief.

"It is time," she intoned. "Come and share what you wish, to gain what you might."

"Um...that seems a little broad," Nikki began, but at that moment, the very air in the room seemed to shudder. The lights jumped in their sconces, and the walls seemed to press inward. A swirling vortex appeared in the center of the circle, but to my surprise, it didn't remain in the circle. Instead, it extended beyond that inner rim, and I saw too late there was a second circle etched on the walls of the room—and that circle surrounded us. We'd fallen into a trap. Again.

"Son of a—" Warrick roared.

We plunged down several feet and landed heavily, all of us in a crouch. Unlike the room above however, this one was already lit with softly glowing stones fixed into the wall. Magic hung thickly in the room, a knot of circuitry so strong, it made my third eye water. The chamber looked like an ancient throne room, with what looked to be two dozen nobles gathered around the dais. An ornate chair carved from gold had been positioned in the center of the dais and a jewel-encrusted chalice stood on one of the armrests. But there was no king.

I tried to parse the magic but didn't get far, other than understanding that this was a heavily warded space. Something had been trapped here and had been meant to stay put.

A man standing near the throne turned toward us. He was short, barely taller than five feet, with dark skin and dark eyes, his head shaven clean. Either they had great razors down here, or there was some serious Nair magic going on. His painfully thin body was draped in a long tunic of pale fabric, his manner alert, attentive. He pinned his gaze on Danae.

"Have you come to free the djinn Qadir or have you come to bind him?" He spoke English, surprisingly enough. His mournful words echoed around the chamber. "You bring warriors of faith we have no quarrel with, sorcerers of a time we cannot fathom. But you are of an ancient coven, and you know the binding spells."

Danae's face remained serene. "I come for the djinn," she said. "That's all you need to know."

The man smiled faintly. "Then you come for all of us."

More of the nobles turned to us, giving me a better look, and I stared in surprise. These were all djinn? If so, Oman had been right. They didn't look at all like the demon creatures we'd fought in the corridors above, and they didn't look like possessed humans, or even demons effecting glamour. They were entities unto themselves, and as I studied them with my third eye peeled wide, I couldn't pierce the veil of their illusion. They were of all ages, despite the fact that they had apparently been trapped in this forbidding space for centuries. Millennia. Who would do that? I found my need to know would not be denied.

"Why are you here?" I asked abruptly. "Surely you weren't all needed to guard a chalice containing this djinn Qadir, a prisoner with no way to escape?"

A ripple of emotion murmured through the room.

"You act as if we are here by choice. We were trapped with the same magic that ensured the djinn Qadir was restrained to this place."

Now Warrick started to rumble his dissent. "Not trapped, I think. It was your magic that kept *him* here, wasn't it. You were complicit in the restraining spell cast by the Queen of Sheba, and then you were caught in a snare as well."

He smiled, and it wasn't a pretty smile. "Does he know?"

The djinn guardian stiffened. "You know nothing of the battles that were fought three thousand years ago. You know nothing of the betrayal or the deceit perpetrated by the queen in ensuring her power. The seat of her kingdom was far from here, but her influence remained long after history swept her name from its records. We were led into this place with a profound belief, and that belief was trampled upon."

"Oopsie-daisy, here you go, buddy. Sorry about that," Nikki said, and I turned to see her helping a slender boy to his feet.

She looked at me, surprise evident in her face. "May not be true, but they believe it," she said softly.

The djinn scowled at her and then looked back to me. "What did she say?"

"She said if what you say is true, you've waited an awful long time for your release. The fact that you haven't turned on us yet is comforting, but I suspect you won't just hand over the chalice and let us go. Though, if that's the plan, we're all for it."

The djinn smiled. It was a weary smile, but I remembered what Danae told me about their kind. Perhaps more than any other supernatural creature, they were masters of illusion. Even the young boy Nikki had handled could just as easily be the leader of their entire operation. I couldn't afford to be stupid.

"Your judgment of us is unwarranted," the djinn said. "It is not for us to give you the chalice, it is for you to take it. We are merely required to defend it once you've made your intentions clear. At this point, you haven't done anything that would require us to act."

Hugh huffed. "Just how bored are you guys? That is some fucked-up thinking right there."

"Hugh," Warrick warned.

"What, am I wrong?" Hugh protested, and he strolled forward through the crowd, as if daring someone to throw a punch. "I mean, I'm a big fan of spoiling for a fight, but you guys are practically begging for one, in the true sense of the word."

"You're not wrong," the djinn responded, his gaze tracking Hugh. "We are trapped with a spell as profound as the one that holds the djinn Qadir. We cannot act unless given a reason. We must use all our resources to protect the djinn we serve. Should we fall, there is relief in death or perhaps in circumstances we cannot fully predict. Such is our fate. Should we succeed, then arguably the djinn Qadir will reward us with our own release, or with the opportunity to serve him in his new capacity."

I narrowed my eyes. "Is there any way we could set you free ourselves?"

Beside me, Warrick hissed a cautionary warning. But the djinn shook his head.

"No. Queen Makeda was no fool. She predicted that time and circumstances might change the opinions of humans against djinn. She knew there was a threat of us being rescued by sympathetic forces. If we leave this room without the chalice being liberated, we will die. If we travel any distance away from the chalice even within these walls, we will die."

Nikki made a face. "You know I hate to ask, but..."

"We have tried," the djinn said, answering her question before she posed it. "There were several who made the attempt over the years, thinking that at some point, the spell would lose its potency. It did not. We were left to mourn the demise of those who sought only to improve our lot. It was... an unkind death."

The djinn fell silent, but Warrick spoke again.

"And a death you will avenge." He glanced at me. "The vengeance of the djinn is well documented and not something you should take lightly. They will turn on you without a moment's hesitation should they feel warranted."

"And I've got to say," Hugh cut in. I was surprised to see

him nearly halfway to the throne. "After three thousand years of hanging out in this basement shithole, watching a few of my bravest friends die in a fruitless attempt to get the fuck out, I'd be feeling pretty pissed off."

The head djinn made no comment, but his gaze tracked Hugh as the demon continued his slow amble. He deliberately jostled a few of the djinns' shoulders, and though they reacted with flashes of irritation and even outrage, none moved against him.

"There's more *to* this," he said in an almost singsong voice, and Raum took up the tale.

"He's right," he said, his voice so melodic that even a few of the assembled djinn looked his way in surprise and wonder. I could relate.

"The djinn are born deceivers," Raum continued, and now he began moving as well. "They were the original sirens of the ancient world, luring unwary humans to their demise. It's why they had to be caught in vessels such as the chalice in order to ensure they would not deceive."

The head djinn scoffed. "Unlike you, who can be constrained with little more than a circle of chalk," he said, his derision plain.

Raum laughed, and both Nikki and Danae jolted, as well as a few more djinn. I didn't know what the beautiful enforcer's story was, but he was by far the most compelling demon I'd ever met. The closest I suspected to a true angel of any of them. I found myself wondering what his sin had been, the crime that had relegated him to the ranks of demons.

As if he could read my thoughts, Raum turned to me, his sea-green eyes flashing in the darkness. Our gazes met, and my throat closed up, my heart quailed. A rush of sadness swept over me, then was gone.

He turned back to the head djinn.

"You struck a second deal," he said, his words low and resonant. "You struck a deal with the djinn Qadir himself. Even as you allowed him to be taken, to betray his first master. There had to be a reason it was even possible..."

As he spoke, he continued moving slowly through the room, and I realized Warrick was on the prowl as well. The demons were circling ever closer to Qadir's chalice, tightening the net. It felt like an Old West shootout with everyone posturing, hands twitching, but not quite going for their guns, knowing that whoever made the first move would be held accountable. The demons certainly didn't care about starting the fight, but they wanted to be in the best position possible before they did it. The djinn *couldn't* start the fight, but they weren't idiots. Eventually, one of the demons would get too close and implied aggression could be justified.

I, on the other hand, simply wanted it done, but I'd spent a fair amount of my life hunting down artifacts. This one had a riddle tucked inside it, I could feel it.

A riddle. Something about that caught at me. Some piece of information. My own fingers twitched down to my side, and I dipped my hand into my pocket again, shaking free a card. The Knight of Swords, and I sighed, tucking it back into place. No matter how this played out in the short term, we were going to be making a run for it, and soon.

As the demons moved forward, I shifted over to Danae.

"What do you think?" I murmured.

She didn't need any explanation. "I've never summoned a djinn before, and I'm still not sure I did here. The circle I activated above was secondary to the one I completely missed. So they are clearly well prepared. The ancient scripts that circle these walls are curses for the unwary, but they aren't typical arcanum to ward off the ignorant. These are quite specifically stated to warn off the educated—but in such a way as to hint at the wonders we will be missing out on should we walk away."

I scowled. "Meaning what, exactly?"

"Meaning that Queen Makeda has been expecting someone to spring this trap for a very long time. And she wanted to make sure they made the attempt despite the obvious dangers."

Raum took another step forward, then seemed to sink slightly into the solid rock. A sudden click and hiss flowed through the room, and everything erupted at once.

"Had to happen sometime," Hugh crowed, while Warrick bit out an annoyed curse. The pack of djinn turned as one, transforming themselves into the hellspawn beasts I was getting to know all too well. Short, thick-bodied ptero-dactyls, lifting up on their skinny, taloned hind legs and taking wing.

"I *hate* these guys," I muttered.

To my surprise, Hugh turned toward Nikki and offloaded two of his throwing stars on her. "This isn't their natural form. They've taken on the glamour of hellspawn because you remember those creatures, Sara—and your memory is stronger than the rest of our fears combined."

"Well, they *sucked*," I protested, but Hugh didn't seem to care.

"Don't let them touch you," he ordered. "These are mean motherfuckers, but they can't hurt you if you have iron."

I widened my eyes. Iron, of course. Raum turned to Danae, tossing similar weapons to her. "You were well chosen, Mistress of the Iron Sea," he said. "Any spell you cast will have a potency a hundred times over. I suggest you get to it."

"Meanwhile..." Warrick wrapped one arm around me and hauled me up high against his chest, the move startling me.

"You're the one with the strength to manage what's about to come out of that chunk of iron up there," he announced, slashing out his free hand to keep the djinn back. "Danae can destroy the cup, but she can't control the djinn. It'd kill her."

"Then go—" I started, but he was already moving, grunting with approval as he sliced through djinn after djinn.

"Their magic is old, strong," he shouted over the din. "The archangel was right to send so many of us. They're not to be underestimated. The riddles of the queen are deep indeed."

Riddles. Once more, that word smacked into the deep processors of my brain, but there was no more time to think. We reached the throne, which now was surrounded by djinn at each of the cardinal points, the one nearest to us the head spokesman for the group.

"You are not worthy," he declared as Warrick set me down.

All four djinn repeated the accusation. I took a step away from the demon enforcer as Warrick laughed in the djinn's faces.

"And you are *failures*," he growled. "Stand back!" His hand swept up, and a moment later, a curved iron blade slashed down into the nearest djinn. As an arc of light flared wide, I burst forward and grabbed the chalice from the armrest of the throne. The weight of its magic jolted through me with such unexpected pain that I nearly dropped the damn thing.

Sariah! The vision was like a firestorm of agony, but I saw her plain as day. Her eyes were wide, her face radiant. She stared back at me with an expression of utter satisfaction, her mouth opening to speak—

Another knife of power stabbed through my hands, and I screamed, the sound rocketing around the room. For the barest moment, I had a vision of Nikki whirling toward me with startled eyes, Danae staring over at me, horrified—and Warrick paying me absolutely no goddamn attention at all. Instead, he redoubled his efforts in gutting the djinn surrounding us, his cry one of exaltation, not worry.

Freaking demons.

I wrapped my hand tighter around the chalice and crackled out of existence.

23

I re-formed in the Magician's penthouse office with a strangled cough a moment later, thrusting out my hands. "It burns!" I gasped.

Armaeus was there, of course he was there, and he grabbed the proffered chalice and sent it spinning off deeper into the room, then pulled me close.

"You're safe. Safe, Miss Wilde," he murmured. "Always safe."

"Holy crap," I managed, collapsing against him. "They seemed so—normal at first. Reasonable. But once they made the switch to hellspawn, it was a freaking zoo. I can't believe I caused that."

Armaeus hugged me close, his soft laugh ruffling my hair. "Despite what the demon Hugh claims, you cannot know what was born of your memory, versus a form they may have been cursed to take on. From all accounts, Queen Makeda's magic ran deep. She could have easily transformed the lesser djinn into hellspawn if she knew the proper spells. It was dark magic, but not inaccessible to someone with training."

"That's even worse," I groaned, remembering the attack at Pompeii. Were those djinn too? Was that magic still surviving, turning magical creatures into ravening bird bats? "Those horrible, pitiful creatures. How could they have lived so long on such a thin thread of hope? How could they have done so much without even knowing they would ever be redeemed? And should they be redeemed?"

Armaeus leaned back from me, his dark eyes glinting with amusement. "Now you understand why the Arcana Council prefers to let mortals find their own way in this world, whether they are gifted with magic or not."

"But these—"

"I know. The djinn are not mortals. They're not exactly demons either, not in the true sense that we have come to know them. They are a kind of creature unto themselves, who dip their hands into both the mortal and immortal realm. But you have done what Ahmad sent you to do, I see. You found the vessel of the djinn Qadir and retrieved it."

He gestured to the chalice, now at a safe remove, caught in a sphere of smoke as it levitated in a corner of the room. "I seem to remember him telling you not to go anywhere with the chalice after you captured it, though."

"Ahmad can go suck an egg," I grumbled. "I happen to know a Magician with a trick for stopping time. If ever I needed a time-out, it was now. Those birds..."

I shuddered again. Armaeus's face softened as he studied me, and unaccountably, I felt tears surge up behind my eyes again. I glanced away, struggling to collect myself. "What's going on with Sariah?" I blurted. "When I closed my hands around the chalice, I—I felt her, suddenly. Her presence. Her strength." *Her pain.*

"She felt you too," Armaeus said. "She is part of the reason I knew to expect you. She woke up not ten minutes ago, doubtless when you first got your hands on the chalice and lifted it from its pedestal. In so doing, you set into motion some very powerful magic—magic I felt. Magic that doubtless Ahmad felt as well."

I grimaced. "The Shadow Court?"

He shrugged. "If they were paying attention, undoubtedly. And I suspect they were. What I saw only made sense because Eshe had prepped me on what to expect. She has provided all the background she could on Ahmad and his story. He served in his position as Sun for over a millennium before I ever ascended. The Council could have tracked him down at any time, but we, in our hubris and isolationism, never bothered to pursue him. If he didn't want to be a part of the Council's activities, we would leave him to his desert idyll and not worry ourselves overmuch with his actions unless and until we needed to call him to a vote. Over the centuries, it proved prudent for us to not do anything that escalated the Council's concern so high."

"Because you didn't want to get involved." It was an accusation, but there was no heat to it. What I'd accomplished today, the Council couldn't have. Not without drawing a whole lot more attention to itself. "You were content to let humanity fend for itself."

"We were." Armaeus nodded. "Then, when I lost my memory of the Sun, the Moon, and Star as Arcana Council members in absentia, it was as if the other members of the Council forgot them, too. When those memories returned, it wasn't a true recollection, merely an absence of forgetting, if that makes sense."

"You didn't think about them before, so you weren't triggered to think about them again." I sighed against him. "The Shadow Court made you forget them? Why?"

"There could be any of three hundred and forty-seven reasons thus far."

I managed a weary smile. "So you have no idea."

"On the contrary, I have three hundred and forty-seven reasons why. The answer will prove most illuminating. It's a curious development, and one which will require much study. But not today."

He turned again to the chalice, his elegant fingers tracing a circle, and the smoke-filled sphere surrounding the chalice gleamed with power.

"It too will require much study. You can't keep it here, of course, and I must remove any trace of my magic from it, but this will provide me with some preliminary information that I need to analyze it. To capture the scrollwork etched into the chalice, understand the intention of the spells that bound the djinn, both those enacted by Ahmad's father and those added by Queen Makeda, you see?"

He pointed, and now that I could study the chalice more closely, I could see what he meant. The heavy markings on the chalice looked as if they'd been filed smooth in a wide band around the base of the cup and its rim, replaced with fine scrollwork. The etchings were too indistinct for me to read at this distance, but they had the unmistakable sense of feminine power.

"And now you must return back to the moment you disappeared," Armaeus said. "Until I can help you more."

"Ready when you are." I braced myself for the surge of power and pain that I'd already come to expect at touching the chalice of the djinn Qadir. Armaeus dropped the magical thrall around the vessel, I grabbed it with a hissed curse, and fled both warmth and comfort...

Only to reappear in the middle of Armageddon.

"*Sara,*" somebody shouted as I dropped to the floor,

rolling away from a trio of attacking djinn in their hellspawn party outfits while I shot out an arcing flare of fire to keep the bastards away from me. Frankly, I was little surprised. As fiercely as the Syx, Nikki, and Danae were fighting, they didn't seem to be making much headway. I struggled upright, and Warrick beat his way toward me.

"Sara," he shouted again. "The Magician? Did he get what he needed?"

"He did. Was I gone for long?" I asked, wondering if Armaeus was losing his touch. I felt the murmur of indignation all the way from Las Vegas.

"No—oof!" Warrick shoved back an entire line of djinn. "Barely a heartbeat or two, but the djinn, we're not meant to hurt these people. They're not"—another punishing blow —"ours to fight."

I blinked, finally realizing the difference in this djinn battle: no black goop. It was a rumble in the ruins, but nobody was losing or gaining any ground. We could go on fighting like this for another millennium and have nothing to show for it.

"So what the hell are we supposed to do?" I demanded. "How are we going to fight something we can't get rid of? It's like an infestation of ants."

"We escape. Legs over there knows the way. Follow her. We'll follow you."

I looked at him and swiveled to where he gestured, where I saw Nikki doing her best impression of Crouching Tiger Fabulous Dragon, flying out with brutal kicks and martial-arts-worthy karate chops. Even though she was doing a fair job of keeping the djinn from harming herself or Oman, she also wasn't gaining any ground. We were stuck on permanent defense.

"Nikki?" I shouted as Warrick shoved me toward her.

She looked up with a bright grin, as if she'd be more than happy fighting back hellspawn for a few hours more. Oman huddled behind her, his face waxy with shock.

"Dollface!" she shouted. "We gotta roll. I've rubbed shoulders with enough of these creepers that I know the tunnels the martyrs took to make their bid for freedom. They didn't make it, but we damned well better. Otherwise, they'll just wear us out. Oman's brain is fried, and I can't take a breath long enough to get a fix on Ahmad's Sun deck, so until we get these bat boys off our backs, we're stuck. I don't like being stuck, gotta tell you." She punctuated this last with a vicious strike of her left elbow, sending a squawking pterodactyl flying.

I redoubled my grip on the chalice, grimacing with pain. "Then let's go."

"Only problem with that is—"

"I don't care," I snapped as I ducked away, a djinn claw barely missing my shoulder. "Let's *go*."

"Roger that."

She turned and collared Oman, who looked ready to follow her anywhere, and shoved him toward the nearest arched doorway, one of easily a half dozen. How confident was she that she'd made the right choice?

Around us, the djinn screamed with eerie, keening excitement, and I understood why Nikki had hesitated. "We go, they can go too," she shouted. "So let's hit it."

We ran. Danae was right on my heels, and I assumed the demon enforcers were following behind us, but I didn't need to worry about them so much. The route twisted and turned and then split off in two directions, but Nikki never faltered. As I drew up close behind her, I realized she wasn't just going on borrowed memories from the djinn. No, in her fist, she held the neck of a small, violently flapping creature, which she clearly had conscripted in the role of guide on her way out the door. The creature squawked and flailed, its eyes rolling, but it didn't slow Nikki down one bit. It took us another five minutes of hard running through ever-tightening tunnels before I sensed the corridor gradually sloping up.

I risked a look back and saw nothing but the flapping of furious wings at first, but fortunately, they didn't seem to be getting any closer. I couldn't understand for a moment why, then spied what was running directly in front of them. Warrick, with Danae hiked up against his shoulders. She faced backward, her hands spread wide, her hair flying. She shouted imprecations and spells I couldn't fully understand, but they seemed to be doing the job. The djinn in their bird-like forms followed us closely, but never too close. Somewhere in their squalling midst, Hugh and Raum ran as well...at least I hoped so.

I stumbled as I turned my attention forward again, jostling the chalice I held tight to my chest. It was definitely reacting, either to my rough handling or the fact that it had been taken from its chamber, not once but twice. Either way, as we turned into a tunnel where the air was decidedly fresher, I could tell it was heating up. I clamped my hands down on it, glaring at it for good measure. I had no interest in releasing this genie from its makeshift bottle a second before I needed it.

We pressed on, the tunnel gradually widening, and the gloom around us lightening as well. Racing beside Nikki, Oman thrust his arm out, gesturing forward. "There—look! This stone, these walls are not man-made. This is a cave. We're nearing the surface!"

His announcement seemed to do more than encourage our small troop. The mini hellspawn in Nikki's hands started freaking out, its wings batting at her in a frenzy, and the screams of the djinn behind us lifted to an unholy roar. If there was anyone around the opening of this cave within a three-mile radius, we were hosed, but there was nothing I could do about that.

I bent double as the chalice in my arms started shaking more aggressively as well. Did it also know that it was nearing its release? Was it reacting to the cries of its fellow djinn? Did the spirit inside, Qadir, have any idea what was going on? These questions kept time with my pounding feet as I rushed up the passageway.

It was only when I glimpsed a break in the unrelenting gloom ahead that I sensed something else. Something bad. My third eye flipped open, and the crisscrossing net of electrical bursts covering the opening ahead of us was another indicator that our lot was not necessarily improving. *Crap.*

I raced toward the opening of the cavern a few seconds longer, then braked sharply and lurched to the right.

"Down!" I shouted. Nikki and Oman heard me, and Nikki yanked him back with one hand as she freed the hellspawn-cursed djinn. It screamed in utter joy and burst forward.

As I hit the ground, I could hear Warrick and Danae crash to the ground behind me. I covered the chalice with my body as a roar of wings flew overhead, trailing talons ripping at my hair and my clothes. But the hellspawn weren't trying to stop me anymore. If anything, they were using my body as a launching pad to move forward as quickly as they possibly could. The entire lot of them soared above me and burst out into the open air as Hugh and Raum caught up to our party. Hugh reached me first and leaned down, yanking me upright. A second later, Raum raced up, and Warrick pulled Oman free from Nikki, now carrying two humans as Raum hauled Nikki to her feet.

But we didn't run any longer. We wanted no part of the carnage going on outside the cave opening.

"Jesus, Mary, and Joseph," Nikki muttered as the exalted cries of the djinn turned to horrifying screams of terror and pain. The sound of bodies crashing to the sand in hideous, crunching thuds came next.

She looked at Warrick, her face sheet white. "I thought no one could kill these guys?"

"You can't," Warrick said, his voice unusually quiet. "But doesn't mean you can't cause them pain. Enough pain to take them back to their most natural forms, no matter how powerful the spells laid over them."

That appeared to be what was happening before us now. Djinn littered the ground outside the cave and lay sprawled like the victims of some apocalypse. They moved, but only barely, their bodies sliced to ribbons, their blood spilling out over the sand. It was golden, I saw, my own horror mounting. The djinn remained in the same human forms they had presented back in their prison chamber. Men, women, children. It was like watching a mass-murder scene unfolding in real time.

"Dollface," Nikki said, and I turned back, knowing what I needed to do. We couldn't rush out into the midst of whoever was waiting for us. It almost certainly had to be the Shadow Court or their minions. "We need to go back to—"

"The palace," whispered Oman suddenly, sounding on the verge of tears. "Yes, *yes*."

Without any further prompting, he flung himself away from Warrick and toward Nikki, practically jumping into her arms and pressing his cheek against her. She swung around, her eyes wide as the rest of us crushed together, and I focused. It was the largest group I'd ever attempted to move, and I felt the strain of it on me. In the last moment, a burst of smoke billowed up from the tomb, the cries of something else stirring beneath the sands, and that was all that was needed to get us underway.

We appeared in the middle of a large, ornate chamber, clearly one of Ahmad's receiving rooms, which was impressive since, once again, I'd never been there before. But such was the intensity of Oman's vision and Nikki's connection to me that it proved to be enough.

We fell apart, the demon enforcers rolling to their feet and brushing the embers away as Oman patted himself down frantically. Nikki pulled off her draping scarf. It had been reduced to a charred and tattered mess at the hands of her djinn guide.

"He better be okay," she muttered, and I grimaced. I'd seen all sorts of carnage in my service to the Arcana Council, Connecteds performing terrible acts of violation against other magical beings, but this attack against the djinn guardians somehow struck me as more horribly wrong than usual.

Ahmad stood at the front of the room, not moving a muscle until I stood. His eyes lit up with joy and more than a little avarice as he saw what I held in my hands.

"The djinn Qadir," he murmured, his voice practically vibrating with awe. "You have brought it."

I'd been through my share of artifact deliveries, and I knew the danger I was in. Suddenly glad for the team surrounding me, I straightened my shoulders. More than a few clients would opt to kill me at this point rather than have any evidence of what I'd brought back to them leak out to others, whether ally or enemy. Fortunately, setting aside my own not inconsiderable skills, with a witch, three demons, and the awesome that was Nikki Dawes, I didn't worry as much about my personal safety. And, too, this time around, it wasn't a question of money changing hands. I almost felt a stab of disappointment at that. I hadn't set any price for the delivery of this artifact. I'd merely done the job to stick it to the Shadow Court and help out a fellow Arcana Council member. I needed to start raising my rates again.

"Come, come," Ahmad said excitedly. He turned to Oman as the guide approached, beaming at him, embracing him with his cheek to either side of his trusted guide. As he pulled back, though, I caught the flash of steel in Ahmad's hand.

My response was automatic. With a flick of my hand, I shoved Ahmad back, using the same energy I'd used to lift Armaeus a few inches. Invisible, but effective. Ahmad flinched back, and the steel disappeared once more into his robes. Oman leaned away from his master, starry-eyed with delight, with no idea of what Ahmad had planned for him. If I had anything to do with it, he never would.

I slanted a hard glance at Warrick. He rolled his eyes, but nodded. The burly demon would see to it that Oman remained safe until we could get him away from Ahmad. I had no doubt that the Sun had his reasons for killing the man, but I had better reasons for keeping him alive. Though he'd been half out of his mind with fear, Oman had fought well and admirably, and had done his job without shirking. He didn't deserve to die for that.

Speaking of...

I fixed my glare on Ahmad as he turned back to me, oblivious to my darkening mood.

"Was that the Shadow Court waiting for us at the mouth of the cave?"

He shook his head and spread his hands, patently confused. "In truth, I don't know. You emerged so far away from where you started that it is only by a slight miracle that I knew where you were, and even that information was relayed seconds before you arrived here. You came in with a rush of wind and the sound of gunshots. I assumed it had to be you."

Hugh snorted. "Generally a good assumption."

"I should never have doubted for a second that you would find it," Ahmad said, his joy palpable as tears glistened in his eyes. "Finally, after so many thousands of years, the djinn of my father is returned to the house of Ahmad to finish his final quest. It is a great gift that you give me, Justice Wilde. My payment to you and the Council shall be rendered tenfold."

Despite the pretty words, I still wasn't feeling all that great about this transaction. Beside me, Nikki remained tense, and even Danae had drawn closer to me as if to render emergency aid. The three demon enforcers stood loose and at their ease, willing to watch mortals sort things out. Until the djinn showed up again or there were more demons to fight, they only needed to stand down.

"Justice Wilde, please, it is time."

Ahmad stepped aside to indicate a small pedestal set on a dais ringed by a half circle of heavy drapes that looked like they'd been made from cloth of gold. I took another step forward, and there was no denying the tremor the chalice gave at the movement.

I frowned. "It's been a long time since anyone's dealt with this particular djinn. Do you have safeguards in place to protect yourself and your people?"

"And us, for that matter?" Nikki asked.

Ahmad beamed like a boy asked to present his science fair project.

"Of course," he said, gesturing around us at the room, with its marble floor inlaid with metal scrollwork and the draped dais. "This entire room was originally constructed to house the djinn. It's warded at all four corners and reinforced for both the djinn's safety and ours. There are doors behind these curtains that go straight to far more comfortable quarters than Qadir has been forced to endure these past centuries. He will be treated like the great and mighty djinn he is."

Ahmad spoke overloudly, and I glanced down at the chalice, wondering if he was pitching his voice to be heard through the thin metal. At this point, nothing would surprise me.

"And you can handle him?" I pressed.

The Sun straightened with imperious authority. "The djinn is bound to my family, and only I can transfer that bond permanently. What Queen Makeda did was a result of her own great power, but it is a spell that is easily broken by a member of my family." He placed one hand on his breast, beaming beatifically. "I am more than ready to release the djinn."

At that proclamation, the chalice trembled violently, almost jerking out of my hand. I found my patience wearing thin with all of Ahmad's dramatics.

"Well then, let's get this over with," I said, my mind already moving ahead to the next challenge. We still had to track down the Shadow Court and neutralize them for good. I couldn't shake the image of the scattered djinn on the dunes at the mouth of the tomb's ruins. I didn't think I could ever shake that image. I reached Ahmad, but to my surprise, he didn't take the chalice from me. Instead, he stepped back and gestured to the pedestal, the small stand ringed with tiny, intricate scrollwork.

Fair enough. Ahmad wasn't taking any chances, and he shouldn't. I stepped forward and placed the chalice on the pedestal. No sooner had I straightened than Ahmad edged close and placed one hand reverently on the lid of the chalice.

"Djinn Qadir, bound to this house. Step forth to serve."

The djinn didn't make us wait a moment more. The lid didn't so much slide off the chalice as burst up in a blast of smoke and sparks. The smoke continued, billowing out of the chalice and roiling over the edge of the pedestal and into the room. Emerging from the clouds was an enormous form that seemed to construct itself out of the mist, a creature as large as the demon enforcers, then larger still, his head and chest expanding out and up until his skull struck the ceiling. His white-hot glowing eyes blinked, and then the creature turned into another whirling dervish of light and smoke, but compressing down, down, until he stood before us, an enormous male, bronzed and fierce. Other than the fancy gold pants and bald pate, he could have been the brother of one of the Syx.

"Djinn Qadir!" Ahmad declared. "Do you serve?"

The genie turned toward Ahmad, his face impassive. If he didn't like his role of cosmic handyman, he didn't show it. "I serve," he responded, in a rush of languages—Arabic, Hebrew, Latin, Aramaic, Greek, Japanese, French, Urdu, German, Hindi, Dutch—even English in the end. As if he was learning all the languages of the world and running through them, one by one. I thought about the djinn in the ruins, who'd picked up our language even more quickly.

What had happened to them out on that killing field?

Had the Shadow Court left them, or were they torturing them still?

"Excellent," Ahmad said, beaming, though my stomach had curdled and I was barely paying attention anymore. "Then I transfer your bond to your new master."

From out behind shimmering drapes, Jarvis Fuggeren stepped forward.

24

I reared back as a dozen armed men flooded out from the drapes—not even men but straight-up demons, their guns trained on Nikki and Danae. I lifted my hands and made my second unfortunate realization. My hands barely crackled enough to toast marshmallows. It wasn't quite a dead zone, but it was close enough. Beside me, Warrick, Raum, and Hugh remained barely constrained. I couldn't tell if they were being held in check by force of magic or by the reality that they couldn't reach all the demons in time to save Nikki's and Danae's lives. Either way, they remained stock-still, though their eyes boiled over with fury.

"You are wise not to strike," Ahmad said modestly, addressing the Syx—and then me directly. "Even you, Justice Wilde. I have never been successful in fully suppressing the magic of the Council, though I have certainly tried over the centuries. Though in Pompeii, I gave you some trouble, no? And certainly here, even my small talents will serve to delay your reactions long enough that your compatriots will fall. First, I have gifted Jarvis with a measure of my own power, so you have not two beings of magic before you, but three."

I shifted my glare to Jarvis, who preened. But Ahmad wasn't lying. As I fixed on Jarvis with my third eye, I could see, for the first time ever, real power crackling off him. *Freaking great.* At least that explained how he'd been able to reach out to me in Hell.

"Secondly, I assure you, the dampening effect of my magic on you will be a quite sufficient deterrent. I will plug these unfortunate souls full of enough holes, they will not survive long enough for you to reach them. Your legs, you see."

I didn't need to move far to confirm his taunt. My feet felt like they were encased in cement. I reached out mentally for Armaeus and felt the pressure weighing down on that attempt, too. Smothering me. Would Armaeus figure out what was happening in time? I doubted it. He had no reason to be tracking me, and he was fascinated by the riddle of the chalice.

"What is *wrong* with you?" I gritted out, staring daggers at Ahmad. "Why are you doing this?"

It was Jarvis who answered. "We so long held out hope of turning you to our cause, Justice Wilde. Despite your position on the Arcana Council, you were never meant to be one of them. And yet, though you claimed affinity with the Connected of this world, you apparently were not meant to be with them, either. That makes you an outcast to both sides, and as such, no use to me. Ridding you from this earth will be my pleasure."

"Good luck with that," I muttered, but I kept my eyes on the djinn Qadir. My third eye in particular. The djinn stood impassively at Ahmad's side, looking bored, but he was possessed of so much magic that my third eye had to squint to fully take him in. This was a being of no small Connected merit...and like nothing I'd faced before.

Ahmad spoke in an overloud, self-important tone, stroking his Sun medallion. "You shall fight the djinn Qadir to allow him vengeance for the deaths of his people—deaths that you caused," he announced.

"*What?*" I pulled my gaze away from the djinn to refocus on Ahmad. "What are you talking about? I didn't kill any djinn—I didn't think I could."

"They will carry their injuries for eternity. Is that not a fate worse than death?" Jarvis asked.

With every word, Qadir grew in stature, his face darkening until he regarded me with murder in his eyes. When he spoke, his words were low and menacing.

"You shall pay for the pain you have brought upon my family, Makeda, you and your king," he promised.

My eyes flared even wider. Makeda? Did this guy not know who I was?

It wasn't an unreasonable mistake. I didn't even know if the Arcana Council had a Justice in place at the time of the djinn's existence. But Makeda? And who the hell was her king? As far as most historians were concerned, the Queen of Sheba didn't even exist, let alone have a husband out there somewhere.

I glared right back at Qadir. "Look, buddy, I don't have any problem with you, and I certainly have no quarrel with your people. Whatever happened to them..."

As I spoke, Qadir's face only grew darker, and I couldn't blame him. Even listening to myself, it sounded like bullshit. This guy wanted a fight. He deserved a fight. I shot a look at

Jarvis. "And so, what. If he kills me, is his service to you done?"

"Qadir shall kill you as his third act to the house of Ahmad and his first to me. When he kills you, his service to Ahmad's house is done," Jarvis intoned. "And you can die knowing you helped usher in a new world order, one that is long overdue. One that is already in motion, in truth. It is only a shame you won't be around to see it."

I opened my mouth to issue another zinging quip when Warrick grunted in pain. Apparently, the dead zone was working its reverse mojo on him, too.

"Sara," Warrick said repressively, his eyes filled with rage and his body trembling with his need to move. "We cannot kill this creature. It is a djinn, not a demon. The difference is enough that we can't strike it dead. We will likely be unable to even slow it down. The demons, though...we can break this hold."

"No," I said, not missing the way the demons were shaking as well as they held their guns on Nikki and Danae, the excitement of the kill wafting off them like poisonous fumes. I suspected there was more than simple bullets in those weapons...and then I noticed something else. Explosives. Wrapped to the legs, arms, and torsos of the demons, enough firepower to rip us all apart. Without warning, an image of Sariah's shattered body filled my mind, making my throat tighten, my lungs burn. The Shadow Court wasn't leaving anything to chance, and a slow, steady fire awakened inside me, ready to set the world ablaze.

Nevertheless, something was screwy here. I glared at Ahmad. "Why aren't we already dead?"

Jarvis answered for him. "Yet another good question. It is *such* a shame that we won't be able to usher in this new world order together," he said with what seemed like real regret in his voice. He turned and favored Warrick with an indulgent smile. "We can't kill your compatriots, or the enforcers here will transcend the restrictions we've imposed. Their dedication is that strong. Commendable, really."

"Fuck off," Warrick said succinctly.

Jarvis sniffed. "I cannot kill you personally because I too am bound to the djinn in my own way. He is a being possessing both great power and a strict moral code. You die by our hands before the contract is complete, depriving him of completing our assignment, he is not only released to his own devices, he has lost faith with us. Fortunately, the moment you die, in the modern vernacular, all bets are off."

"In other words, don't lose, dollface." Nikki drawled the words with such exaggeration that I had to smile. I refocused on the djinn, who still stared right through me, as if he could see out into Ahmad's grand estate as it rolled down to the beach. Ironic that, after three thousand years locked away from the world, he still hadn't seen the open sky.

"All right. So we fight here?" I focused hard and was able to move one foot, then the other. It took all my energy, though. So even if I could access some of my magic, I'd have to sacrifice mobility to do so. Nifty.

In my mind, I could hear Sensei Chichiro urging me to strike, to kick, to slash. I hoped she planned on sitting on my shoulder and yelling instructions in my ear when things got real. I needed all the help I could get.

"You'll fight here," Ahmad said.

"Now, now, we should give them some space, shouldn't we?" Jarvis countered, turning to Ahmad. He flicked his hand toward the walls, and Ahmad hesitated, a slight flush rising in his cheeks, but Jarvis's eyes were on Qadir. Ahmad glanced to the djinn as well, and there was no discounting the mulish look on Qadir's face as he stared at the walls, despite his overall passivity. Clearly, the djinn wanted some air.

"I assume there's no problem with that?" Jarvis pushed, and now it was Ahmad's turn to look mulish.

"Of course not," he said pompously. He gestured with a rich man's indolence, and the entire northeast wall of the receiving room fell away, retracting back into pockets that allowed the room's light to spill out onto the wide flat surface paved with stone. It ran all the way to the beach and was bordered by gently flowing palm trees, an oasis at the water's edge.

Beside Ahmad, the djinn stirred to life, staring out at the wide-open sky with such naked longing, my own heart caught.

"Yes," Jarvis murmured, his tone almost wheedling. "See what you are fighting for, Qadir." Then turned to me with a smirk. "You see, I've even given you a sporting chance. Ahmad's magic is strong and his wards are great, but under the stars, anything is possible, no?"

I narrowed my eyes. Jarvis was smart, and I could almost smell the duplicity rolling off him. He didn't want me to win, so what was he doing here? Because he had to know...

He had to know...

I didn't have time to work out all the angles. Qadir rushed forward, moving with a speed that I should've expected in a supernatural creature half made up of wind, but somehow, I'd overlooked that detail. The djinn caught me before I could draw my first breath, and we went tumbling end over end. With my hamstrung abilities, I couldn't defeat this creature with fire, but instead, I made note of my position within the cartwheel and rolled a few more rotations toward Hugh. The demon enforcer was no idiot. He might not be able to take out the posse of demons while Ahmad's wards kept him restrained, but he could still help me.

As soon as I got close enough, Hugh wrenched his hands forward, and two shining iron-bladed scimitars blew through the air, aiming directly for me. I even caught one. The other one passed harmlessly and buried itself in the wall. Still, one iron pointy thing was better than none, and when I came up again, I shoved the blade into Qadir's shoulder with a satisfying thunk, then jerked it out again as the djinn reared back.

"Drop your weapons, Syx, or the women die," Jarvis ordered, a single shot ringing out to punctuate his words. I didn't have to look to imagine it flying by either Nikki's or Danae's face, and I heard the clatter of iron against tile. The Syx weren't taking any chances either, preferring to wait until the situation fell in their favor.

Meanwhile, Qadir's eyes went wide, his mouth curving —but not in dismay, unfortunately. Way more like a delighted grin. "That's right, Makeda—*fight*," he snarled.

"I am *not*—oof—"

My protest was cut off as the djinn bent forward and rushed me again, this time catching me right in the solar plexus, knocking all the wind out of me. I went flying, barely managing to hold on to my scimitar, and crunched to the ground at Warrick's feet. Fortunately, he'd seen fit to drop his weapons as instructed, and I grabbed two of them before struggling back upright. I staggered to the side a little, but the moment I stepped beyond the border of Ahmad's magic-warded room, I remembered Jarvis's remark, and at the same time, Sensei Chichiro's voice filled my mind.

"Qadir is old and fat, slow," she said tersely, her voice as clear as if she really was sitting on my shoulder. "He has lived in his chalice too long, plotting his poisoned revenge. He has forgotten to stay strong and ready. That is why he fights the way he does, seeking to knock you off your feet, to beat you by blunt force and not skill and subtlety. And do not forget, he has named two parties in his grievance, not one."

Before I could process what she was saying, Qadir was on me again. I barely got off a few defensive slashes before he was too close to my body, defeating my advantage with the blades. I stumbled back a few more steps, and another voice came to me, this one as welcome as rain in the desert. *"Miss Wilde."*

Armaeus didn't need to say any more. His smooth, confident voice reminded me of who I was and what I was capable of, out beyond the direct pull of Ahmad's wards.

I stretched out my hands, my blades still in place, but this time, they were electrified with my magic and anger in equal measure. I threw the mother of all fireballs at Qadir, and it was my turn to knock him off his feet. He went sprawling, his body disintegrating into wind, his scream rising into the heavens. I didn't give him a chance to react any further. I raced forward, both hands together, my scimitars twin blades of destruction as I swept them down and through his body, cleaving him in two.

He stared up at me with clear surprise. Then to my horror, he ripped the rest of the way, the bottom half of his ruptured form dissolving into mist while the top burst apart in a rush of color and fire. A moment later, I realized my mistake. Two djinn stood in front of me now, both looking equally pissed.

"Son of a—"

"You will not defeat us, you wretched queen!"

"I am not the freaking *queen*," I snarled. I brought my

weapons down again. As I did, I finally remembered my wits. A second later, fifty blades hung in the air, all of them wrought from pure iron.

"*Witch*," the second Qadir snarled, and Danae's laugh rang out, sharp and fierce.

"I'd be real careful of your tone if I were you."

Her bold voice caught Qadir's attention for a half second as I set the knives to flight, but the two djinn dissolved into themselves and then, with a gust of wind, reappeared fifty times over, one for each of my blades.

"Will you *stop*," I snapped as the Qadir collective rushed forward. Easily a third of them dropped with the first assault, but it wasn't enough. One of the djinnlets reached me, and the moment it did, the mini genies coalesced back into one, and it was with all his reconstituted might that Qadir bore down on me, wrapping his hands around me, choking me half to death.

"You *bastard*," I gasped. "I'm not who you think I am. You're fighting the wrong battle for the wrong guy."

"I will defeat you, and I will defeat your king," the djinn roared, three thousand years of bad breath blowing back my hair.

Well on the way to losing consciousness, I sent out an appeal I knew Armaeus would be more than happy to answer. I was right. In less than the blink of an eye, the Magician rose up beside us in a rush of smoke and fire, and the battle waged anew. He pulled Qadir off me, ripping him apart, clearly not having been watching the fight up to now. When one djinn once more became two, however, I ended up with the stupid one. He crunched his heavy body into mine while out of the corner of my eye, I watched the second djinn and the Magician trade light-ning bolts.

As they fought, my version of Qadir decided to wrestle with his inner demons on my time.

"*Witch!*" he seethed, his black eyes haunted with pain. "You kept me from my third and final act. The act that would have freed me and all people. The act that would have seen a father kill his only son, drain his power, and take dominion over all the land the Sun touched. And you stopped me. *Why?*"

Somewhere far back in Ahmad's warded chamber, I heard a strangled cry, but I had problems of my own.

"I am not your *queen*," I tried again, but that argument was clearly getting me nowhere. There was an air of desperation about this djinn, a need for freedom and self-determination. To not be bound by those who believed themselves stronger than he was, to live his life. Ordinarily, I would've supported that, but as it happened, I currently had mixed feelings.

"Die," Qadir howled as he scraped his hand toward me, clipping my jaw. The blood that spewed out across his face refocused me—mainly because it was my blood. Sensei Chichiro's admonitions roaring in my head, I surged forward. As I shoved him backward, I assembled a bed of iron spikes for the bastard to land on. They pierced him through from shoulder to hip, and he screamed with infernal pain. But he didn't get up. I staggered back, staring down at him, and dragged in ragged breath as I heard Nikki shout, "Sara!"

I whipped around to see more of Jarvis's men entering the room, as the gun-toting demons crowded around Nikki and Danae, even edging closer to the Syx. The security guards had devices in their hands—detonators? I couldn't tell. Behind them, Ahmad's counselor Hassan stood tall, his hands up. So it was the warlock who was managing the horde so effectively...here, and in Pompeii too? Just how deep was Ahmad in with the Shadow Court?

Either way, surely he wouldn't kill Nikki and Danae and the demon enforcers while I was still fighting the djinn. Not like this. Not like—

"You'll need to drop the wards," Hassan announced, and I felt more than saw Ahmad lift his hand as Jarvis gestured to his men, thumbs depressing buttons and the spark of electricity flaring—

I didn't think. I didn't breathe. *Armaeus!* I roared in my mind, and the Magician turned, instantly assessing the situation and—for the barest moment as Ahmad dropped the wards—he stopped time.

In that tiny moment, no more than a heartbeat, I rushed forward, ripping the explosives free from the demons and the detonators for good measure, then disintegrating away, reappearing in the bowels of Queen Makeda's cellar domain. This was a place that mankind did not deserve to see, and this was a place to which the djinn would never return. They had suffered enough here. I dumped the triggered explosives and wrenched myself away again, propelled by the force of the explosion as Armaeus set time once more in motion. I blew back onto the plaza outside Ahmad's home, staggering as I took up the fight again.

This time, however, when Armaeus struck at Qadir with his iron scimitar, Qadir stood firm and took the cut, a wide gash opening from neck to hipbone to bleed golden blood. He clasped his hand over his breast, blood spilling through his fingertips, and his eyes turned to smoke.

"Enough!" he hissed. "I cannot win unaided. It is finished." He turned and, with a mighty roar, swept Armaeus and me back into Ahmad's chamber...where the dead zone crashed down over us. Both of us. Armaeus cursed, driven to his knees.

"Return to the chalice," Jarvis ordered, and Qadir's eyes shot wide even as his body turned into smoke. He could not defy the charge of his owner, however, and a moment later, as if a great wind had been sucked from the sky, he vanished into the chalice, the lid clattering closed.

25

My third eye still remained fixed open, and there were more gyrating energy circuits rocketing around the room than I could fully process.

"What?" Ahmad's wail startled me, and I whipped my gaze toward him. He continued to stare at the chalice as if it were going to render him a response. "My father wanted to *kill* me?"

I threw my own question out, my voice cold with rage. "You were going to allow him to *murder* us? Are you insane?"

It was Jarvis who answered for Ahmad, however, since Ahmad was clearly still reeling from his admittedly legitimate daddy issues.

"You aren't the only member of the Council who has chosen to stick your head in the sand, Justice Wilde. We made our first pleas to the Emperor, never suspecting he would turn us down, and to the High Priestess. The other members of the Council, while strong, did not possess the requisite darkness within them to carry out our tasks. And though your strength is undeniable and your darkness ever growing, you were a failure as well. So our work continued.

And we encountered Ahmad during the course of our search for the hidden storehouses of magic that would help turn the tide of the battle that is even now being fought."

"Once more for the cheap seats?" Nikki asked. I glanced her way—and stopped. She and Warrick had edged ever so slightly closer to the chalice. Warrick was a demon enforcer, and only a demon could kill another demon—but he couldn't kill a djinn. So I wasn't sure what he was up to, but I would take his protection of Nikki however it came.

Speaking of demons...

While Jarvis chuckled indulgently, I glanced around. Other than the Syx, all the demons in the room had gone eerily still, as if someone had turned off their electricity. Just how sophisticated had the Shadow Court gotten in their demon-control tactics? Hassan still stood at the doorway, but his hands were down, his gaze on Ahmad.

Jarvis's unctuous voice recalled my attention. "I think Justice Wilde understands me well enough. A meeting is taking place even now, a show of faith, if you will, between our strongest allies, our most highly placed politicians and military directors, seeded all over the world. And as it happens, I have my own personal show to bring them. I'll arrive with my newfound magic *and* my warrior djinn to seal the deal. I thank you, Justice Wilde, and you as well, Armaeus, for making all this possible."

"We live to serve," I said drily. With the double whammy of being in Ahmad's dead zone and Jarvis's unmistakable flush of power, I didn't know quite how to play this. Meanwhile, Armaeus knelt, his expression almost distracted, as if he was working out all the various mathematical possibilities of different courses of action. I tried not to tell him to hurry it up already. There would be no point in us making a stand if our magic wasn't sufficient to the task. We were immortal, but not unkillable.

Strangely enough, I didn't feel particularly worried. I felt nothing but an ever-quickening anger that seemed like it might never burn out. I needed a trigger to light things up, a lever I didn't yet have. But it was coming. And when I blew...

I refocused on Jarvis. "So you're just going to have a little meeting, give them a PowerPoint display of your new magical skills, trot out your new little buddy in a bottle, and the world is going to kneel down to you? That's all it'll take?"

"No," Jarvis said. "The world won't kneel, and we don't want it to. We need perhaps two billion humans on this planet, no more, and then we can build a new Atlantis. We can start over with the force of magic to guide us and the remaining population of souls separated into their proper places. They won't know what happened, and they don't need to know. There will be tragedies. There will be wars. With the swift cruelty of fate, merciful death will roll out across nations large and small, and those who are left to pick up the pieces will not much mind being taken care of."

"You've given this a lot of thought," I said, not trying to hide the sarcasm in my voice. Ahmad staggered to Jarvis's left. "My father..." he murmured again, the words practically a sob.

"Your father is the least of your concerns," Jarvis said curtly, turning on him. "The magic you've given me as part of our agreement is not sufficient, I'm afraid. I would take it all."

"You can't," Ahmad protested as I glanced sharply at Armaeus, who still seemed locked in a game of internal *Jeopardy*. I tried to reach out mentally to poke him, then remembered the dead zone. "You don't have the power."

"Fair enough," Jarvis said. "But then, I don't need the power, do I?"

He spoke laconically and strolled over to the chalice to drift his hand lightly along the rim. Holding their positions, Nikki and Warrick went still as statues. That's when I noticed that Danae had shifted toward the pedestal as well, but was now studying the floor.

"Unlike you, your father, and so many before you, with the possible exception of the actual Queen of Sheba, *I* fully understand the power of the djinn captured in this fragile vessel," Jarvis said. "Its bonds are eternal until it is granted clemency. The greatest oracle in the modern world told me this, so I know it to be true."

I blinked and glanced again at Armaeus. Still out to lunch. "Eshe?"

"We didn't truly think she would come to our side, but she is proud, and she doesn't get out all that much. It was, in the end, easy enough to sway her into a trance state. Her visions were extraordinary and varied, and we assembled interpreters from all corners of the earth to work them out. As with all prognostications, they were a jumble of possibilities, but once we separated the main threads of her predictions, we knew what was possible. And we were willing to take the steps to make some of those possibilities happen."

He turned back to us and smirked, which was lost on Armaeus in his glassy-eyed state. "The Arcana Council could not countenance a member of our organization killing a member of the Council. But up to that point, it seems, anything was fair game. Even the desecration of Justice Wilde's own flesh and blood was not sufficient to move the Council and their feet of clay. So, no. I won't kill the Sun and take his remaining magic for my own. I won't have to."

With an elegant flick of his finger, Jarvis slid off the lid of the chalice. Smoke and fire immediately billowed forth, and even I stepped back, witness to the impressive display of Qadir's might.

"Another small detail I forgot to mention," Jarvis said, his words flush with excitement. "Should Qadir refuse any command I give him, he will *never* be set free."

The djinn slowly took form once again as the bigger, meaner cousin to the Syx. His face was a glory to behold, his body straight and firm, his chest massive. Only his eyes remained vacant pools of smoke for the moment as Jarvis continued. "The djinn cannot refuse a command from its owner, on penalty of remaining trapped forever in its vessel, without even the hope of being called forth in service to interrupt its exile. Queen Makeda knew this. She also knew the third wish of Sheikh Iman, Ahmad's father, and the profound destruction it would cause Qadir. As it turns out, she herself was part djinn, and understood the moral code. A father killing his own son is a violation most foul, one that Qadir would pay for far more than Iman ever would. She would not have wished that fate on any of her kind, and she despised Iman for placing such an onus on Qadir. But place it, Iman did."

Ahmad issued a choked moan, his face naked with horror. "She saved my life."

Jarvis shrugged. "I wouldn't go that far, but she certainly extended it. Now, however, I'm afraid your amnesty is at an end." He turned to the djinn. "It's time, Qadir, for you to complete the task you have avoided these past three thousand years. You are bound to me, and I have no problem with the stain you so fear. Complete the request of Sheikh Iman, and kill his only son."

Qadir's eyes cleared, and as he turned his head to sweep the room with his gaze, they met mine. In that moment, I could see the torture in his soul. This djinn had killed scores and would kill more without compunction, but there was something about this request that still haunted him, all these centuries later. Despite the djinn's dismay, however, there was also grim resolve. Before today, it had been three thousand long years since Qadir had last been summoned from his prison. He would not relegate himself to a second eternity of entrapment.

"Now," Jarvis ordered.

"*No,*" Ahmad whispered. The djinn turned toward him, pulling an enormous scimitar from his waistband.

"No," Ahmad said again as Qadir approached him. I didn't like Ahmad, but even I didn't want to see him go out this way. I struggled against the layers of magic that draped over me like a lead blanket. Out of the corner of my eye, I saw Nikki and Warrick shift again, still edging toward the now-empty chalice that sat on the gold-draped pedestal. But all the other eyes in the room were on the djinn and Ahmad as they met in the center of the chamber.

"No," Ahmad said again—but this time, there was a firmness to his tone. A certainty. The djinn halted at it, but Jarvis merely chuckled.

"Ahmad, you are long past the time of taking a stand yourself. You know that."

"I do know that," Ahmad said, and once again there was the flare of haughtiness I'd first seen in the lounge at the Dubai airport as he'd flashed the medallion of the Sun at me. He stood straighter, and his eyes burned with both deep pain and deep knowledge. "I know a great deal. Not the inner workings of your infernal Court, but certainly your plans, your ideas. And I *agreed* with them. I, too, wanted to see magic return to the world in a system of order, of right-eousness. So that the lowly, vulgar Connecteds who ruined the divine nature of our ability would be put in their place or wiped from the earth. So that those humans without any magic to them at all would *know* our strength and bow to us, just as the flowers in the meadow turn their faces to the sun, welcoming it for the strength and the nourishment it brings. These are the things you promised me, Jarvis, and I believe you will grant them, whether or not I am here to see it. But you are without honor to force this djinn into fulfilling my father's wish. With the stain of that request on his soul, even if the directive comes from you and not my father, he will suffer. For all his murders, all his many sins, he does not need that added to the pile."

Then Ahmad turned to me. "I betrayed you many times over, Justice Wilde," he said. "I helped the Shadow Court twist the weather to speed its agents into the most vulnerable Connected communities. I gave Jarvis the power he needed to command the hellspawn to rip your sister limb from limb. It was the price of my entry into this foul arrangement with a Shadow Court. For that, I deserve to die."

He turned back to the djinn. Qadir remained motionless, watching him. "But you, djinn Qadir, you do not deserve to kill me."

In a movement that was startling in both its swiftness and brutality, Ahmad lurched forward, grabbing the scimitar from the djinn's grip. Without hesitation, he turned it and plunged it into his chest, piercing himself through. An explosion of magic shot from his body, sending us all reeling. Even the djinn disappeared in the burst of smoke, as Nikki, Danae, and Warrick leapt toward the pedestal that held Qadir's empty chalice.

It was a testament to Ahmad's personal power that the dead zone held even as he fell, and after the first bolt of power, his magic burned like an incarnate flame, immediately consuming him and the djinn, who stepped forward and wrapped Ahmad's body in his arms. Qadir spoke words I couldn't translate with the roaring in my ears, but within seconds, the fire dimmed, gradually seeming to vanish altogether inside the djinn's body.

"Uh...oh," Hugh muttered beside me, but I didn't understand why, and Jarvis didn't waste any time.

"It is finished," he said, his face flush with excitement. He lifted his arms and turned toward Armaeus and me with exultation in his eyes. "I can feel the rush of the new magic filling me. Magic that Ahmad grants me through the agency of the djinn under my control."

Across the room, Armaeus's brows tented, this new piece of information apparently interrupting his playlist of crazy.

"And now, Qadir and I will finish what the djinn could not finish alone," Jarvis crowed.

"Whelp, that *would* make for an awesome fight," Nikki allowed, drawing our attention. "I think you're missing something, though." She nodded toward the center of the room.

Qadir stood up from where he'd laid Ahmad's body to the ground, a body that was now nothing more than the golden robes of Ahmad's position. In his hand, he held Ahmad's medallion. He turned toward Jarvis.

Jarvis thrust his shoulders back, beaming. "Yes. Yes, I should wear the medallion of the Sun. It is well past time. Bring it to me," he commanded. His eyes were only on the djinn as Warrick and Nikki took their last steps toward the chalice. Danae, her forehead bloody, had finally crawled to the pedestal as well. Warrick helped her to her feet. Then Qadir started speaking.

273

"Jarvis Fuggeren, you hold my bond. You do not, however, hold honor," he rumbled, his voice heavy.

"I'm sorry to hear you feel that way," Jarvis sneered. "Alas, you are my servant, bound to all I command. Such was your dishonor that you have no recourse. You have earned the ultimate curse."

"I have," Qadir sighed. "And I will pay its price."

He reached Jarvis and draped the medallion over Jarvis's head. Then, with a brutal lurch, he grabbed the long chain in his hand and twisted it tight.

Jarvis's newly enhanced magic was nothing to take lightly. He practically pulsated with rage, Ahmad's borrowed power once more rocking through us, but this time, Armaeus and I bent against it, even made headway. The dead zone was cracking as Ahmad's stolen magic was tested in the djinn's grasp.

"You will return to your prison attended by the hounds of hell," Jarvis screamed.

"You attacked my people," Qadir shot back. "I heard their cries and their horror as they lay naked and bloody on the sands of our homeland. You have *no* honor in you."

"You will submit," Jarvis choked. "You will return to the vessel which—"

A small crash sounded at the back of the room. The sound that should've been so indistinct as not to be audible over Qadir and Jarvis's shouting match arrested us. Danae stood above the chalice, Nikki and Warrick flanking her, and she held shards of the chalice in her hands. It was destroyed.

I caught only a glimpse of Jarvis's horrified expression as Qadir stared at Danae, his eyes flaring wide. "My *queen*," he gasped, then turned back to Jarvis, roaring with delight. Another ball of magic burst from the two men, exploding out across the sand and sea.

"Miss Wilde," Armaeus alerted me, but I felt it, too. The destruction of the dead zone. A wave of fire swept through the room, setting the demons into motion, which in turn triggered the Syx. As they set to battle, Armaeus and I, our free hands up, built a web of magic that arched over the two battling figures in the center of the room—

And then suddenly, there was only one.

The djinn threw Jarvis Fuggeren's desiccated form to his feet, whirling on us. His eyes glowed gold, smoke pouring from him, his form shifting back and forth in a hundred different incarnations, each scattering to mist. Finally, he settled on the form he'd taken most readily, the giant burly chested demon with golden skin and fiery eyes. He stared down at Jarvis's smoking body, then back to us.

"That was a freebie," he muttered.

26

A rmaeus gestured with a sharp flick of his hand, and Ahmad's golden medallion skittered across the floor to him, but none of us moved. The djinn Qadir stared at us, oblivious to the battle going on around us as the Syx dispatched the remaining demon army of the Shadow Court.

"I have broken my bond," Qadir said, his eyes returning to smoke. "I am at my weakest. If you would strike, you should do it now."

"You are a djinn of great power," Armaeus countered. "Perhaps one of the strongest magical beings in the world. You didn't drain Ahmad's magic from him. He gave it to you."

Awareness and sorrow flickered in Qadir's expression. "He was a man of honor in the end. He lived a long life. He will be judged, but yes, there was grace within him."

"That's not what I'm talking about," Armaeus said. "You know what he did. And so now you possess not only the power he granted you, but the power you've liberated from Jarvis as well."

Qadir's mist-filled eyes narrowed. "Which is, as I said, a good reason for you to act and act quickly, while the weight of my deceit still cripples me."

Armaeus shook his head. "I don't think so. We have a need for the magic of this world to be bent to good purpose, not to hide in the shadows any longer. What Jarvis has planned is already in motion."

Qadir gestured toward Jarvis's body with one meaty hand. "I have no quarrel with mortals, other than this one, who willfully attempted to slaughter those who stood guard with me and over me these long centuries. The world of your kind is not my world, nor my interest."

"Yet I would like to make an offer to you," Armaeus countered. "An offer that, of course, you can refuse."

Qadir said nothing, his eyes still filled with shifting smoke, and Armaeus continued. "We have gone for three thousand years with the Sun remaining hidden from the Council, whether due to pride or foolishness. I would raise you to that position in Alsain Ahmad's place, if you would take it."

I sent a startled glance Armaeus's way. He was no longer the head of the Council. Did he have the power to raise anyone anymore?

I kept my thoughts to myself, however, as Qadir straightened. "You would make me the Sun? But I am a demon to you."

"Not cool enough to be a demon," Warrick commented from across the room as he sent another creature back across the veil in a splatter of black goop. "Don't get ahead of yourself, bright boy."

The Magician's gaze never wavered. "You are a djinn, and within you is a power that transcends time. Power born in the ancient world, that we have forgotten how to wield. And in the coming battle, such power will become important. Will you join us?"

Qadir stared at Armaeus, then back to the chalice, still broken in Danae's hands. His gaze lifted to her face, and his eyes cleared.

"You *freed* me," he murmured. And though his words were quiet, they pierced through the noise of the battle to reach Danae. She shrugged, clearly unimpressed by the emotion in Qadir's voice. To her, at least, he was still a demon, and her disdain and distrust remained written all over her face.

"It wasn't my idea," she said.

The two of them stared at each other a long, fraught moment, while the chaos of the Syx raged around us. Then Qadir smiled, slowly and deliberately.

"You are on the Council?" he asked her.

Danae scoffed. "Hardly. I stand with Sara, nothing more."

Qadir shifted his glance to me. "*You* are on the Council."

I nodded, and he returned his gaze to Armaeus. "I will become your Sun, though I don't know what that means, exactly."

"A whole lotta meetings, I'm telling you right now," Nikki said, crossing to me from her position at the pedestal as Armaeus stepped forward.

I couldn't help it, I felt compelled to explain to the djinn what the Magician would not. "You will be held under the control of the Council," I said, drawing Qadir's attention. "They have the authority to restrain your actions should they wish to do so. You won't be able to harm others without someone knowing."

Even as I said the words, I felt a new truth behind them. The Council sat on the sidelines, governing from the shadows. But who was to say there weren't even deeper shadows they never looked toward? And who was to say what wrongs could be righted in those shadows? If the Council wanted to come after me, maybe I should let them. Or maybe I should send out the night witch to do her worst.

For his part, Qadir studied me another few seconds, then nodded.

"And I say, let them come," he said, as if responding to my thoughts. I blinked, not missing Armaeus's hard smile. Was this why he'd been lost in such deep thought while Jarvis had been pontificating? Did he know something about Qadir I didn't?

Armaeus stepped forward and slid the medallion on its chain over Qadir's head, the gold of the amulet sizzling as it connected with his flesh. Beside me, Nikki winced.

"That's gonna leave a mark," she muttered.

"It is good to have you with us," Armaeus said, stepping back again. "And now, I think, in all the confusion of your ascension and Jarvis's departure from the Shadow Court, we have the advantage of time and surprise. There is some work that can be done."

"Miss Wilde." He turned to me, and I felt an unusual pressure at my wrists. I glanced down. The cuffs of Justice were now around my own wrists. Not constraining me, exactly, but definitely exuding a menacing appearance.

Armaeus's lips twitched into a dark smile. "I think that will work nicely." He turned back to Nikki. "You have the situation under control?"

"Are you kidding? I've got a date with the spa in about thirty minutes, give or take." Nikki grinned. "I'm just sad I'm gonna miss the show."

I blinked as the Magician shifted slightly. Suddenly, standing between Qadir and me was Jarvis Fuggeren, his smile smug and aristocratic, his elegant suit perfectly pressed.

"I believe there is a meeting we should be attending," he said. Qadir flinched as a set of heavy gold manacles appeared around each of his wrists, a third yoke around his thick neck. "Together with the spoils of war."

"The blond fool would have liked the shackles," Qadir grunted. "But I drained his thoughts as well as his power. He no more knows his keepers than you do, Magician. He hoped to meet them this night, or to impress their proxy."

He blew out a long breath. "The place we go is a private chamber in a building he calls the Palais des Nations. You know it?"

"Intimately," Armaeus said in his smooth, smarmy Jarvis Fuggeren voice. If the man's corpse wasn't still steaming halfway across the room, I couldn't have said for sure it wasn't Jarvis in the flesh standing next to me. I fought the urge to edge away.

"His allies there are people he wished to impress, particularly the woman, this proxy," Qadir continued, tilting his head as if trying to hold onto fading memories. "He wants her body, but there's more to his quest than that."

"Cut to the chase, Qadir. You're going to make me sick," I muttered, and the djinn looked my way without fully seeing me.

"He seeks her approval. She is the gateway. The gateway to the very gods—the masters of the Shadow Court."

"Bingo," I breathed, and beside me, Armaeus grinned.

"Then, as Miss Dawes would say, we will do our best to give her a show," he promised.

We vanished into smoke and reappeared moments later in the midst of an amphitheater-like hall. I'd never been to the UN's official base of operations, but this room certainly looked like some side chamber of a yesteryear political palace. The gallery was filled with rows upon rows of VIPs—and to my surprise, some of them I even recognized. The rich, the famous, and the well connected of multiple nations, from diplomats to debutantes. If this was a sampling of whom the Shadow Court had drawn into its circle...damn. We had our work cut out for us.

And apparently, we made quite the spectacle. The assembled guests collectively gasped as we appeared in their center, then burst into remarkably enthusiastic applause.

"Gentlemen, ladies," Armaeus began in his best Jarvis voice. "It is with great pleasure that I bring to you the evidence of our success. Many of you know Justice Wilde?"

There was a gratifying ripple of conversation through the room. It appeared that my reputation had preceded me with the assholes of the world. Good to know.

"Then you will appreciate that she is constrained." He lifted his hand, and mine followed without me doing anything, as if we were bound by an imaginary chain. Armaeus-as-Jarvis smiled, clearly enjoying this part a little too much. Something we would need to talk about later.

He gestured to his left. "And with me as well is a creature of profound power—a creature who is my slave." Qadir dropped to one knee and then the other, and bowed almost to the floor. As he did, he exhaled heavily, and a rush of colored mist flowed out to fill the room, billowing up in shades of maroon, blue, and green. This guy would be amazing at a thirteen-year-old's birthday party.

Around us, the murmuring grew more intense.

"So you see. It is *all* coming together," A woman spoke out, and she strode forward, her power so evident that my third eye shot straight open, and I marveled at the gyrating electrical currents that rolled off her in waves. I didn't recognize her, but I felt like I should. She was tall, as pale as Jarvis, but with a shock of deep black hair that was swept back in a sleek fall over her shoulders. She was beautiful and aristocratic and entitled, I could see in a flash. No wonder Jarvis liked her so much.

Now she continued. "Your commitments are all made, and the weapons of our revolution are in place. The secrecy will be held. No one will know where the strikes come from, as they will come from everywhere at once. It cannot be stopped."

"We'll be safe?" a blonde woman in a deep-crimson business suit asked, her voice both cold and excited, the fever of bloodlust as thick as her Southern twang. "Throughout the whole of it?"

"You'll be safe," the elegant brunette confirmed, radiating confidence. A second later, I understood why. "We have our own army of mercenary soldiers, culled from the deadliest military forces in the world. They're on their way here right now to ensure your safe transport. Nothing has been left to chance."

I barely managed to avoid glancing at Armaeus. A cabal of highly trained mercenary soldiers descending on us didn't sound all that awesome. *Why can't anything be easy?*

A chill snaked through me as another man stood forward, bulky in his designer suit.

"We are ready. You have only to say the word," he announced. He had a smooth Belgian accent, and practically oozed money. In fact...they all did in this room. I felt like I was staring out at a nest of gold-plated vipers. "When does it begin?"

The woman smiled. "It already has."

Armaeus inhaled a long breath, and I saw the subtle

shift in the djinn smoke emanating from Qadir. My eyes widened slightly. Were those two working in tandem with each other to...what? Gather intel? Mark the attendees? Fumigate the room?

"You are all members of the Shadow Court," Armaeus said in Jarvis's smug drawl. "The first time you ever dared to assemble."

The woman's chin lifted. "A show of faith was important for what was to come," she said, a touch of warm approval in her tone. "We all believe—as *I* believe in you, Jarvis."

I forced my lips not to twist at her clear affection. Somewhere, burning in Hell hopefully, Jarvis must be seriously pissed. *Sucker.*

Qadir, still on his knees, lifted his bound hands, and blew a soft whisper across his palms. A new puff of smoke billowed upward, creating a screen against which the plans of the Shadow Court erupted like a rushing storm.

War, sickness, death. I watched with growing horror as the same people who stood in front of us emerged from the wreckage, blood on their hands and their feet, striding forward, glowing with magic. Magic they'd taken from the victims strewn around them like scattered straw.

Even worse, among the victims' corpses were thousands of figures destroyed the way Sariah had been. Their bodies literally ripped apart in a bid to permanently destroy and dispel their magic. Fury spun within me, coalescing into a hard ball.

The picture changed, but the group before us remained together, lifting goblets in some sort of future celebratory toast. Applause broke out in the room, a patriotic fervor to a twisted cause.

We all had seen enough.

"It is perhaps not fair to judge you for an atrocity you

have not yet committed," Jarvis drawled. For the first time, the woman running this little show looked at him with something other than smug superiority.

"What?" she asked, but Armaeus was already changing—and Qadir as well. As they did, the shackles fell from my wrists.

"But I think we can overlook that, this once," the Magician said.

"Attack! Guards!" the woman shouted, twisting into a pillar of smoke. By then, we were already in motion. My hands snapped apart, and a thousand sets of bracelets leapt into view, cuffs that would allow me to send every last one of the Shadow Court's minions to Gamon for judgment.

I sent them flying—but not here, not in this gallery. We knew our enemies here. Instead, I directed the cuffs to go streaming through the night *outside* this place, to find their targets wherever they lurked. As steeped as I now was in the stench of the Shadow Court, surrounded by its magic and its foul intent, I could recognize its members anywhere—if only for a little while. It was enough. The Shadow Court would be bound, once and for all.

But even as I pressed into the chaos of the gallery, I knew what Gamon would see in whatever bastards I did choose to send to her. Abuse. Violence. Death.

Fury roared through me. Was this the moment for the night witch to strike? For who was I to let the blood from this battle only be borne by others? Who was I not to commit, when I had asked others to stand?

A man rushed toward me out of the darkness, shoving a gun in my face.

Time seemed to move forward a frame at a time—each second a decision, each move a declaration. In my mind's eye, I saw myself striking out, crushing the man's skull. Saw him falling to the ground, dead.

It would be so easy, I thought. It would be right, even good. It would be exactly what the night witch would do —should do.

Was I the night witch, truly? Both light and shadow, right and wrong? Was that my path, now?

A voice cried out a half a world away, my voice. My soul. "*Yes,*" shouted Sariah, lost in her delirium. "*Yes, this. This!*"

"*Yes,*" echoed the memory of Gamon in my mind.

No, came another voice—a multitude, an army. The roar of the Connecteds I had pledged to serve. They did not need a murderer to lead them. They needed honor. Possibility. Hope.

No.

I didn't strike.

Time raced forward once more. I ducked away from the man's attack, and he disappeared into the chaos, only to be replaced with another—and then another. They didn't— couldn't touch me. I was Justice, and they were not mine to Judge. Not yet. Maybe not ever.

But I could—would—make sure they never harmed another soul again.

It was another several minutes before it was done. The mercenary soldiers the elegant woman had spoken of never arrived. Maybe because she'd called them off? Maybe because they'd called themselves off? They were mercenaries, after all. Either way, the gallery of glitterati no longer stood in their resplendent business suits and elegant evening wear. Bodies littered the space, most of them not moving. Qadir and Armaeus, apparently, had no such restrictions on who they saved and who they spared. The ones that remained were trembling in fear in the cuffs of Justice, moaning for release.

"These would be more useful alive than dead, at least in the short term," Armaeus said. His voice was cold, and his eyes gleamed black, their red rims shot through with gold. I looked over the group, but I didn't see the sleek-haired woman. Maybe Armaeus had taken her out?

Qadir grunted beside him. "You should have a care, Magician. They cannot be trusted not to recall—something. Even if you wipe their memories, there will remain a terror of what transpired this night. A terror that will never leave them."

"Then I chose well," Armaeus returned. "Because this particular handful of Shadow Court members employed that very trick. They each utilized a particular technoceutical in their campaigns of terror to ensure their victims could not remember...but also could never forget."

He turned to me. "Miss Wilde? You can take them now."

I stepped into the fray and set us all on fire.

Gamon was waiting for me when I rematerialized in the stark amphitheater of her intake bay. She nodded at me, but there was no joy in her expression as she took in my captives. "You could simply have sent them."

"No. They need to know it was me who sentenced them." I gestured to the huddle of prisoners. "So they carry that memory forward too. How much do you know?"

"All of it." She gave me a steady look. "You didn't kill. Actions have consequences. Your position has responsibility. It was your right to kill them, to protect the greater good. And you didn't."

The haunting lyric whispered through my mind. *I lost my power in this world...*

I pushed the thought away and focused on Gamon. "Do

we have any way of knowing how much of what they were planning was bullshit and how much is real?"

"It was real, as far as their intentions were concerned." Gamon shrugged. "But as to their readiness to act, it gets murkier. Simon's been tracking down every player to their base, both the ones in the gallery, and the ones you cuffed remotely. Where'd those people end up anyway? Not here."

"I didn't have time to fetch them." I shrugged. "If their magic is strong enough, they can get rid of the cuffs, but if they're part of the Shadow Court they're marked either way. I'll find them all eventually."

"Good, because there's no mention of any nefarious plot in any official channels anywhere. The terrible tragedy of this meeting and the terrorist attack that cost the lives of so many great leaders, military, and celebrities, blah blah blah, is being met with confusion in official circles. Most of the attendees of this Girl Scout meeting were here on the down low, with not even their official security details involved. There will be hell to pay and an outcry against terrorists, but so far, we've seen no evidence of the war laid out so prettily before you."

I scowled at her. "All that was a lie?"

"Far from it," Gamon said. "It's an indication that the Shadow Court had its talons dug deep, guided by subtle hands. There are doubtless active cells already in place. We just haven't found them yet. Hopefully, the information I can pull out of these guys will be worth it."

"I think Armaeus already read their minds. He would have found something that major."

"Armaeus and I use far different tactics," Gamon said. "You never know which one will be more effective until you try."

"How long will you need?"

Another shrug. "A day, maybe two. No more than that. It'll take you that long to get your own head on straight."

She wasn't wrong. Even now, with the rush of the fight leaving me, I struggled to understand how I truly felt. It didn't feel good to have stepped back from revenge, to have remained in the shoes of Justice and not the night witch, but it didn't feel wrong either. It would have to be enough.

"I'll let you know what I find out when I find it," she said.

She lifted a hand, and a door at the far end of the bay slid open, grim-faced minions hustling out, pushing gurneys and wheeled chairs. We watched silently as they loaded the day's work, and the haunting lyrics washed over me again. *I lost my power in this world...*

"You know, the rules of Justice don't have to apply to you," Gamon said quietly. "You're more powerful than any Council member who ever walked the earth. Powerful enough to be Justice—and the night witch too, maybe. Think about it."

I didn't know if her words were intended to comfort me or indict me, but she'd already turned away to follow her fell cargo into her domain. I turned away as well. I had other places to be.

But as I disintegrated into nothingness, I heard her murmur drift across the open space between us.

But you could still use it.

27

I didn't return to the chamber of horrors where I'd left Armaeus and Qadir. Instead, I hung, unmoving and unformed, transfixed in the space between being and nothingness. In all my adult life, I'd never felt so unmoored. Something had changed within me, and I didn't know how to process it. I didn't know who I was anymore, or who I wanted to be.

A voice broke across my thoughts like waves crashing on a distant shore, a cry of rage and vindication in the darkness. A cry I knew. Sariah. Unlike the moment during the battle at the Palais des Nations, she wasn't shouting for me, or even at me. She was simply challenging the night with the same demanding, forthright anger she used to face everything in life. Constantly needing to move forward, never taking respite. Had I been like that as a child, before the horrors of my seventeenth year split me away from Sariah's spirit? Was I becoming like that again? Should I?

Power crackled around me, the urge to remake myself, to re-form as a Justice Wilde who no longer passed the worst offenders to others to face the consequences of their actions, but who held those offenders accountable myself. Was this truly the right path for me? Would it lead me to become as dangerous as some of the criminals I hunted down?

Was this who I really was?

And if not me...who?

I didn't know how long I hung in that space—minutes, hours. Finally, a new demand teased at the edge of my senses, a call that broke through my fog, urging me into the fight again. Another cry for Justice from a victim looking for deliverance? Oddly, I didn't think so. This was something sharper, clearer. This was a call not for aid, exactly, but...to come home?

"Dollface!" The words exploded in my mind. *"For the love of brats and sauerkraut, get yourself here already!"*

I slapped my hand to my arm, pressing into the tattoo that Death had inked into my skin what seemed like a millennium ago. I rematerialized in a puff of smoke and scattered embers, not much the worse for wear despite my prolonged stay in the ether.

"Boom," Nikki said, finger-gunning the burly Mongolian general who sat across from her on the broad, sunny patio of Danae's House of Swords. She wore a bright red minidress, cowboy hat and tasseled boots, a vivid white kerchief around her neck—daywear for her. Ma-Singh's attire was decidedly more subdued—his usual dark-hued military gear. A crowd of silent figures stood some distance away, all of them dressed in military gear. "You totally owe me a pony ride."

"Chono is no pony," Ma-Singh shot back. "He'll just as soon eat you as let you on his back."

His grin faded as he turned to me. "Justice Wilde. Thank you for coming so quickly. This meeting we must have is...

unexpected. With Mistress Danae traveling, I did not know where to begin."

I scanned the patio again, but I didn't recognize any of the assembled men and women, other than they possessed the kind of fierce intensity I'd grown familiar with during my tenure as head of the House of Swords. "What's going on?"

"The army of Swords has been called to battle. But we don't know by whom."

"And Danae is out of commission," Nikki put in. "Armaeus whisked me back to Pompeii, where we found Eshe's trio of virgins locked up in a caravan near the ruins and guarded by idiots. He left me there with a Council plane at my disposal to sort out the mess, and poofed out just as quickly. I jetted the girls back to their families on the double —and you've now got one happy wizard willing to follow you anywhere, by the way—but I haven't heard from Armaeus since. That was yesterday. I think he had to work through the mess of demons we left behind..." she paused. "You know, what *do* you call a group of demons? I've never asked Warrick. Gotta be a horde, right?"

"A legion?" Ma-Singh offered.

"Something with a D would be good, for alliteration," Nikki mused. "A den? Dominion? Diaspora?"

"Nikki," I broke in sharply. "What's going on here?"

"Well, we need Danae, speaking of important D words," she said. "And you. But she's gonna want to hear this pretty much pronto. I was thinking you could, you know..." She tapped the side of her head. "Phone a friend."

I barked a sharp laugh, but obligingly opened my mental barriers to Armaeus. *You there?* I asked.

A huffed, surprised breath met my query, a breath that

was decidedly not Armaeus's. *"The Magician is...thinking. He seems to do that a lot."*

My brows shot up. *Qadir? You can intercept our communications?*

"You've made a connection?" Ma-Singh asked, hope ringing in his voice. "Please. Tell her it's urgent. The battle cry has sounded from the four corners of the Connected world, and our troops are mobilizing—but here at the House of Swords base of command, we have received no such call for help. We don't know where this is coming from. We need Mistress Danae."

"I can see that," I said, eyeing the grim-faced assembly of warriors. They certainly looked like they meant business. *Ahhhh...Armaeus?* I tried again.

"He is very committed to thinking," Qadir observed in response, a touch of awe in his words.

Well, knock him over if you have to. Is Danae with you?

"Oh, yes..." There was no denying Qadir's rush of emotion, so intense, it rocked me back on my heels. *"She stands in sunlight, straight and fierce. A glowing beacon in a shadowed—"*

Got it. I need her here. Las Vegas, Nevada. She'll—

"I know where you are." Qadir sounded like he was moving. Good. *"Never forget, I am wherever the sun's bright rays caress the earth, whether in full day or in reflected moonlight."*

I blinked at that, but needed to focus. *Great. I still need her here. Get Armaeus to help.*

Qadir drew in a long, shuddering breath. *"My queen,"* he said, the words a tortured whisper, and I had to smile as I imagined Danae's most likely reaction to his approach.

She didn't disappoint. Her sharp, cutting tones ripped

across my mind. *"Qadir. Stop. Exactly* what *do you think you're—"*

A moment later, two figures burst onto the bright, sun-swept patio, forcing me to step back. The giant djinn Qadir, still bare-chested and sporting glittery gold pants and the heavy medallion of the Sun strung on its thick chain around his neck, immediately stepped back and opened his arms wide, releasing Danae. She spun toward him.

"Doing!" she spluttered. "Get *away* from me."

"My queen," Qadir said again. He brought his hands together in front of his mouth, as if in prayer. Never taking his adoring gaze from her face, he dissolved into light.

Danae turned back to us, barely giving me time to wipe the smirk from my mouth. "What?" she demanded, and she glowered at Ma-Singh. "I'm *busy.*"

Then she scanned the patio with sharp eyes, immediately seeing the crowd of warriors, who as one had lifted their right arms to their chests, their hands clenched into fists. "What is going on, Ma-Singh?"

"A battle is at hand. The call has been put out, and you can believe that the houses of magic will answer it."

"A battle against whom?" Danae asked sharply. "The Shadow Court? We don't know who they are. Jarvis is dead, but he wasn't the head of their group. No one believed that."

Nikki put her hands on her hips. "We've got some data coming in on that. The woman that Jarvis had the hots for—she apparently belongs to some highly placed family, but she has no name, operated only under an alias. We can't trace her. Yet. And we don't need to trace her. We should fight the enemies we have already unmasked. According to Simon, we've already got a pile of them."

I sighed. "Speaking of Simon, we're going to need to inform the Council of this battle cry. We would be better served if we had their weight behind us, but that's not going to happen. The Council will have to maintain an air of plausible deniability."

"And they'd slow us down," Ma-Singh put in.

"That's true enough," Danae said, shrugging as I glanced at her. "But something is going on in the Connected world. It has been for a while . There are deeply embedded cells of activity in the arcane black market being funded by unknown sources. We've resisted acting, preferring to watch and prepare, but make no mistake, we have been preparing. And we're not afraid to act. We don't have the luxury of time like the Council does when the threats hit this close to home."

"If it's war these bastards want, they'll get it," Ma-Singh said.

Nikki crossed her legs, swinging her boot almost playfully. "If it's war, then the Connecteds of this world will need to be given a reason to act on their own behalf. Singly, even in small groups, they can do a great deal of damage. With a champion, or two champions, willing to strike in the shadows, giving them hope..."

I narrowed my eyes at her. "You volunteering? Because I already have about three thousand years of backlog to work through."

"And we're telling you that the Connecteds' problems are now far beyond psychics harming other psychics," Nikki countered. "It's escalated to the brink of a systemic attack. *That* is the legacy of the Shadow Court. And we've got to fight it."

"She's right," Danae sighed. "Far more people know about us now, people in power, who are threatened by the existence of Connecteds. They don't understand them, and they wish to control that which they don't understand.

Worse, they're eager to act. The work you and the Council did at the Palais des Nations helps, but at best, it only buys us a short amount of time. The vacuum left by so many critical players in the Shadow Court is going to be filled, and soon. When it is, we must be ready to act."

We stared at each other a long moment, then Danae squared her shoulders. "I stand with you," she said simply, though I hadn't asked the question. "You fight—I'll fight."

I blew out a long sigh. "Fair enough," I said, shifting my gaze back to Ma-Singh. "When?

"Sooner than any of us would wish," the general replied. "Be ready."

28

This meeting of the Arcana Council was decidedly exclusive. Kreios stood at the head of the room, gazing out, not over the expanse of the Las Vegas Strip, but the people he had assembled. The Fool, the High Priestess, the Magician, and me. Gamon had returned to her lair to more fully interrogate the members of the Shadow Court who had survived the "terrorist attack," and we were left to sort through the rest of our infiltration of their organization.

A glint of gold caught my eye, and I blinked, squinting into the bright daylight. A new domain now stretched high above the Sahara Las Vegas casino, looking like a mirage in the radiating heat that shimmered above the sunbaked streets. An enormous collection of white and dusky-tan tents, topped by poles as thin as lightning rods, from which flew narrow, pennant-style flags of every color, flapping stiffly in an unseen wind. The entire setup looked like, well, a mirage. I glanced down at the Mirage Casino, but the airspace above it was empty.

Simon caught the angle of my gaze. "Too crowded," he

explained. "Qadir decided he needed a little more space, and that the end of the Strip has it."

I couldn't argue with the logic. With a residence over Sahara Las Vegas, the closest Council member to the Sun would be the Hanged Man, and Tesla wasn't likely to show up with pie. "I take it Qadir is settling into his new role?"

Armaeus fielded that one. "He is, and we have started the process of tracking down the Moon and the Star. The energy signatures that accompanied their votes for the Council disappeared as quickly as the Sun's had. But with the memories that Ahmad provided to Qadir, and with the Sun taking up such a visible role again on the Council, it's possible they'll take note. It's equally possible it will drive them further underground."

"We do have some anomalous information, though, that could prove useful," Kreios put in, nodding to me as I glanced his way. "For which we have you to thank."

That sounded promising. "What kind of information?"

"The cuffs you sent out to tag the members of the Shadow Court did not always find their marks," Kreios said. "They also targeted the highest-level Connecteds on the planet, who were most assuredly not in the Court, namely other members of the Arcana Council. The only difference being as soon as the cuffs skimmed those worthy souls, they sheared off just as quickly, as no Shadow Court affiliation could be established. But they still tagged them. It was only for a moment, but it was a moment we took note of."

He gestured to Simon, who swiveled on his chair, a wide, satisfied grin on his face. "I had energy signatures popping out all over the place," he said. "Basically, anyone with any intense amount of magic in them, whether or not they were trying to keep it hidden, got pinged. Totally better than Google."

"Without the tedious concern for privacy rights," the Devil agreed.

"So we *do* know where they are," I pressed

"More correctly, we know where they were," Kreios said. "Most of these high-level Connecteds were tagged and dropped so quickly that in most cases, they weren't aware it was happening. They simply didn't notice. The members of the Arcana Council who were fully aware of your actions understood the touch of your cuffs for what they were and continued on with their business. It certainly helped, of course, that the connection was so brief. The cuffs bound them only briefly, then left for other marks."

I snorted, conjuring up an image of any of the Council members suddenly finding themselves locked by the cuffs of Justice, even for the barest second.

"Trust me, I'm putting together a video montage." Simon grinned at me. "It'll be epic."

"But there are certain sets of cuffs, it would appear, that were annihilated almost immediately upon reaching their targets," Kreios continued. "They didn't shear away, but took off like bottle rockets and were destroyed."

I grimaced. Poor little cuffs. "And that helps us how?"

"It helps us in the same way that the last known location of a precious artifact helps us," Armaeus answered with an amused smile. "We don't know where the cuffs of Justice are, but we know where they were, and whether they brushed up against Connecteds of unexpected depth or hidden members of the Arcana Council, given the nature of the challenge that lies before us, we need to find them. Especially if they found hidden members of the Arcana Council who are also the hidden leaders of the Shadow Court. That, as you'll appreciate, changes everything."

Our gazes met, and I didn't miss the gleam in his eyes. "Well, finding stuff is always fun," I allowed.

"I agree. It would appear your skills remain in high demand, Miss Wilde."

The conversation turned to tactics and potential targets, but Simon insisted there remained far too much data to crunch to set any initial course. He'd need at least a few days. I suspected I'd need every bit of that time to sort through the newest round of complaints thudding into Justice Hall. I'd also be spending some considerable time in the library, tracking down more information about the actions of the houses of magic over time. There was something I was missing in all this. Something deeply rooted in the Connected communities far away from the soaring towers of the Arcana Council. Then too, there was the elegant woman who had so captured Jarvis's attention.

Speaking of...

"What about the woman we saw in the gallery?" I asked. "The one who seemed to run the show, this supposed representative for the leaders of the Shadow Court. Do we have a line on her?"

"Madame X. We're working on that," Simon said. "Interestingly enough, the data is all over the place. She was known by thirty different names, a true cipher. Nobody ever met any members of her family, though she referenced them by that term in most of her conversations as her source of information and financial support. Given that she was a high-level Connected, she could and probably is effecting a disguise. I'm tracking standard surveillance as well as those put in place by the houses of magic, but I'm not getting anywhere fast. I can tell you this, though. That army of mercenary soldiers she promised? The biggest, meanest bad guys in the land?"

"Oh yeah." I nodded. "What happened to—"

"Dead. All of them. Slaughtered in their cars."

That...wasn't what I'd been expecting. "Seriously?"

"Straight up," Simon said, leaning forward again to type on his laptop. "I'd show you what was left, but it isn't pretty. All of them knifed in their cars, heads taken clean off in some cases. No weapons, no survivors, no witnesses. Cars were found stopped in traffic not three blocks from the Palais des Nations. Switzerland is a polite place—most people just drove around them. But someone finally looked and...the shit hit the fan."

"They were knifed to death. In their vehicles. And no one saw."

"So far as we can tell, yep." Simon grinned. "So either they all spontaneously decided to shuffle off this mortal coil, or we've got a friend in high places. Something *else* we need to investigate."

"No doubt," I said, the same chill sweeping through me that I'd felt in the Palais des Nations when Jarvis's girlfriend had mentioned the soldiers. Had I known then they were marked for death? And if so, how? "Maybe put that at the top of your list."

More discussion ensued, but the reality was—we needed more information. Until we understood what lurked in the shadows, we couldn't strike. The only difference now was...I *wanted* to strike. It was a swelling need within me, sharp and hot. Was that the desire of Justice, of the night witch...or both? I couldn't say. But I was finally ready to find out.

We broke up shortly thereafter, and despite the fact I knew my way to Justice Hall without the benefit of walking, I left the Arcana Council conference room on foot, needing the heat of the unforgiving sun to sear some of the unease out of me. Armaeus fell into step beside me the moment I reached the sizzling concrete of the boulevard. We moved along the sunbaked sidewalk beneath the looming, iconic casinos, passing doorways that beckoned with the whoosh and clatter of slot machines and fanning cards.

"You know what the House of Swords is planning, right?" I hadn't kept my line of communication open when I'd spoken with Ma-Singh, given that I didn't know how to mute my feed from Qadir yet, but the Magician had his own unique set of skills. He probably had tapped into Danae's mind when he saw she was being whisked away. "They believe a war is coming. They may be right."

"Now you know why the Council never embroiled itself in the maintenance and direction of the houses of magic," he said. "Those houses are made up of mortals, and therefore, they face the challenges to their power and their very survival with a uniquely mortal viewpoint, the immediacy of which is not always effective or prudent. As a result, their solutions are born of emotion more so than strategy. They react and do not think of the long-term impact of their actions."

"To be fair, they weren't exactly put in this position of their own volition," I countered. "Their hand was forced by us."

The Magician only smiled. "Was it, though? Actions have consequences, even those we feel we have no choice but to make. The Houses will take actions that will bring the Connecteds into the full glare of awareness—exactly what the Shadow Court wanted, in the end. And of course, they are not my only concern, Miss Wilde."

I looked at him, surprised. "You don't need to worry about me."

"Oh, do not misunderstand. I don't *worry* at all. In fact, I couldn't be happier. With each new act I'm able to under-take free of the strictures of the Council, I recognize what can be done. But we will both be watched."

"By Kreios?" I protested. "I have a hard time believing that."

Armaeus laughed softly. "You'll note I didn't say we'd be stopped. But the wheels of government are already moving, and some of those Connected with the highest level of power even if they are not tacitly members of the Shadow Court, are moving and acting. Whether they seek to draw us out by attacking the weak and the vulnerable, or whether they come at us more directly, through official or unofficial channels, remains to be seen. But what we are approaching is a battle not with the gods, but with a far less predictable foe. It's a war that's been waged against Connecteds in secrecy up to now, but...no longer, I suspect."

"Great," I muttered. "And where do the other outlying members of the Council play into this?"

"An excellent question," Armaeus said, excitement edging his words. "If the Sun can be moved to join us, who's to say what the Star might do, if she—or he—is not already guiding the Shadow Court? The Moon, by its nature, will prefer to remain hidden...but working for us or for another, darker force? It's impossible yet to say. There will be much research to be done, shadows to pierce, and many long, dark nights to search for them."

I looked up at him, feeling a now-familiar flutter of excitement rising within me. A sudden, unquenchable yearning to stretch the fiery wings that simmered against my shoulder blades even now, to fly into that night at Armaeus's side. A deep and powerful need to confront whatever evil awaited us in the dark and shifting gloom...and drag it screaming into the light.

Fire crackled along my nerve endings and made my fingers twitch. "I look forward to the hunt."

Armaeus smiled and reached for my hand, drawing it to his lips. Then together, we walked onward, beneath the bright and burning sun.

EPILOGUE

I found Sariah sitting on the wall beside Bellagio's famous fountain, watching the play of water in the shimmering lights. It was a bright, star-filled evening, and the crowd oohed and ahhed at all the appropriate places as gusts of water arced and twirled in perfect time to the familiar strains of a Frank Sinatra standard.

She didn't glance over to me when I settled beside her, merely took a long pull on her bottle of beer. I was pretty sure there was a strict glass container law in force on the Strip, and was equally sure Sariah didn't give a shit.

"Does Sells still think you're asleep in your bed?" I began. She laughed, the sound low and raspy. I suspected it would be some time before she lost the gravel of the pits of Hell from her voice.

"Nah, she gave me the all clear. Probably knew she couldn't hold on to me anyway."

"Probably." I doubted, really, that anyone could. Not anymore.

A long silence stretched between us, and I watched the water dance. I'd once fought a battle with a fiery dragon beside this fountain, at almost this exact spot. I figured Sariah knew that too. We had a habit of knowing a little too much about each other's battles, it seemed.

"I couldn't do it," I finally said, the words coming out far sadder than I intended. "I couldn't outright kill those people in Geneva. Even though they deserved it."

She took another long drink, then wiped her mouth with the back of her hand. "I know," she said.

"It's not who I'm supposed to be, in the end. As much as I sometimes want it to be. The night witch...it's not who I am."

She'd stopped drinking now, staring at the gusts of water shooting up. "I know," she said again. There was no judgment in her tone, or even resignation. She was simply stating a fact.

I thought about the faces that had flashed by me at the Palais des Nations, hatred in their eyes. The same faces I'd seen in the horrific images that Qadir had projected for all to see. Murderers. Anarchists. Oppressors. I had to fight them, without question, but I had to do more than fight. I had to protect. I had to bring hope to a people who had long ago forgotten what hope meant. I had to lead.

When I spoke next, my voice was barely audible over the sweeping pop standard that seemed to push the bubbling streams of water out of their placid pool and send them sparkling across the night sky. "I got to thinking, though... maybe the night witch could be someone else. Maybe she already was someone else. Someone I could work with. Someone who could help me do the things I'm going to have to do."

At that, Sariah looked over to me, her face so much like my face, her smile so much like mine. Only in her eyes, the twisting flames of Hell leapt high, clawing, scrabbling upward, a thousand roaring demons, desperate to break free. This was my sister, my other half. The twin who'd run back into the fires when I'd first confronted my dragons, while I'd raced forward into the wide, wild world that awaited me.

I'd missed her, all these years. Far more than I'd ever realized. And as I noticed the long, wicked strips of steel that now hung from the loops of Sariah's jeans, the jagged, lethal blades she'd carved for herself from the cuffs of Justice, I was fiercely proud to have her by my side once more.

She smiled and tipped her beer toward me in salute.

"I know," she said.

~

THANK you so much for reading **The Night Witch**! I sincerely hope you enjoyed the book. If so, I welcome any and all reviews on the book retail site of your choice!

To keep up with the latest on Sara Wilde's next adventure, sign up for my mailing list here. If you're feeling social, you can find me online at my website, or follow me on Twitter, Facebook and/or Instagram (though, to be fair, I'm terrible at Instagram. Don't go there.) I look forward to seeing you online!

AUTHOR'S NOTE

In *The Night Witch,* I reference a song that teases at Sara, but don't name it specifically. For the curious, that song is *Go Insane,* by Lindsey Buckingham. If you haven't read the lyrics in awhile, they contain a bit of a spoiler for the story, so I am putting this note at the end of the book. The haunting nature of the song echoes the sense of uncertainty in Sara's constant quest, and helped make writing this book a unique and unexpectedly poignant experience for me... which after sixteen books in Sara's world, is saying something!

Speaking of, if you're reading this book, chances are good that you've been on this journey with Sara from the very beginning. Thank you for allowing me to share her story with you...and for being part of that story as well. Without you, there would be no artifacts to find, cards to decipher, or adventures to undertake. I love you all.

ANOTHER NOTE FROM JENN

The Sun is a big bouncing ball of happy, even though in this book, the Sun took a long stroll down some dark paths. For a more traditional interpretation of the card, read on for a full description!

ALSO: Interested in learning more about the Tarot, upcoming book releases, and other bits of arcana and mayhem? Get Connected (heh) and sign up for my mailing list here (www.jennstark.com/newsletter).

THE SUN

The Sun is Trump 19, taking us almost to the end of the Major Arcana cycle, with only Judgment and the World after. It is a card of tremendous bounty, eternally positive and radiating with vitality. It's the card of joy, abundance, good health and good luck. Get the idea? When you draw the Sun, throw open those curtains and expect to spend some time in the great outdoors, or in the limelight—all eyes will be on you, and you will truly shine! This is an intensely creative card, and bodes well for any artistic pursuits as well. Be lighthearted, open-minded, and filled with good cheer—the Sun is telling you that it's time to celebrate!

BOOKS BY JENN STARK

Wilde Justice Series

The Red King

The Lost Queen

The Hallowed Knight

The Shadow Court

The Wayward Star

The Night Witch

Immortal Vegas Series

(series complete!)

One Wilde Night (prequel novella)

Getting Wilde

Wilde Card

Born To Be Wilde

Wicked And Wilde

Aces Wilde

Forever Wilde

Wilde Child

Call of the Wilde

Running Wilde

Wilde Fire

The Demon Enforcer Series

ACKNOWLEDGMENTS

THE NIGHT WITCH turned out to be a fascinating book to create, as it took me down new paths for Sara I didn't originally plan. She never fails to surprise me! Thank you to all my readers for continuing to read my books, which allows me to write these stories for you. I remain ever grateful to Elizabeth Bemis for her beautiful work on my books and my site—especially my fantastic series covers. My editorial team of Linda Ingmanson and Toni Lee are absolute troopers, and I couldn't do this without their amazing work. Judi Soderberg also went above and beyond copyediting this book. Any mistakes in the manuscript are completely my own! Thank you to Edeena Cross and Sabra Harp for their insightful, careful beta reads, and to Kristine Krantz, whose guidance remains extraordinary, sixteen books in. And, of course, thank you to Geoffrey, who makes every story better than it was before. It's been a *Wilde* ride.

ABOUT JENN STARK

Jenn Stark is an award-winning author of paranormal romance and urban fantasy. She lives and writes in Ohio. . . and she definitely loves to write. In addition to her Immortal Vegas and Wilde Justice urban fantasy series and Demon Enforcers paranormal romance series, she is also author Jennifer McGowan, whose Maids of Honor series of Young Adult Elizabethan spy romances are published by Simon & Schuster; author Jennifer Chance, whose Rule Breakers series of New Adult contemporary romances are published by Random House/LoveSwept and whose modern royals series, Gowns & Crowns, is now available; and author D.D. Chance, whose paranormal romantic fantasy series, Twyst Academy, is now available.

Visit her online at www.jennstark.com and sign up for her newsletter to keep up with all the latest information about upcoming releases and special events!

www.ingramcontent.com/pod-product-compliance
Lightning Source LLC
Chambersburg PA
CBHW061934170626
46813CB00006B/2386